D0028396

Tunnels *of* TERROR

ANOTHER MOOSE JAW ADVENTURE

TUNNELS
of TERROR

ANOTHER MOOSE JAW ADVENTURE

MARY HARELKIN BISHOP

COTEAU BOOKS
WWW.COTEAUBOOKS.COM

© Mary Harelkin Bishop, 2001. Second Printing, 2002.

All rights reserved. No part of this book covered by the copyrights herein may be reproduced or used in any form or by any means – graphic, electronic or mechanical – without the prior written permission of the publisher. Any request for photocopying, recording, taping, or storage in information storage and retrieval systems of any part of this book shall be directed in writing to CanCopy, 1 Yonge St., Suite 1900, Toronto, Ontario, M5E 1E5.

This is a work of fiction. Names, characters, places, and incidents either are the product of the author's imagination or are used fictitiously. Any resemblance to actual persons, living or dead, is coincidental.

Edited by Robert Currie.

Cover image and interior map by Dawn Pearcey.
Cover and book design by Duncan Campbell.

Printed and bound in Canada at Transcontinental Printing.

National Library of Canada Cataloguing in Publication Data

Bishop, Mary Harelkin, 1958-
Tunnels of terror

ISBN 1-55050-193-3

I. Title.
PS8553.I849T84 2001   jC813'.54   C2001-911217-3
PZ7.B573Tun 2001

COTEAU BOOKS
401-2206 Dewdney Ave.
Regina, Saskatchewan
Canada   S4R 1H3

AVAILABLE IN THE US FROM
General Distribution Services
4500 Witmer Industrial Estates
Niagara Falls, NY, 14305-1386

The publisher gratefully acknowledges the financial assistance of the Saskatchewan Arts Board, the Canada Council for the Arts, the Government of Canada through the Book Publishing Industry Development Program (BPIDP), and the City of Regina Arts Commission, for its publishing program.

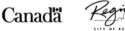

TABLE *of* CONTENTS

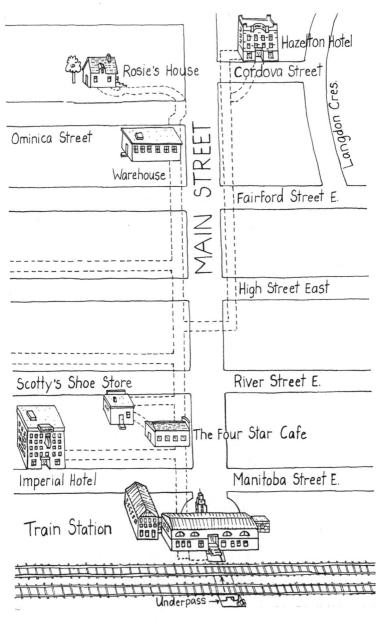

ABOVE GROUND

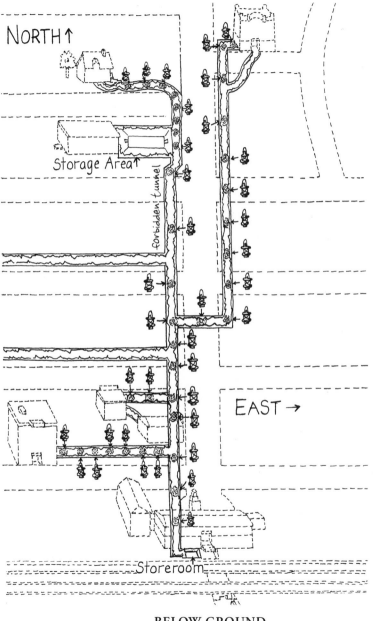

NORTH↑

Storage Area↑

Forbidden tunnel

EAST →

Storeroom

BELOW GROUND

for Eileen

PROLOGUE

"He's coming after me! Help!" Andrea was frozen to the spot, her face ghostly pale, her mouth hanging open in shock. "He's after me!" The armoire stood open, revealing a gaping hole in the wall in front of her. The air sizzled with an electrical aura. She willed her feet to move, to carry her to safety, but they refused to obey. A long arm snaked out of the darkness and clutched her shirt, dragging her into the black hole. She couldn't see the face; it was shrouded in the inky blackness, but she recognized the menacing laugh and it sent chills of fear chasing up and down her spine. "Help!" she screamed. Another hand clamped itself over her mouth as she was pulled down the few stairs and into the dank tunnel. She whipped her head around and managed to free her lips. "Leave

1

me alone!" she yelled. Using her feet, she aimed a kick at his shins. He cursed loudly in her ear and loosened his grip, and she slid to her knees on the tunnel floor.

Andrea heard the rustle of clothing and then an ominous click, the sound the hammer of a gun makes just before it is fired. In the faint light of the lantern hanging nearby, she caught the glinting of metal as Ol' Scarface pointed the gun at her head.

"You were bad news right from the start, girlie. Ya caused me and my gang a heap a trouble. I don't know why I waited this long ta do ya in. I'm just sorry I have ta do it myself. I don't like ta get my hands dirty."

Andrea cowered at his feet. Her heart pounded in her chest so loudly that the vibration echoed in her eardrums. She was a goner this time. Her luck had run out. She would die in this filthy tunnel under Moose Jaw, and no one would ever find her. Her parents would never know what had happened to her.

Sudden fury at her no-win situation and the injustice of it all caused Andrea to act. Even before she knew what she was doing, she had picked up a handful of dirt and whipped it into his face. He yelled and cursed, coughing on the dust.

It was the chance Andrea needed. She scrambled to her feet and ran through the narrow tunnel, fleeing for her life. Panic made her feet fly, but the tunnel was endlessly long and there was no place to hide, and nowhere to turn. She didn't recognize this tunnel. It should have twisted and curved, joining the larger one. This was one long tunnel that seemed to go on to infinity and she was sure that she was lost.

With no place to hide, and no way to get to the surface, she knew Ol' Scarface would catch her eventually, for she was weakening and growing tired. "Grab her!" She heard him yell. She turned to stare into the black void. Another man materialized from the tunnel wall, reaching out to grab her as she passed. His rough hand snagged her wrist. He stared at her with beady eyes, a thin black moustache accenting thin lips. She didn't recognize him. He held her prisoner as Ol' Scarface approached, every step causing panic to flood her stomach.

"I've got ya now." Ol' Scarface sneered, reaching out to grab her by the throat with one beefy hand. He whipped her around and stared into her panic-stricken eyes, a snarl curling his lips. "I wanna watch you die," he said. His fingers tightened around her slender neck.

Andrea felt her Adam's apple constrict. She tried to swallow but couldn't. Her windpipe collapsed under his strong hands as she dragged in one last gulp of air. It made a high-pitched whistling noise. She pummelled his chest with her small fists in a futile attempt to gain her freedom.

Suddenly a young girl was standing beside her, calling her name. "Andrea, Andrea! Come back! Come back! I need your help. We all need you, Andrea. Please come back."

Help me, Andrea pleaded silently. Her hands gripped the man's white tailored shirt. The girl didn't seem to hear, for she turned and disappeared, a disappointed expression on her face, pleading as she went. "Please, Andrea. Help me!"

"Goodbye, girlie."

Andrea turned horror-filled eyes on Ol' Scarface, silently begging for her life. He gave one last squeeze, his evil laugh echoing inside her oxygen-starved brain. The fragile bones in her neck gave way with a sickening crack, and Andrea felt her body begin to slump toward the tunnel floor....

BAD DREAMS

Now was his chance! It was perfect timing, as long as Andrea stayed asleep. Tony glanced up over the top of his comic book to see his older sister Andrea reclining in the big seat beside him. Her eyes were shut, but she looked tense. Once or twice she muttered, restlessly twisting her head this way and that. It looked as if she was having a bad dream.

The motion of the huge Greyhound bus, as it rumbled over the prairie landscape, had finally lulled Andrea to sleep. Her head was turned slightly away from Tony, cushioned from the vibrations and bumps on the road by the dark sweatshirt she had placed between the window and her forehead. They had been travelling for several hours and Tony figured that they were already more than halfway to Moose Jaw. If he was going to succeed this time, he knew he had better do it now.

"Andrea," he called softly, his voice full of the eagerness of a nine-year-old about to embark on an exciting and dangerous act. The sound was lost in the roar of the engine. He tried again. "Andrea?"

She didn't stir. He tried once more, for good measure, calling more loudly this time. "Andrea?" He poked her arm a few times. She muttered in her sleep, pulling her arm around her body. He froze, holding his breath until she settled back into a deeper sleep. The woman on the seat across the aisle turned to study him. Tony wanted to stick his tongue out at her and tell her to mind her own business, but he didn't. Turning away from her, he poked Andrea once more. She muttered again but didn't move. She was sound asleep.

He could see her knapsack unzipped on the floor in front of her; its gaping mouth yawned invitingly at him. It tempted him, made him forget the many promises he had made to Andrea about never reading her diary. He knew just where she kept it too, in the medium-sized pocket on the front of the knapsack. Over the last few months he had made it his business to know. Finally his patience and keen observation skills would pay off.

Taking a deep breath, Tony moved cautiously forward to the edge of his seat. Andrea didn't move. He slid his short legs closer to the bag, and casting a glance at her slumbering form, he bent over and slipped his hand around the bag until his fingers touched the zippered pocket. His heart thumped in his chest, reminding him that he really shouldn't be doing this. A diary was a private thing. How many times had Andrea caught him looking for it this winter? How many times had she had to find a new hiding place? She had finally given up hiding it at home and now took it with her everywhere she went. It was safer with her, she had told him angrily the last time she had caught him rifling through the desk in her bedroom. Since then she always carried it in her knapsack.

Tony stealthily unzipped the smaller pocket on the front of the pack. He could feel the outline of the thick diary through the canvas. He knew it was there. The zipper slid open and he stuck his hand inside, his fingers latching onto the locked clasp meant for keeping secrets safe inside. The lock wasn't a problem for him, either. He knew where the key was kept. Beating back his conscience, he carefully reached around to the other side of the backpack. There he knew he would find a tiny Velcro flap. This was where Andrea kept the miniature key, the key which would reveal the secrets long kept hidden from him.

Diary in his lap, key in hand, Tony glanced over at Andrea once more. It seemed too good to be true.

Here, on their second trip to Moose Jaw in just over a year, he would finally get to read about everything she had been keeping secret from that first trip.

Something strange had happened then, he knew it. He had seen the way Grandpa Talbot and Aunt Bea had hovered around Andrea after her accident with the mirror at Cousin Vanessa's wedding rehearsal dinner last year. Andrea had run headfirst into the mirror that was used to block the entrance to an old tunnel. The tunnels of Moose Jaw were famous now, and this particular restaurant had two of them. Somehow Andrea had managed to run into the mirror. For several minutes, she had lain on the thick grey carpet, pale and still, a large bump forming on her forehead. After she had come to, she, Grandpa Talbot, and Aunt Bea had huddled in a corner of the restaurant, ignoring the rest of the family. They had been talking excitedly, but in whispers, as if they didn't want anyone else to hear. And they wouldn't talk about it with Tony, no matter how many times he had badgered them with questions, pleading to be let in on it all.

It was Aunt Bea who had presented Andrea with the diary the day after Cousin Vanessa's wedding. "To write down all of your memories, my dear Andrea Talbot," Tony had overheard her tell Andrea. They had shared a secret smile that had nearly driven him crazy with curiosity. It still bugged him when he thought about it. He wanted to know what had happened in Moose Jaw last year. He had a right to know! He was part of the family, but sometimes he didn't feel like it. He hadn't even gotten to be in Vanessa's wedding party! He could have carried the rings, or ushered people in, but no one had thought of that. And Andrea had gotten to be a junior bridesmaid, even though she didn't really like Cousin Vanessa. Andrea had teased and tormented Vanessa while they were growing up, even going so far as to cut off one of her pigtails in the middle of the night, and she still got to be in the wedding party! Life sure wasn't fair.

Sometimes, Tony wondered if he really was part of the family. People treated him differently now, like they were afraid he was going to break or something. He hated that. He didn't want to have to worry about what people thought about him, or about how they looked at him these days – like he was an invalid – like he couldn't take care of himself.

Pushing aside those bleak thoughts, he concentrated on opening the diary. Even though his fingers were shaking, the key slipped easily into the tiny slot. He turned it and the golden clasp popped open. Carefully pushing the key back into the small pocket in the knapsack, he securely closed the flap. Andrea would never know that he had read all of her secret thoughts. Glancing at her once more, he grasped the diary and slid carefully back into his seat. Opening the book to the first page he began to read....

Andrea awoke with a start, the remnants of a bad dream still clinging like a spiderweb to her sleep-fogged mind. Hot and sweaty, she pushed shoulder-length blonde hair out of her face and sat up, looking around, trying to remember where she was. The continuous, soothing motion of the Greyhound, like that of ocean waves, had finally lulled her to sleep in the big seat and she remembered that she was on the bus heading to Moose Jaw.

"Was I asleep long?" she asked in a hoarse voice. Her younger brother Tony sat in the seat beside her, reading a comic book.

Tony stared at her, eyes almost popping out of his head. His cheeks were flushed.

"Are you all right?" Andrea asked, concern in her voice. She turned and put her hand on his forehead, checking his temperature.

"I'm fine." Tony stumbled over the words, shrugging her hand away. He continued to stare at her, blue eyes wide, his mouth hanging open, but when she met his gaze with her concerned one, his eyes suddenly skittered away.

"What's with you?" Andrea studied her brother, alarm making her voice high-pitched. "You look as if you've seen a ghost!" She stared hard at him, brown eyes narrowing. "What have you been up to?"

"Nothing! And I told you I'm fine," he replied, his voice rough and angry. "You know I hate people asking how I am."

"Well, you don't look good. I'm worried about you."

"You're just worried because you don't know how to help me if I get into trouble on the bus," Tony sneered.

"I do so know how to help," Andrea returned, brushing tangled hair out of her face. "I went to the classes too, remember?"

"You just don't *want* to help me." He shook his comic book indignantly and went back to reading it, ignoring her, a scowl on his face.

Andrea sighed and turned back to face the window, watching as prairie farmland zipped past. There was no reasoning with Tony when he got like this, and it happened a lot these days. That was why her parents had gone to Victoria for the week. They hadn't had a break since the problems with him had come to light a few months ago. They needed a chance to get away for awhile. Besides, Grandma and Grandpa Talbot were going to be there. They had taken the classes, too. They would know how to handle Tony.

She didn't like to admit it, but he was right. She wasn't sure if she could help him. It wasn't that she didn't know what to do, and it wasn't that she didn't want to help. It was that she was afraid. She was terrified of what helping Tony meant.

She sighed as the bus took her ever closer to Moose Jaw. Now she had two big things to be worried about.

Life sure wasn't simple. People said that teenagers were the most carefree people in the world. At fourteen, she definitely didn't agree. She had way too much to worry about these days, and her worries about Tony and about being back in Moose Jaw again weren't helping to ease her mind.

She looked out of the bus window, catching a quick glimpse of a highway sign. With a sigh of resignation, she realized that it was only a matter of minutes before they reached the small city on the Saskatchewan prairie and pulled into the bus depot where her grandparents were going to meet them.

"You were muttering in your sleep," Tony commented vaguely, his nose still buried in the new comic book. "It was like you were having a bad dream or something."

"Yeah, or something," Andrea sighed, using both hands to smooth her hair back into place. She was obsessed with her hair these days, now that she had let it grow down to her shoulders. It was a lot different than the short, boyish haircut she had sported last year at this time.

"I called you a few times, and poked you –" Tony stopped reading long enough to demonstrate. "I tried to wake you up, but I guess you were really tired."

"Thanks," she replied. Well, that explained it then, she decided with relief. She had heard a persistent voice calling for help over and over in the dream. It must have been Tony. Only the voice hadn't sounded like Tony's at all. It had sounded faint but sweet, a trace of desperation echoing from the past. It sounded more like that of a frightened young girl, someone who really wanted Andrea's attention.

"You kept repeating a word over and over again. It sounded like 'scar' or something close to that." Tony was watching her very carefully, and it made her uncomfortable. It was as if he knew something that she didn't, but she couldn't figure out what. She was the one with all of the secrets these days.

She tried to forget that word, *scar,* and all of the images it conjured up. Unfortunately those images never disappeared entirely. They seemed to hover in the deepest corners of her mind, waiting until she least expected them. Then they would jump out, bringing scary memories that were best forgotten.

She did not want to think about Beanie, or Vance or anyone else from the past. She especially didn't want to think about Old Scarface and all of the problems and dangers she had encountered because of him. On the other hand, if she hadn't gone back to the past she would have never spent the wonderful time with her Great Aunt Bea, alias Beanie, or her Grandfather Talbot, whom she'd known as Vance. Together, they had had a wonderful, but often frightening time in 1920s Moose Jaw.

Andrea pushed these thoughts out of her mind.

"Pack up your things," she instructed Tony. "We're almost there." She watched as Tony dutifully tucked away his comic books alongside his laser gun, a remote car and the control, and a set of walkie-talkies – his favourite toys these days. She wondered what he would need them for, with no one else to play with, unless he met new friends in Moose Jaw. "What's this?" She picked up a thin booklet he had forgotten on the seat beside him.

"That's part of my birthday present from Grandma and Grandpa Talbot, remember?"

Andrea studied the small paperback book. It was titled *Moose Jaw Remembered* and showed a picture of the majestic-looking old post office which now served as city hall. "Why would he send you this for your birthday?"

Tony shrugged his shoulder. "What's really weird is what he wrote inside." He took the booklet out of Andrea's hand and opened it to the first page. "It says, 'To Tony, Study up on the history of Moose Jaw, you may need that information some day soon. Love, Grandma and Grandpa.'"

"That is weird," Andrea agreed, taking the book back and reading the inscription for herself. A tiny chill of apprehension ran down her spine and she squirmed. Grandpa Talbot was up to something. She could think of only one reason that he would want Tony to be knowledgeable about Moose Jaw's colourful past, and she refused to think about that. She quickly flipped through the booklet, noticing that there were a lot of photographs, which were grainy and dark. They were arranged in chronological order.

Skipping through the early history of Moose Jaw, she slowed down when she came to the 1920s. Having spent time there, she wondered if she might recognize some of the faces in the photographs. She turned the pages more slowly and came face to photograph with a scary-looking man who seemed vaguely familiar. Even through the old photograph his eyes felt cold and calculating, and Andrea shivered. The portrait showed a frowning man with a thin black moustache. Just looking at him gave her the creeps. Reading the caption below the photograph, she realized that he was a Sergeant in the Moose Jaw police force. He must have been good at his job, she thought, studying the old photograph once more. His eyes seemed to pierce her heart, and she quickly turned the page. She wouldn't want to run into him in some dark alley, and she was positive that most bad guys would have felt the same way. He sure looked mean. She couldn't shake the scary feeling that she had seen him somewhere before.

"There's a cool biplane near the back of the book," Tony told her, reaching to turn the pages. "See. Isn't it great?"

Andrea examined the photograph of the old plane,

a shiver of excitement running down her spine. The people in the picture looked very familiar, especially two of the kids. She bent her head to look more closely just as the bus driver sang out, "Next stop, Moose Jaw." Snapping the book shut, she thrust it in Tony's direction. She would study the photograph later, when she had time.

She grabbed the few items she had left scattered around her on the large bus seat and began stuffing them into her knapsack. Her hand went unconsciously to the side pocket, checking to make sure that her diary was safely tucked inside. Breathing a sigh of relief, she felt its square corners pushing against the fabric. It was safe and sound, zipped into the small pocket. Checking the seat around her, she made sure that she had picked everything up, trying hard to shut the door on her thoughts, but that door refused to stay shut. No matter what Andrea did, something always reminded her of her Moose Jaw adventure. When that happened, the door would spring open again, spilling secrets and memories into her troubled mind, bringing back names and faces which she would rather not remember.

Old Scarface, that was the name she didn't want to think about. She had been trying for a whole year to forget that one fateful night in Moose Jaw, and she had almost succeeded. But recently the dreams had started again in full force. Those frightening yet wispy bits of fantasy seemed so real. They robbed her of her sleep, left her sweat-drenched and tight-fisted, clutching the twisted bed sheets to her chest. At least she didn't remember her latest dream. Maybe it hadn't been about Old Scarface at all. She usually remembered those, waking up with a start, a scream lodged in her throat.

She shuddered and shook off the horrible images. She didn't know which was worse, Scarface, with his dangerous, cruel laugh, scaring her awake at night, or the sudden and determined voice of that young girl, plaintive yet demanding, calling through the years. That voice seemed to be reaching to draw her back to that surreal time, the night that she wished had all been a dream, the night that she wished she could forget.

The voice echoed in her head again, sounding hauntingly familiar. Whose voice was it, she wondered. She wracked her brain, trying to remember. Suddenly a picture of Beanie, hunched up against a huge armoire, thin arms encircling her knees, sprang into her mind. The voice belonged to Beanie! The dream swirled vividly again and she heard Beanie's voice pleading with her to return to the past. She saw the two men holding her in the tunnels, felt fingers pressing against her throat. Goose bumps popped out on her forearms. Was Beanie really trying to call her back? And what about those horrible men? Was

Beanie in some kind of trouble with them? Maybe the person getting strangled in her dream wasn't herself at all! Maybe it was Beanie! Andrea was torn. She sure didn't want anything to happen to Beanie, but she still didn't want to return to the past.

She hadn't wanted to return to Moose Jaw at all. She had fought and complained, cried and begged and pleaded with her parents until they were beside themselves with frustration. Then her grandfather had called, his cheerful, still boyish voice ringing in her ears. Andrea could never say no to Grandpa Talbot. She had always had a soft spot in her heart for him, but it had grown since their Moose Jaw adventure last year, when she had gotten to know him as the teenager, Vance. He had gently reminded her that her parents needed a break from the stress of Tony's ailment, and that it was best that she and Tony come to Moose Jaw for a few days. That way her parents could go away knowing that he would be safe. She had finally, reluctantly, agreed to return to Moose Jaw.

As the bus pulled into the city, the tiny voice continued to call for help in the deepest parts of Andrea's mind. It seemed to be growing louder, more persistent, demanding attention. A sense of dread filled her soul as the bus rumbled down the long hill at the end of Main Street, drawing her ever closer to the bus depot and closer to the past. She had a feeling that this might turn out to be the kind of holiday she had been hoping to avoid. She really didn't want to spend a minute in Moose Jaw this summer. She especially did not want to end up in the past again, not with the nightmares and bad dreams she'd been having. They must be an omen of some kind. With a sigh of resignation, she picked up her backpack and prepared to follow Tony off the bus. Like it or not, she was here for a few days. She just hoped that she could keep the past where it belonged, down in the tunnels and safely away from her.

WHERE IS EVERYONE?

"Somebody had better pay me back that wad of money I just spent on the taxi ride over here!" Andrea stood in the afternoon heat, glaring down the street at the departing vehicle. The driver had dumped the luggage on the sidewalk, grabbed his money, and jumped into the waiting car. She kicked childishly at the pile of bags at her feet; she was hot, cranky, and miserable, and a weird feeling of doom hung over her like a sheet ready to engulf her. "I didn't want to come here in the first place! I didn't want to spend my babysitting money on a cab. And I especially don't want to spend my vacation here with you."

Tony rolled his eyes. "Don't be such a grouch, Andrea. It's not *my* fault that you had to come. If I'd had my way, I would have left you at home! I'm sure I'd have way more fun without you breathing down my neck all day!"

Andrea shot daggers at him with fierce brown eyes. "Be quiet, Squirt. I'm not in the mood to argue with you right now. We've phoned and phoned! Where is everyone?" She had asked that question at least a hundred times since the bus had deposited them on the hot dusty sidewalk almost an hour ago. "What's going on around here? Why didn't anyone meet us at the bus depot?"

Tony stared at the house. "I saw a movie like this once. The relatives the kids were supposed to visit were missing! No one believed the kids so they had to solve the mystery all on their own. It was great."

"That won't happen to us. That was just a dumb movie." She studied her watch, then looked up to see Tony sprint along the sidewalk. He bounded up the stairs and pounded on the screen door, then turned back to look at her, shrugging his thin shoulders, a frown worrying the corners of his mouth.

"I wonder where they could be?" Andrea asked as Tony trudged back toward her. "They wouldn't leave us alone unless something bad happened to them." They both studied the big house from the street, wondering what to do next.

"You know, that movie started out with the main character having bad dreams, too. I wonder if your dreams are a sign, you know, an omen or something like that. I wonder if they're about some mysterious, secret past."

Tony's seemingly innocent words shook Andrea. That was exactly what she was afraid to admit. She had hoped that her dreams were just something left over from her strange trip the summer before. She didn't want to think that she might have supernatural powers that allowed her to communicate with another world.

"What's the matter?" Tony asked, his voice sly. "You look like you've seen a ghost."

"I think I have," Andrea admitted, staring up at the vaguely familiar-looking house. Sure, it was her grandparents' house, but somehow it was more than that to her. Grabbing a piece of luggage from the pile at her feet, she marched up the walk, feeling confused and worried. A big sigh escaped her tense lips as she climbed the wide steps to the porch and sat down on the top step to wait for Grandpa or Grandma Talbot to return home. "I'm worried about Grandpa and Grandma," she said softly, staring out across the street. "Something isn't right around here. Can't you feel it?" She rubbed at the goosebumps on her skin, feeling herself shiver even though the blistering sun shone down upon her. "It feels like that time just before a bad storm. You know, don't you? The air feels thick and the wind gets really still and it's as if – as if everyone is waiting for something bad to happen."

She looked around. "That's how I feel right now, like I'm waiting for something bad to happen."

Tony put his face up and sniffed at the hot afternoon air like a dog trying to catch a scent. "I can't feel anything," he commented, "and the only thing I smell is smoke. It smells like someone's having a barbecue." He licked his lips. "I wonder if Grandma will make her famous barbecue chicken for us for dinner tonight. That's my favourite." Tony sat down beside her, looking at her with a strange, appraising glint in his eyes. "Whatever is worrying you, you can tell me, you know," he said, trying to sound grown-up and sincere. "I might be able to help. I'm not a kid anymore."

"You're right," Andrea said softly; maybe Tony could help. She had kept all those feelings and memories trapped inside for a whole year, her only outlet, her diary, which she wrote in daily. Mostly she wrote about the events of the day, but at least once a week, she wrote about her fantastic time-travel visit to Moose Jaw. Even after a whole year, the past wouldn't leave her alone. She had to keep revisiting it, trying to make sense of what had happened to her, trying to understand why she was the one who had been given the chance to travel back in time. She hadn't told a single person about her incredible journey. Only her Aunt Bea and Grandpa Talbot knew exactly what had happened and that was because they had been there.

When Andrea didn't answer Tony spoke. "I know

when those dreams started," he asserted. "It was just after Vanessa's wedding; just after our last trip to Moose Jaw." He rubbed his hand over his chin, a knowing look on his face. "I wonder what could have happened to make you have all those bad dreams."

Andrea's eyes narrowed into tiny slits as she studied her brother. What had she been thinking? She couldn't share those dreams with him, she had promised. He was just scheming again, trying to find a way to get her to talk. "Get off those dreams, will you? They're just stress because of school and – and other things," she said. Suddenly she had had enough. She was angry with Tony and was looking for a way to shut him up, to make him leave her alone, and she found it. "Those dreams are because of the stress you've caused this family too, you know!" Her voice was heavy with innuendo and accusation.

"Me?"

Andrea wished she could take back the hateful words the moment they flew out of her mouth. Tony's face turned pasty white, tears forming in his blue eyes. He slumped down on the stairs, as if his body was suddenly very tired and would no longer support his weight.

"I didn't do it on purpose," he cried, tears slipping down his cheeks. "It's not my fault! I don't like it any better than you do! I hate it! I wish it hadn't happened to me."

"Oh, Tony," Andrea sighed. She tried to hug him,

to comfort him. She wanted to take back the terrible things she had said, but he pushed her roughly away.

"Leave me alone," he yelled. "Just leave me alone. You don't like me anymore! No one likes me! I'm a problem for everyone and I hate it!"

Andrea stayed beside Tony and tried again to put her arm around his shoulders. She realized with a gulp of concern how thin he was. His shoulder blades felt sharp, and he was small for his age. "I'm sorry, Tony," she whispered, tears gathering in her throat. "I really didn't mean it. It just slipped out. I'm sorry."

Tony let her arm stay in place, his face buried in his hands. "Yeah, you meant it. I am a problem now. Everyone has to be worried about me."

"I was just angry," Andrea argued, snuggling closer to him. "I was looking for a way to hurt you. It wasn't fair. I'm sorry."

Tony scrubbed at his face with his fists. "I hate this! I don't want people to be worried about me! I just want to be me! I just want to be healthy!"

Andrea had no reply for that. She wanted him to be healthy, too. "Come on, let's go see if that secret key is still hidden in the back stairwell. Remember? The one Grandpa told us about?"

"Yeah," Tony sighed, wiping away his tears. He stood up and walked slowly down the stairs and onto the lawn, his feet dragging. He stopped suddenly, staring up at the house. "Are we sure no one's home?"

he asked in that smart-aleck voice that only a younger brother could excel at. "After all, Grandpa and Grandma may have gotten back by now, from wherever they've been. Maybe they came in the back and they're inside taking a nap. Or maybe they've been kidnapped!"

Andrea rolled her eyes and punched him lightly on the arm. "Come off it, Tony," she said, looking at the house, searching for any sign of life. "I don't think they're home." She looked around, noting trim grass and lush flowers in the front flower beds. Everything looked normal. "Something just doesn't feel right. Somehow the house looks as if everyone's gone away on vacation or something. I just don't like the feeling I've got right here." She pointed to her stomach. "As if something's going to happen."

Tony stared up at the old three-storey house that belonged to his grandparents. "Yeah, I know what you mean." Tony rubbed his tummy. "I can feel it, too."

"Things sure aren't starting out well here. It's almost as if they weren't expecting us or something."

Andrea stomped off around the side of the house, frustration, anger and worry gnawing at her. She knew she was acting like a spoiled brat and she was having trouble understanding the emotional roller coaster she was riding. If she wasn't arguing with Tony, she was hurting his feelings, or she was mad about something else. She had been in a foul mood since her parents had put her on the bus that afternoon and her bad dream sure hadn't improved her disposition. It wasn't like her to be grumpy for long, and she didn't usually pick on Tony any more, not since he had gotten sick and had to spend so many days in the hospital. She tried hard not to pick on him. Usually she just ignored him. It was easier to deal with everything that way, but Tony and his condition and being in Moose Jaw were big problems pressing urgently against her.

This definitely wouldn't turn out to be a good time, she was sure of it.

ALL ALONE

Pushing worrisome thoughts out of her mind, Andrea concentrated on finding the key. She remembered Grandpa Talbot telling her about it once when she had come alone to stay with her grandparents for a few days. But that was at least two years ago. Would the key still be there? She remembered that her grandfather had said it was hidden in the outside stairwell around the back of the house. It was an old-fashioned entrance that led directly into the basement. It was covered by a heavy wooden door, which lay slanted over the aging cement steps.

As Andrea rounded the corner of the house, pushing open the white gate, a sense of déjà vu washed over her. She stopped short, staring hard at the huge door that lay at a lazy angle over the basement stairs.

Her breath caught in her throat and a familiar feeling of panic settled in her stomach. She glanced up to study the windows looking out over the backyard. In the middle of the house, three windows, one on each floor, stared back at her. In a sudden flash of memory, she saw dark windows with curtains blowing in the night breeze. She could see herself throwing pebbles up at the third-floor window to get Rosie's attention.

Why, of course! This was the house Rosie had lived in! Why hadn't she realized it before now? Rosie had rented a few rooms on the third floor of the house. Andrea and Vance had had to climb out that very window on the night Andrea had gone back in time. Vance, with his wounded arm, had wanted her to break his fall. She grinned now, just thinking about how she had promised to catch him. Instead he had bumped her and they had both fallen to their knees. She could smile about it now, but she knew that Vance had been in a lot of pain that night.

Why hadn't Grandpa Talbot told her that he had bought Rosie's house? It was amazing to think that he and Grandma Talbot actually lived in what used to be the rooming house where Rosie lived. What was more surprising was that Andrea hadn't even recognized it. She guessed that was due to the stress and excitement of the night. Besides, it had looked very different then; after all, the house had aged more than seventy years!

Andrea remembered it from the 1920s as a tall

wood frame house painted white. It was now sided with blue-grey aluminum siding and had a metre-high white fence wrapping the property. A large carport had been built on to the side of the house and a huge garage had been added at the back of the lot. Andrea wasn't observant at the best of times, and the last time she had been in Moose Jaw she had had so much to think about. Too many strange incidents had taken place so quickly that identifying a house was the last thing on her mind.

This was the only house Andrea remembered her grandparents ever living in. It made Andrea feel more worried than ever to think that she was actually in the exact location where so many bizarre things had happened last year. She was back in the house that held at least two entrances into the Moose Jaw tunnels. Andrea knew this for a fact, she had used those two tunnels several times herself the night she had been transported back in time. One of the tunnel entrances was in the basement of the house, hidden behind the huge armoire that she and Vanessa had pushed away from the wall the night before the wedding. That was the tunnel entrance she almost always dreamed about. The armoire would often mysteriously slide open, revealing a gaping black hole. Long arms would coil out to grab her, pulling her into the tunnels, trapping her until she awoke, panic stricken and sweat-drenched in her bed.

The other tunnel entrance was located in the back

stairwell, which was an outside entrance into the basement. Andrea remembered that the tunnel passageway was located on the left-hand side of the stairs as she faced the basement wall. A small wooden door hid the tunnel entrance from view, and Andrea was sure that most people using the stairs would never see it. They would be looking straight ahead at the larger door, which led into the basement. These two tunnels actually joined up very quickly just a hundred metres or so from the house, when the smaller tunnel turned sharply. Rosie had said that Ol' Scarface and his business partner had had the second tunnel entrance built directly into the basement as a way of getting into the house undetected.

Andrea shuddered as she got closer to the slanted door covering the back stairwell. The tunnels scared her, especially after all the bad dreams she had been having. She was afraid that they would lure her until, like a fish caught on a line, she was trapped, stuck back in time.

Remembering how heavy the door covering the outside stairs was, Andrea bent and reached for the handle with both hands. The key was all she wanted. With a loud grunt she heaved the door open. The hinges were stiff from disuse and squealed loudly in the quiet afternoon air. As the door settled open in a wide lazy V, Andrea's hands tingled. It was as if an electric shock had run through them. Nerves and apprehension tightened into a knot in her stomach. Moose Jaw held far too many memories for her, memories of too many freakish events that she didn't want to relive. She had tried to convince herself that it had all been a weird dream, but she knew that it was real. What were the chances of it happening again, she wondered. Was it possible to go back to the past twice in a lifetime? It would be like winning a lottery or getting struck by lightning, she decided; a pretty minuscule chance. Those kinds of things just didn't happen, and certainly not to the same person.

"Hey, what's with you?"

Andrea jumped. She hadn't realized that Tony had followed her into the backyard. He was getting hot and cranky and was tired of standing in the glaring sun. "You're staring at the house as if you don't recognize it or something!"

"Keep your shirt on, Brother," she retorted irritably as she gazed down the cellar stairs, searching the dark corners created by the angle of the door against the foundation of the house.

Tony peered around her into the gloomy space. "There's something shiny hanging way back there." He jumped down the stairs, landing with a bang. "It's a key!" He grabbed it from a tiny nail near the low ceiling. As he turned to head back up the stairs, Tony saw the faint outline of a rectangle in the wall. "Look Andrea," he called excitedly, pointing to the ancient and decaying wall. "There's a door down here! Where do you think it leads?" He reached for the rusty latch.

"Don't touch that," Andrea yelled. She flew down the rotting steps, grabbing at his clothes, and pulled him up into the bright afternoon sunlight.

"All right, all right," Tony muttered, twisting out of her grasp. "Keep your shirt on." He knew what would make Andrea jumpy and nervous. Smiling, he watched her slam the heavy door shut and march stiffly toward the front of the house. He gazed back at the door. That mark on the wall, that old wooden door was a tunnel entrance, one he had read about in the diary. He couldn't wait to open the door and start exploring!

"Tony," Andrea yelled impatiently from the front yard. He sprinted around the large house. Tunnel exploring would have to wait until big sister wasn't around.

"Let's go see if this key fits. If it doesn't we're in big trouble."

"It'll work." Tony was certain. Something inside told him it would. He walked out to where the cab driver had left their luggage and picked up the rest. Bags hanging from both arms and one suspended around his neck, he struggled up the walk.

"How do you know it'll work?" Andrea asked.

Awkwardly climbing the stairs, Tony dropped the luggage on the porch and shrugged his shoulders.

"Some things I just know, and I know that key will work."

Andrea wrestled the old key into the lock. "It works," she called as she turned the knob. She glanced over her shoulder at Tony, a puzzled look on her face. The door opened into the large house and they stepped inside. "Hello?" Her voice echoed up the wooden stairs against the wall and drifted into the living room off to the right and down the narrow hallway and into the big kitchen. Everything looked normal, as if Grandma and Grandpa Talbot had just stepped out for the day. Still, something didn't seem right. It was as if the old house held more secrets than even she knew about.

"No one's here," Tony reported. He walked into the kitchen. "Hey, here's a note!"

"What does it say?" Andrea had been grabbing the luggage off the porch and lugging it into the hallway, a small pile collecting at her feet. She set the last piece down and shut the screen door, leaving the old-fashioned wood door open to coax fresh air into the house.

Tony quickly scanned the note and then handed it to her, his eyes large with concern. "Grandma and Grandpa Talbot had to take Aunt Bea to Edmonton for that de-defib –"

"Oh no," Andrea moaned. "You mean, they got the call?" Snatching the note from Tony's outstretched hand, she quickly scanned it. "They just got the call today to take Aunt Bea to get that defibrillator for her heart! They tried to get in touch with Mom and Dad but missed them. Aunt Bea has been on that waiting list for months and her turn finally came up."

Tony grabbed the note back. "Vanessa is supposed to be here to look after us." He made gagging sounds and laid his head on the table. A small stack of bills caught his attention. "Look! They left money, too." He held up a fistful of green paper dollars and a couple of red ones. "I'll bet it's for us to do fun things with around here."

"Give me that note back!" Andrea grabbed it again, leaving him to count the money. "It says it's for groceries, Tony." She scanned the note again. "But does it say when they'll be back?" She tried to keep the worry from creeping into her voice. Her grandparents must have been desperate to go and desperate to find someone to look after them, if they'd left Vanessa in charge. She was about the most unreliable person Andrea knew, always going back on her promises.

"No," Tony whispered, his luminous eyes staring at her. "And where's Vanessa? She's better than no one, even if I don't really like her. I like her husband, Greg. He's a cool guy. He plays baseball with me." Tony's face brightened. "Maybe he's coming, too."

Andrea heaved a huge sigh. "I hope so, but I wouldn't count on Greg if I were you. He's in the air force and he's stationed somewhere else right now."

"Look," Tony pointed to the answering machine on the desk next to the fridge. "It's blinking. There's a message on it." He walked over and stood staring at the machine. "Do you think we should listen to the messages? They might be private." He felt a pinch of guilt as he remembered the diary. He hadn't worried about privacy then.

Andrea reached over Tony's shoulder and pushed the button. "Yeah, we'd better listen to the messages. I have a feeling one of them will be from Vanessa, and it won't be good news."

"We're not going to like what she has to say," Tony predicted.

Andrea squeezed his shoulder, dread making her breathing shallow. Instinct told her that he was right.

There were four messages on the machine. The first two were for her grandparents. The next message was from Grandpa Talbot saying that they had arrived safely and giving the telephone number of the hotel in which they were staying. They promised to phone again soon to see how everyone was making out, and to give an update on Aunt Bea. The last message was from Vanessa, her cheerful voice filling the kitchen:

"Hi, Gram and Gramps. I'm sorry, but I can't be there for Andrea and Tony like I said I could. Something has come up. You'll just have to make other arrangements. I'm off to see Greg. He just got a surprise leave. Anyway, bye...I love you...."

Andrea and Tony stared at one another as the afternoon sun filtered into the large windows around them. Even in the bright kitchen, Andrea felt troubled.

Tony's mouth hung open in fear. "Oh no, Andrea. We're all alone," he gasped. "What are we going to do?"

ANDREA – IN CHARGE

Andrea gathered up her courage. "I'm fourteen," she reminded them both, trying to make her voice firm and confident. "We can stay here alone for a few days. I'm sure we can manage." But could they really, she wondered.

Tony chewed on his lower lip, tears filling his eyes. "I don't think we can, Andrea. Don't you know what that means?"

"What does it mean?" Her voice was sharp with impatience. "It means that we're here alone for a few days. Big deal, Tony! I am fourteen," she repeated, as if that answered every concern they might have. "I can handle things around here for a few days."

"But who will help me?" Tony whispered. A huge tear gathered in the corner of his right eye. It slid over the lid and rolled down his pale cheek, magnifying each freckle as it slid past. When she didn't reply he grabbed the phone and began to push the buttons.

"What are you doing?" Andrea asked, snatching the phone from his grasp. "Who are you calling?"

"I'm calling Grandma! She's supposed to be here to help me!"

"No!" Andrea yelled, keeping her hand firmly on the phone. "Don't call Grandma. She needs to be with Aunt Bea right now!"

"Then I'll call Mom and Dad! I don't care who I call, I just need help!" Tony tried to wrestle the phone from her grasp. "Give me that! I need someone! You can't help me! You don't know what to do! You've never done it before!"

"You can try to phone Mom and Dad, but they're probably flying over the Rockies right now, so you won't be able to reach them!" Andrea slammed the phone down. "Anyway, I can help you," she said quickly, before she had time to comprehend what that would mean. This was her chance to show everyone how grown-up she had become. She should be able to look after Tony for two or three days. It shouldn't be that difficult. "I'll do it," she said more loudly. She wondered who she was trying to convince, herself or Tony. "I said I can do it for you."

"You?" He almost laughed in disbelief. "You're a chicken! You hate this kind of thing almost as much as I do! How can you help me? Besides that, all we do these days is fight. I don't think we'll be able to get along for even two minutes! I want to phone Mom!"

Andrea felt her heart beating loudly and took a deep breath. "Look, you can't phone Mom and Dad right now. And I can help, Tony. I know what to do." She tried to calm herself down. "I promise not to argue with you for the next three days, Tony," she said. "Scout's honour." She held up the appropriate fingers.

He eyed her warily, his grip on the phone loosening. "You were never a Boy Scout," he said.

She rolled her eyes. "I'm making a promise, all right? Come on," she urged.

"I don't know," he said, tears brimming. "Do you really think you can do it?"

"Look, I'll try. I'll try really hard. I just think that we can do this alone. We don't need to bring Mom and Dad back from their vacation just for this. And Grandma and Grandpa Talbot are obviously very worried about Aunt Bea or one of them would have stayed. And Tony, I'm sure I can do better than Vanessa!"

He smiled, a tentative smile. "Yeah, I know you can do better than her. She'd probably faint. I wonder if she knew exactly what she was in for when she agreed to stay with us. Maybe that's why she chickened out."

I might faint too, Andrea thought, but she didn't

say the words aloud. There was no sense in getting him more upset than he already was. "Please, Tony," Andrea pleaded. "Let me try." She wondered why she was begging so hard. She really didn't want to do this for Tony. It scared her silly to think about what it meant, but she had to press on. "We can manage, Tony. I know we can. Let's give it a try."

Tony's quick breathing filled the kitchen. He was silent for so long that she was beginning to think that he hadn't heard her. Finally he took a deep breath and sat up, clutching at her arm. "All right," he said, "if you think you can do it."

"Sure I can do it," she said with bravado. She squeezed her cold fingers together into fists, hiding them behind her back so that he wouldn't see them shaking.

"Well, we have to do it now," he said as he searched her eyes.

"Now?" She drew back. It was too soon. She needed time to psyche herself up. She saw him begin to pull away again, reaching for the phone. "N-now," she agreed, trying to keep her voice from shaking. "I forgot, we need to do it before you eat, and I'm getting hungry." She coughed to clear her clogged throat. "Go get your stuff. Where do you want to do it?"

Tony went in search of his luggage, still piled up by the front door. "I like to lie down. I always feel faint afterwards." He stood looking up the narrow wooden staircase that led to the bedrooms on the second floor and then turned away. "Let's use Grandpa's office in the basement. That's where I want to sleep."

"Not there," Andrea protested. She was hoping to avoid that room on this trip. That was where the entrance to one of the tunnels was located, and she didn't want to be reminded of it every time she went in search of her little brother.

Tony looked defiant again, a scowl darkening his face. "That's where you and Vanessa got to sleep last year," he accused. "See, I told you it wouldn't work. We can't even get along for two seconds. We're fighting again! I'm calling Mom and Dad."

Andrea sighed. "All right, all right. You lead the way down to the basement."

Tony gathered up his things and headed back through the narrow hallway to the kitchen. "You know, you'll have to cook the meals around here."

Andrea gaped at him. She hadn't thought about that. "Well, you can help too, you know," she retorted. She saw a look flash over his face. "We'll make your favourite foods, Tony," she said. "It'll be fun, you'll see."

"I can't eat my favourite foods anymore. Not the way I want to, anyway!" Tony grabbed his bag and hauled it toward the basement stairs in the kitchen, tears making his blue eyes glisten. "I am sleeping in Grandpa's office downstairs," he roared. "And you can't stop me!" He ran noisily down the wooden steps, threw open the office door and then slammed it shut with a resounding bang.

Andrea stood alone in the kitchen, shaking her head after Tony. It was so hard to reason with him these days. She never knew what would set him off. Hadn't she already agreed to let him sleep in the office? Andrea wanted to argue with Tony. She wanted to plead with him to stay anywhere in the house, anywhere but in the basement. She wished that she could push the stove or refrigerator in front of the basement door so that nothing could get up or down the stairs. But it looked as if Tony had his heart set on staying down there and she could tell by the mood he was in that he wouldn't change his mind, so she was stuck having to revisit the basement after being away from it for over a year.

She picked up the phone, deciding to try her parents and see if they'd arrived. She found the number to the hotel on the message board near the phone and punched in the long series of numbers. The call was brief. Her parents hadn't checked in yet. "No, I won't leave a message, thanks. I'll try again later," she said. She was hanging up when she heard Tony's voice calling from below.

"Andrea." He still sounded irritated. "Are you coming any time soon, or what? See, I told you this wouldn't work."

"I'm coming, I'm coming," she shouted, then muttered, "Hold your horses." She had heard her grand-parents use that expression; it certainly fit Tony today. Taking a calming breath, she pulled the door farther open. Two frightening things awaited her arrival in Grandpa's basement office: the procedure that she had to do on Tony, and the huge wooden armoire that stood in the corner of the room. She wasn't sure which she feared the most. She wished she could run away from her fears, but like it or not, she had to enter that basement room and face them.

She put her foot on the first step.

A tingling feeling immediately spread up her spine. It was as if an invisible force was reaching out to sur-round her. She walked slowly down the wooden stair-case, her fingers gripping the worn rail. Each step down toward the basement intensified her sense of being pulled back into the past. She felt her heart speed up as her foot touched the hard cement floor. She skirted the old-fashioned furnace and came face to face with the closed office door. She took a deep breath to steady her nerves and slowly let it out, then she knocked politely on the door, and only entered the room when Tony gave a curt reply.

She pushed the door open, her breath coming out in soft gasps. She didn't want to be in the basement at all and she certainly didn't want to be in this room, not after what had happened last year. The huge wooden cupboard leered at her from across the small room, taunting her to look behind it, if she dared. She took another deep breath and turned her back to the mocking armoire. "Okay," she panted, out of breath, nervousness making her hands shake. "Here I am. Let's get it over with."

Tony was madly searching through his knapsack, pulling out comic books and toys and tossing them right and left onto the tile floor. "I can't find my stuff to do the tests," he muttered as he searched.

"Here, let me look," Andrea said, noticing that he already had tiny beads of sweat forming on his upper lip. That wasn't a good sign. "I'm sure I can find it." Tony dropped to the edge of the bed, waiting. Andrea could feel his tension as well as her own. She wondered when they would get used to this procedure that had to be carried out daily.

She found the necessary items at the bottom of his knapsack and pulled them out. "Are you ready?"

Tony took a deep breath and lay back on the bed against the pillows, his face pale. He squeezed his eyes tightly shut. "I'm as ready as I'll ever be," he muttered savagely. "I hate this. I hate having diabetes. Why did it have to happen to me? Why now?"

"I don't know, Tony." She was trying to sound calm, while her nervous fingers fumbled with the small zippered bag. She had never actually done this before, except on oranges. Truth to tell, she had only watched the procedure once and it was all she could do not to be sick. She sure didn't want to be a nurse. "Okay, Tony. I've found the blood-testing meter and the bottle of lancets." She unscrewed the lid and pulled one blue plastic lancet out. She broke off the small circular shape, leaving a sharp needle exposed. The lancet looked like a small piece of blue Lego with a very sharp needle sticking out of one end. "How do you load this thing?" she said.

Tony sighed noisily. "You forgot to load the blood glucose sensor. You have to get that ready first."

"Oh, that's right," she said, feeling foolish and awkward. She picked up the black, wallet-size pouch from the bed and opened it. Inside she found the sensor that would measure the amount of glucose in Tony's blood. The plastic device fit nicely in the palm of her hand. She found the foil-wrapped blood glucose electrode strips and tore one open. She pulled the tiny strip out and inserted it into the blood glucose measuring device, making sure to leave the small oval exposed. This was where Tony's drop of blood would go, if she was brave enough to poke his finger. "Okay, that's all ready to go." She put the sensoring device down on the bed, noting that the word "ready" had appeared in the small display window. "Now I just have to load this thing."

Taking a deep breath, she picked up the plastic pen-shaped lancing device and unscrewed the top, which fell from her nervous fingers onto the bed. She carefully pushed the lancet into place and screwed the top back on. "I've loaded the lancet. Now to get a sample of blood."

"Just call it a 'poker,'" Tony said between gritted teeth. "That's what it does, it pokes me and makes me bleed, and it hurts! I don't want to know what you're doing. Just do it!"

Andrea squeezed her eyes shut for a moment and willed her thumping heart to be still. She was already a nervous wreck and the worst part was yet to come.

Keeping her fingers steady, Andrea massaged the middle finger on Tony's left hand. She took another deep breath, exhaling loudly into the silent room. Everything seemed to be holding its breath, waiting to see if she could continue. She placed the poker against the pad of his finger and pushed the small button. Nothing happened. "Sorry, Tony," she muttered, "I forgot to spring-load the device." She wiped clammy hands on the bedspread. She pulled the top of the poker back until it clicked. Tony winced at the sound. She squeezed his finger again.

"Ouch," Tony complained, pulling his hand away. "You're hurting me! This never happens when Mom does it."

"Sorry," Andrea said, her own patience growing thin.

Tony squeezed his eyes shut again. "Do it," he said flatly. Andrea jabbed the poker against his finger,

47

squeezing her own eyes shut. She pushed the button. A small click was heard in the deathly quiet room as the spring released the needle, sending it into Tony's finger.

Tony jumped from the pain. "Ow-w-w," he complained. "I think you bruised the bone. You were pressing too hard."

Andrea ignored his whining complaints. She had enough to worry about. Wiping the sweat from her brow with a shaking hand, she took Tony's finger and pressed near the cut. A bright drop of blood formed on the pad, which she smeared onto the strip sticking out of the blood glucose sensor, watching as it counted down the seconds. She handed Tony a cotton ball, which he pressed against his sore finger. "You'll have to help me read this, Tony," she said. "I don't have much experience at translating the information."

"Me either," Tony admitted. "Grandma was the one who was supposed to be doing this. Here," he sighed, reaching for the machine. "Let me see it." He reluctantly took the small machine from her cold fingers. "I think I'll need 15 units of insulin." He picked up a syringe from the case on the bed, showing her the gauge on the side of the tube.

"I hope you're right," she said as she carefully picked up the bottle of insulin and pushed the sharp needle into the rubber top. She held the bottle upside down, as she had seen her mother do, and watched carefully as she slowly pulled the plunger on the syringe. Insulin flowed into the narrow tube. With shaking fingers she set the insulin bottle down. "Okay," she whispered, "ready?" Her heart felt as if it was going to beat its way out of her chest. Sweat formed droplets all over her face. They began to roll down her forehead and into her eyes. She brushed at the sweat with her sleeve. "Wh-wh," she cleared her throat noisily and tried again. "Where do you want me to give you this?" Her voice squeaked and she wiped sweating palms on her jeans.

"In my leg," Tony answered. "Remember, it's supposed to be in a place where I can give it to myself." He was wearing jeans, which he pulled up further on his skinny thigh. "I hate this part the worst."

Me too, Andrea thought. She was panting now, and she wondered if she was going to faint. She felt light-headed and her hands were shaking so badly she doubted that she'd be able to get the needle into his leg properly. After swabbing at a spot on his thigh, she squeezed her fingers tightly and shook them out. They felt nerveless and dead. "I don't know if I can do this," she admitted, tears gathering in her eyes. "I'm scared, Tony. I'm really scared!"

Tony's eyes were shut tight, his freckles standing out starkly against ashen skin. "You have to, Andrea," he replied, a tear rolling out of the corner of one eye. "It's too late to get anyone else. You have to do it.

You've done it before."

"Not for real," she reminded him, wiping the tears from her own face. "I-I only practiced on the oranges at class that day, and that was hard enough. I never thought I'd actually have to do it, Tony. I just went in case there was ever an emergency and you needed me to do it. That's all. It was never supposed to be for real!"

"Well, this *is* for real. This *is* the emergency," Tony's voice was urgent, coming in sharp breaths between clenched teeth. "Do it, Andrea, or I'll end up in the hospital! How would Mom and Dad feel if you refused to do it and I had to go to the hospital?"

Andrea knew what they would think and feel about that, and it made up her mind. Hands shaking almost uncontrollably, she swabbed the spot again. Holding the dispenser in trembling fingers, she gently placed its sharp tip against Tony's skin. She took a deep, deep breath and slowly exhaled. Her heart thudded in her ears. There was no one else to do this, she reminded herself. Tony needed the insulin or he'd be in big trouble.

She held her breath, feeling more tears well up in her eyes and spill over her cheeks. It took every muscle in her body to control her quaking hands, but she did it. She applied some pressure, watching through squinting eyes as the needle slid under the skin. She pushed the plunger down and counted to ten, just to be sure all of the insulin went into Tony's body. Then she pulled the needle out and laid it on the desk beside the bed and collapsed in a quaking heap beside a weeping Tony. She pulled him into her arms, crying and comforting them both.

TROUBLES WITH TONY

How long they lay there, wrapped in misery and exhaustion, Andrea wasn't sure. She suddenly came to, realizing that her eyes were riveted to the armoire. Memories assailed her. She willed herself to get to her feet and move toward the door, to leave this room, to escape the pull of the armoire. But something held her captive. Perhaps the cupboard was enchanted, she thought fleetingly, before all logical thought escaped her.

The need to remember, to relive those amazing events of last year was so strong that she could no longer resist. She sank farther down upon the pillows and was immediately lost in a world that should not have existed, but did exist. She let the memories that she had kept locked away in her subconscious for over a year come spilling out. Memories of Prohibition and rum-running, memories that drew her back to the incredible journey that she had experienced a lifetime ago, just last year.

It was like watching a speedy rerun of an all-too-familiar movie. Andrea saw herself in the restaurant with her family, waiting for dinner. She heard, again, the spiel the restaurant owner gave about the days of Prohibition in Moose Jaw in the 1920s when alcoholic beverages were illegal and gangsters from Chicago rode the Soo Line trains to Moose Jaw, searching for liquor and places to gamble. She felt again the fear and panic after she had hit her head on the mirror and woken up to find herself back in time in the dark and dangerous tunnels. It was there that she had met Vance and become a tunnel runner, taking the gangsters through the tunnels to various hotels or other businesses where they'd find booze and card games. With a quiver of remorse, she recalled how the dark side of the law had taunted and enticed her until she felt herself being swayed. In that claustrophobic underground world the lines of right and wrong had blurred in her mind.

Her memories of Vance and Beanie and the help she had given them made her feel proud. It was because of Beanie that she had finally come to realize that one needed to have a clear understanding of good and evil and stick to a strong set of values. Andrea's last memory, as she fell into an exhausted sleep, was of Old Scarface, immense and terrifying, standing over her, hands reaching for her throat. She managed to escape, and again found herself running for her life down the endless tunnel, terror squeezing her heart. She could see a faint light in the distance, an escape, and she raced toward it, her feet pounding on the gravel.

Suddenly a second man materialized out of the tunnel wall. He grabbed her and yanked her off her feet and onto her knees. Eyes beady and intent, he grabbed her around the neck and began to squeeze while Old Scarface looked on, his frightening laughter bouncing off the tunnel walls....

THE DREAMS ALWAYS FRIGHTENED Andrea into wakefulness with terrifying images of Old Scarface. He represented everything evil she had encountered in the tunnels and he continued to haunt her dreams and steal her sleep, becoming more realistic and frightening every time she dreamed, and now she had something else to worry about. Who was this other man who was suddenly stealing her sleep, too? He looked vaguely familiar. She lay on the bed beside Tony, puzzled about him. Fresh tears dotted her cheeks.

"Why are you crying?" Tony asked as he wiped his

own tears away. It seemed as if they had been asleep for a long time. His voice made Andrea's thoughts of the past evaporate.

"I guess I'm crying because I just hate that you have to have this done every day," she said, wishing she could forget the memories that had become a bad dream.

"Thanks," Tony said, turning his head on the pillow to smile at her. "I know I'm a baby," he admitted. "I know some kids my age who do all of this themselves – even the shot part. But I hate the idea. I hate having diabetes. I mean, I know that it's not the worst thing I could have, and if I control it and learn to live with it, I can have a good life. I'm just really angry that it had to happen to me! Why me?"

"I don't know," Andrea answered quietly, hoping that she wouldn't make him angry again. She got up from the bed, pointedly avoiding the corner where the armoire stood. "It just happened, I guess. Aunt Edna has it, so it does run in the family."

"Yeah, well, that doesn't make me feel any better. I hate having to count my starches and choose what I'm not going to eat and substitute something so that I can eat something else. I hate having to keep track of every little thing! You don't have to do that." Tony's voice was reproachful and angry.

"No," Andrea said, feeling terribly guilty about being healthy while Tony struggled with this new complication in his life. She had felt that way since he was first diagnosed and her parents had begun to make nutritional changes in the family's meal plans. She felt guilty every time she snuck a chocolate bar or a slurpee, knowing that for the rest of his life, he would have to be careful about what he ate. It just didn't seem fair that he should have to grow up so fast, worrying about glucose levels and how much insulin he needed in order to live a healthy life. "I wish it was me, Tony," she said, tears smarting her eyes.

She slumped into the wooden chair beside the desk. Keeping her head down, she studied the white tile floor, hiding her face behind a thin curtain of hair. "If I could, you know I'd switch places with you." She figured that at her age she ought to be able to handle the situation better, although she doubted that she would be able to inject herself either.

"Yeah, I know." Tony sidled off the bed and came to stand beside her chair, leaning against her shoulder.

Their mother had often told her that Tony was in denial about his condition, that he didn't want to admit that he had it. The last few months had been hard on the whole family, but especially tough on Tony, who had spent several days in the hospital getting his body regulated. The nurses had taught him how to test his blood and then inject himself with insulin. They had made him do it at the hospital, but he adamantly refused to do it for himself at home.

Andrea figured that it was his way of trying to hang onto the way he used to be. If he didn't have to do it himself, then it wasn't real and it wouldn't last a lifetime. That would make sense to a nine year old, she thought. She could understand that herself.

"I know how you feel," she said, patting his arm. "I think I'd feel the same way, too. Now, if I remember right, you need to eat soon," she said, changing the subject.

Tony nodded. "That's right. But I feel strong right now." He stood, flexing his arms in the air. Another insulin session was over and he promptly put it out of his mind. "I feel strong enough to...to...." He looked around the room, his eyes falling on the old wooden cupboard standing against the wall. "I feel strong enough to move this all by myself!" The armoire reminded him of the diary he had read.

He flashed knowing eyes in Andrea's direction as he put his hands against the armoire. "Watch the world's strongest boy move this heavy piece of furniture," he taunted. "I wonder what I'll find behind it? Another coin...a door...."

Tiny pricks of apprehension tingled along Andrea's spine and up her neck. A strange fear ran through her, along with a sudden certainty. Tony knew! Tony knew her secret! Only she and Vanessa had been in the room when the coin had rolled under the armoire. There was only one way he could know about that!

He had read her diary! Sick with dread, anger beginning to boil in her veins, she decided to bait him, to trap him into confessing the truth. "This armoire looks very familiar, doesn't it?" she said, keeping her voice neutral.

"Yeah," Tony grunted, still endeavoring to push it away from the wall. "It looks like the one in the restaurant, you remember? The tunnel was hidden behind it. I'll bet there's a tunnel hidden behind this one, too."

"There is not," she retorted, her voice mocking him. It was the tone of voice he hated, the one she often used to make him mad. "Only an idiot would think that."

"There is too," he shouted, straining hard against the cupboard. It didn't budge.

"There is not, there is not," she taunted. "There is not and you're crazy to think that there is!"

Tony whirled around, eyes blazing, hands clenched into fists. "There is too, Andrea, and you know it! You wrote about it in your d-"

Silence fell as he clapped a hand over his mouth, frightened eyes peering over it.

"Ah-ha! You did read my diary, you little weasel!" Andrea advanced on Tony, hands ready to strangle him. "How could you do that? What a low, stinking thing to do!" Blood drained from his face when he realized he'd been caught.

She was so angry her head spun. "I don't even want to talk to you! I'll never speak to you again! How could you do that?" Her voice broke and she spun away from him before he could see the tears. She dashed out of the door and banged up the staircase. "I don't care if I never see you again!" The door slammed shut and she was gone.

It's Magic!

Tony's breath was coming in painful spurts. He wiped sweating hands on his shorts and blinked away tears. It's all Andrea's fault, he reasoned. If she had told him in the first place, he wouldn't have resorted to reading her diary. It was all her fault.

He heard the faint sound of the front door opening and then slamming shut again. A feeling of abandonment filled his stomach and he tasted fear. What if Andrea never came back? What if he was left here all alone? What would happen to him?

He threw himself face down on the bed, total despair washing over him. He had gotten himself into some pretty bad situations before, but this one seemed to top them all, and he didn't know how he was going to get out of it. Still, it was Andrea's fault, he reminded himself again. She was to blame.

If only he could find a way to move that cupboard and get into the tunnel. He was sure that would teach Andrea a lesson. He could explore the tunnels and show her that she didn't need to hide them from him. She would see that he was just as smart and capable as she was, even if he did have diabetes.

He was still having trouble believing everything he had read that afternoon in Andrea's diary. He had known that she had had some kind of wonderful experience in Moose Jaw last year, but he had never dreamed that it was as awesome as she had written. He had wondered at first, as he read it, if she had made it all up just to teach him a lesson about snooping. But too many things made sense for it not to be true.

The armoire was real. It still stood in the corner of the room, just as she had written. Moose Jaw did have tunnels that had been used by gangsters from Chicago and by Chinese immigrants. Everyone knew that. They were finding more and more tunnels every day and excavating them. No, that all made sense. The weird part was believing that Andrea had actually gone back in time to the days of prohibition and rum-running. That was the part that was difficult to believe. Still, that made sense too, in a strange sort of way. He remembered the coin that Andrea had saved. She had gotten it last year in Moose Jaw, although she never told him the details. She had written in her diary that the coin had been given to her by Ol' Scarface, the meanest and most dangerous of the bad guys that she had worked for.

Tony wanted to have an adventure, too. He wanted to go back in time and do something fabulous, just as Andrea had done. Hopping off the bed again, he hurried over to the armoire and leaned against it, hoping against hope to push it open. His fingers tingled as they touched the worn wood. It didn't budge, of course, and disappointment settled with a lump in his stomach. He remembered reading in Andrea's diary that it had taken both Andrea and Vanessa to move the heavy cupboard. No wonder he couldn't move it all alone. Tony could kick himself for falling for Andrea's trick and spilling the beans about reading the diary. What if she never came back? Then Mom and Dad would be angry with her, he decided smugly. Let her get in trouble, who cared? He sure didn't. It was all her fault anyway.

He stood back, studying the armoire, trying to think of a plan for moving it. It seemed to glow, surrounded by a soft aura of shimmering light. He wondered why Andrea had never mentioned that. She didn't mention either, the fact that your hands tingled whenever you reached out to touch it. The aura around the wooden cupboard seemed to crackle and buzz. It was as if an electrical current surrounded the piece of furniture.

Feeling frustrated and sad, he got back onto the bed, yawning widely. He would have to figure out another way to get that armoire moved. He remembered a book he had read. It had been so simple, really. The kids had been playing hide-and-seek and had found an old wardrobe to hide in. One of them had just walked through the huge old wardrobe, pushing through thick, heavy fur coats, and suddenly she was in another world. There was snow on the ground, and a lamppost standing in the middle of nowhere. She had met all kinds of wonderful creatures and had exciting opportunities to visit new places. He wished it could be that simple for him. He lay back against the pillows, studying the armoire through half-closed eyes. He knew that an exciting world awaited him; he just had to find a way to get behind the armoire.

Tony grew tired as he thought up and discarded idea after idea to get that huge cupboard moved. After awhile, his mind went blank. He merely studied the old armoire, watching the electrical field shimmer and dance in the dusky basement light. It seemed to be glowing more brightly, although he couldn't understand why that would be. An energy field glowed and pulsed, green and blue waves, small tentacles reaching out toward the bed. He smiled. He knew it was all his imagination. It had to be.

He wasn't sure how long it took for him to realize that something in the room was different. Suddenly he became aware of a loud humming noise and the crackle of electricity in the air. Feeling a cool draft, he wondered where it could be coming from. He lifted his head just in time to see the armoire moving slowly away from the wall. It was magic! Behind the armoire was a gaping hole. Carefully he sat up on the bed, sure that the illusion would vanish with any sudden movement and he would find the armoire still sitting tightly against the wall.

The armoire stayed ajar. He moved around the edge of it and peeked inside. The tunnel beckoned. Here was his chance to explore the old tunnels under Moose Jaw. Would he too go back in time?

His heart in his throat, he rubbed his hands together, dancing a little jig of excitement. He would need a few things, he decided. What should he take with him? A flashlight! He remembered reading in the diary that Andrea was forever wishing that she had brought a flashlight. Well, he wouldn't make her mistake.

Running quickly out of Grandpa Talbot's office, he hurried across the cement floor to the workbench. There he found two flashlights lying on the wooden surface. Picking one up, he tested it. A bright beam of light bounced across the room, shining on the opposite wall. Good, it worked. Back beside the armoire, he wondered briefly if he should leave a note for Andrea. No way, he decided. Let her worry about him! It was all her fault anyway! She'd be to blame if he got into trouble! Their parents would hate her forever! He smiled thinly. That ought to teach her a lesson!

He forgot about his part in the fight, forgot about feeling sorry for reading the diary. Pushing his guilt to the back of his mind, he locked it away there. Now was the time for exploring the tunnels! He stared into the black hole again. Something seemed to pull at him from within, urging him inside. It spurred him into action. He wouldn't wait for Andrea. That would ruin everything. Maybe he could disappear into the tunnel fast and she wouldn't realize for awhile that he was gone. That would give him a chance to sniff out a real adventure, one just like she had had. It was his turn now, and he wouldn't share any of it with her, either. She didn't need to know anything about this.

He took a step toward the entrance and then turned back to grab his backpack. He kept a treasure store full of odds and ends in there. You never knew when something might come in handy. Hooking it around his shoulders, he turned and stared at the tunnel.

Its pull was like a gigantic magnet. It caught at his imagination and began to reel him in. Taking a deep breath, he switched on the flashlight. Its beam seemed to focus automatically on the black void inside the dark tunnel. I'll just go down the steps and a little way, he promised himself.

Excitement pumping through his veins, Tony put his foot on the first step. His body felt strange and tingly, almost as if he had touched something electrical. The tunnel seemed to welcome him, pulling him down the other wooden steps and onto the dirt floor. A feeling of motion, like the fast-forward button on the VCR machine, pulled at his limbs, and he thought he saw bright flashes of light behind his eyes. What was going on? His heart pounding wildly, he shone the light deep into the black space.

It felt as if he was going on a quest. He was a knight, searching for the lost treasure or the answer to a puzzling question. He was a hero, sent to save the people with his courage and fighting skills. Images of dangerous criminals with huge shiny guns filled his head as well. Something was going to happen soon. He could feel it.

He shone his light ahead into the darkness. Earthen walls and ceiling, roughly hacked out, greeted him. Here and there wooden timbers were planted to help hold the earth above. About ten metres ahead the small passageway twisted to the left and the light shone against a dirt wall.

Tony wanted to see where this went. Bravely he moved through the small space, turning this way and that with the tunnel. Since he had read Andrea's diary he knew the tunnels were narrow and cramped and kind of creepy. He could see why Andrea screamed in terror when she first went. He felt closed-in and claustrophobic too, as if the walls and the ceiling above were slowly pressing in on him. He touched his pants pocket and felt the reassuring crinkle of paper. Good, the map that he had hastily copied from the diary was still tucked safely in his pocket. That should keep him from getting lost.

Mustering all his courage, Tony continued creeping forward. What kind of hero would admit he was frightened to be down here alone? What kind of hero would he be if he wasn't brave? All heroes were brave. He pushed on, fueling his anger at Andrea. He was annoyed that the time travel adventure had happened to her last year and not to him. It should have happened to him. He should have been the one whacking his head and going back in time.

His flashlight shone ahead, bouncing off a pile of dirt and debris. It looked as if part of the tunnel had caved in. A thick beam lay across the mound of earth, blocking the way. Heart sinking, he crept forward to investigate. Was this the end of his foray? He hadn't gone far and he was already stuck. According to Andrea's notes and the map, this tunnel should join with a larger and straighter tunnel. How could he ever get through a cave-in?

Tony reached the mound of dirt and the big piece of lumber. He knelt down and shone the flashlight underneath the beam. He could feel a cool breeze on his cheek from the other side. There was a small opening just at floor level. It wasn't a very big cave-in. He would have to crawl through to reach the other side. He hesitated, not sure what to do, and then pulled off the backpack, letting it drop to the dirt floor behind him. Kneeling, he began to crawl forward on his hands and knees, excitement and fear mingling in his blood. What would he find on the other side?

He wriggled through the small space and stood up, shining his light around. A lantern hung on a nearby post. It was lit and he stared at it and then laughed with glee. He had made it! He was in the larger tunnel, the one that, if he turned left, would lead to the backstairs at Grandpa Talbot's house. Thinking about the tingling sensation he had felt when he slipped down the steps and into the tunnel, he was sure he had travelled back into the past! That must have been how he got back in time. He was glad he hadn't had to whack his head and pass out like Andrea had done.

Turning right, Tony forgot all about being quiet and careful. As he hurried through the longer tunnel he felt excitement making his heart pound. Where did these tunnels lead, he wondered. He couldn't remember exactly what Andrea's diary had said; he had been reading it too fast, worried that she would wake up and catch him at it.

The tunnel suddenly opened into a large underground cavern and he stopped short in surprise. He recalled that the map had a large space, too. Was this the same underground storage area? If it was the same cavern, then the tunnel, the one Andrea called the forbidden tunnel, should be over that way. He shone his light ahead. The opposite wall was far away and he wasn't sure if he saw a tunnel opening or not.

The bright beam from his flashlight bounced off boxes with articles of clothing falling over the sides. They were strewn haphazardly about the storage area. This was strange. Clothes and things were scattered all over the place. Andrea had written about the storage area being used for illegal liquor. She had described bottles and cases and big barrels strewn about – not clothes. This looked like someone's laundry business, or a warehouse for a clothing store. This mess wasn't anything to be excited about. But the forbidden tunnel – now that sounded like an adventure waiting to happen.

Deciding that he would press on, Tony shone his powerful light around the walls of the storage area as he walked toward where he thought the forbidden tunnel should be. Piles of boxes, heaping over with merchandise, cast eerie shadows against the walls. Raising the flashlight, he aimed it in one direction and then another. A black void suddenly loomed up. That had to be a tunnel opening leading away from the underground cavern, he guessed. Forgetting about the clothes and boxes lying about, he hurried toward it. It was much narrower and scary looking. Recalling Andrea's diary, he decided that this must be the forbidden tunnel. It was just as the diary had said it would be, claustrophobic and cramped, the lanterns spaced far apart.

Tony walked on for several minutes in the confined passageway. He didn't know what to expect, but he knew that something exciting would happen soon. When the forbidden tunnel ended, he felt a sense of disappointment wash over him as he stepped into a larger space where a lantern sputtered weakly from a wooden pole. Then he saw with delight that he had another tunnel to choose from. He could turn around and head back toward the large underground cavern through the forbidden tunnel, he could travel straight ahead in a larger and brighter tunnel, or he could turn left into a slightly smaller one.

Tony remembered from the diary that the long straight tunnel eventually led to the train station at the end of Main Street. He turned left, his intuition telling him that something exciting would lie in this direction. He figured that true adventure couldn't be found on the larger, safer-looking path and he hadn't found it in the storage area. It must be waiting for him in this smaller tunnel to the left, the one which Andrea had described running under Main Street. He noticed with satisfaction that this tunnel was not as tall as the other one. Shining his flashlight straight ahead into the darkness, he stepped into the tunnel.

He had walked about three paces when he felt something grab his arm. "Hey! What are you doing down here?"

MORE TROUBLES

Tony jumped, feeling his heart lodge in his throat. It was one thing to go looking for excitement, but quite another to be grabbed by it.

"I know it's you." The voice was deep and stern and full of anger. "I thought Ma told you never to come down here!"

Tony spun around and shone the bright light full in the face of the person who had grabbed him. "Who are you?" he demanded.

"Hey!" Hands moved quickly to cover eyes. "Get that light out of my face."

Tony lowered the light only slightly, realizing that it was a weapon of sorts. He could use it to blind this guy if he needed to make a quick getaway. "Who are you?" he demanded again, feeling confident and in control.

"Who are *you?*" the voice growled back. A hand snaked out and latched onto the arm that held the flashlight. It twisted painfully until Tony groaned and dropped the light with a thump. The bright beam shone up from the ground, casting a circle of yellow light around their knees. Eerie shadows reflected on their faces. "I'm not going to ask you again," the larger figure threatened, curling his hand into a fist. "Now, tell me who you are. I thought you were my sister," he said, looking Tony up and down. "I can see that I've made a mistake. What's your name?"

"T-Tony," came the scared response. He stared at his captor, a teenaged boy a little older than Andrea. He was a bit taller than Andrea, with shaggy hair that had a slightly unkempt look to it. His shoulders were broad. His arms looked strong and muscular. He towered over Tony, who was short for his age, and Tony cringed. This guy could really hurt him if he decided to. "I'm not doing anything wrong. I just wanted to explore these tunnels."

"The best-kept secret in Moose Jaw, these days," the boy answered, his voice as dry as the parched prairie soil. "How did you find out about them?"

"My sister told me."

"Your sister!" The older boy was shocked. "The next thing you know we'll have more girls running around down here, afraid of the spiders and rats. She's probably a friend of my sister. That kid could talk your ear off sometimes.

"It's dangerous down here," the boy continued. "You shouldn't be here exploring. I'm taking you out of here and don't you ever come back again!" He grabbed Tony by the shoulder and reached an arm to pick up the flashlight that had fallen to the ground between their feet. "Where did you get this fancy lantern?" The boy shook it, testing the weight of it in his hand.

"It's not a lantern," Tony replied, studying the boy closely. "It's a flashlight, and it's not fancy at all. It's just an old camping flashlight."

The boy continued to stare at the object, turning it this way and that in his hand to get a better look at it. "It's great," he said. Then he looked at Tony, a frown on his face. "Come on." He grabbed Tony's arm, propelling him through the tunnel. "I'm taking you out of here and you'd better stay out!"

Tony felt his body pushed forward by a strong hand around the back of his neck. His feet tried to resist the pressure, but his running shoes merely slipped in the gravel on the floor of the tunnel. He sputtered and flailed his arms, trying to explain, but the older boy wouldn't listen.

The mismatched pair came to an intersection and Tony found himself pushed into another tunnel. They walked a long, long way like this, Tony protesting with every step he took. How could he have an adventure if this big kid was getting in the way? Tony began to seethe, anger boiling in his blood. Who was this kid to push him around like that? Did he own the tunnels? Of course not! Tony wondered what he could do to escape. If he didn't act fast he would find himself outside the tunnels and he didn't want that to happen.

Thinking quickly, Tony realized how he could escape. He'd seen it in a movie. The big kid was expecting him to continue to resist, making the boy push him forward with a lot of force. What if Tony suddenly ran ahead?

After jamming to a stop, Tony took off running straight into the darkness.

"Hey!" he heard the older boy yell, followed by a rattle of gravel and rock. He saw the beam from the flashlight bounce wildly off the narrow walls and low ceiling of the tunnel before hitting the ground, its light continuing to shine against the dark floor. The boy must have stumbled, for Tony managed to get well ahead of him. The tunnel grew darker and darker as he outran the beam. The lanterns, which hung on the tunnel walls at intervals, gave little light, and he wondered how Andrea could have stood it for so long in the dark.

It was getting so black that Tony couldn't see ahead of him at all. He wondered where he was and where he was going. What if he became lost in this creepy underground world? The thought worried him, but he tried to push it away. He needed to be brave to venture forth into the unknown. Hadn't the knights of the Middle Ages been brave when they went out to slay the dragon? Isn't that what space travellers were when they entered hyperspace? And what about the cops searching for the bad guys? He pressed on, his heart thumping wildly against his ribs.

"Hey, kid! You're going the wrong way! Wait!" The beam of the flashlight was level again and moving quickly toward him. Already the sides of the tunnel were growing lighter, distorted shadows dancing ahead. Tony ran a few more steps and found himself trapped. He was facing a dirt wall. It was a dead end. There was nowhere for him to go, and nowhere to hide. He turned around to face his pursuer, adrenaline pumping through his veins.

The boy caught up to Tony, the beam from the flashlight lighting Tony's chest and the dirt wall behind him. The bright circle of light caught Tony, standing, feet apart, hands clenched into fists in front of his chest, a mean scowl on his face. The teenager studied him in the circle of light. "Look," he said, some warmth creeping into his voice. "I don't want to hurt you; it's just not a good idea to play down here. You don't know the kind of things that go on here. You could walk into real danger and not even realize it. I've been beat up a time or two myself. I'm not supposed to be down here either. I'm just looking for my pest of a sister, Beanie. Have you seen her?"

"Beanie?" Tony gulped. It was the name Andrea had used in her diary. "Did you say, 'Beanie'?"

The boy nodded. "Yeah, Beanie, as in Beatrice Talbot. You look about her age. You must know her."

Tony stared at the bigger boy, his fists relaxing as his arms slid down his sides. "If Beanie's your sister, then you're...." Tony began to grin, a huge smile splitting his face from ear to ear. "Grandpa Talbot!" he shouted. He threw himself against the boy, grabbing him around the middle and squeezing tightly. "Grandpa!"

The boy was so surprised that Tony knocked the flashlight out of his fingers. It bounced to the floor, making a pool of light at their feet. "Grandpa?" The teenager struggled to unclasp Tony's arms from around his waist. "Have you gone nuts? Do I look old enough to be a grandfather?! Let go of me!" He released Tony's hold, pushing Tony roughly against the wall. "You're nuts, kid!"

"No, I'm not!" Tony did a little victory dance of excitement. "I'm Tony Talbot, and you're my Grandpa. I've found my adventure and I'm back in time!" He continued to dance, his feet making large shadows on the tunnel wall behind him.

"I am not your grandfather," the boy said hotly.

"Oh, yes you are," Tony replied in a singsong voice

of delight. "And I can prove it."

The boy folded his arms and looked at Tony, a threatening scowl on his face. "Go ahead," he muttered between clenched teeth. "Prove it."

Tony took a deep breath and calmed down, but the smile never left his face. "Well, let's see, what did my sister say?" He thought for a moment. "Oh, I know. If your sister is Beanie, then that makes you Vance. You're a Talbot and I'm a Talbot."

The boy nodded. "So?" he said. "My name is Vance Talbot, big deal. That doesn't make me your grandfather. Where did you get such a crazy idea, anyway?"

"Your sister has a middle name," Tony continued, ignoring Vance's comments. "It's a name which she's probably just adopted, I think. It's Andrea."

Vance looked taken aback for a moment. "That doesn't prove anything," he said, leaning against the dirt wall in the tunnel. "Beanie could have told you that herself."

Tony nodded, still grinning hugely. "She probably did," he said, laughter creeping into his voice. "She probably did when I was a baby and couldn't remember anything. I wonder if she used to tell me all those tunnel stories when she rocked me to sleep. And maybe you did too, Grandpa," he couldn't resist adding.

Vance's big shoulders came away from the wall and

he advanced upon Tony. "You're not making sense again, kid," he said. "Just forget this whole 'grandfather' thing. Don't say it again and I'll forget all about the way you threw yourself at me. Don't call me Grandpa again if you value your life."

"Your sister's middle name is Andrea," Tony said. "She adopted that name after she met a girl named Andrea who claimed to be from the future." He got brave. He stabbed Vance in the chest with his finger. "That girl saved you after you got that horrible beating down here in the tunnels."

Vance grabbed Tony by the shoulders and pushed him up against the dirt wall. "Where did you hear about that?" he said. "And don't tell me that Beanie told you. She and I promised never to tell a single soul and Beanie wouldn't break a promise like that. How did you find out? Did you torture my sister? Where is she?"

Tony realized that he had gone a little too far in teasing Vance. He felt cold fingers of fear on the back of his neck. Bits of gravel and dirt were falling onto his shoulders as Vance pushed him into the wall. He held Tony pinned against the wall with one hand over his heart; the other he balled into a fist and aimed at Tony's face. "Start talking, buddy," he demanded in a threatening voice.

Tony gulped, feeling fear form a lump around which it was hard to swallow. Boy, his grandfather had a short temper. "Beanie didn't tell me," he managed to squeeze out. "My sister did. She told me everything," Tony lied. He didn't want to admit to anyone that he had actually gotten all of his information by reading Andrea's diary.

"And just who is this sister who knows everything?" Vance sneered, the fist now mere centimetres from Tony's nose.

"A-An-Andrea," Tony choked out around the huge lump. "Andrea Talbot." He watched as shock and recognition flashed across Vance's features.

"Andrea," Vance breathed. He fell heavily against the dirt wall and slid down to the floor. "Your sister is Andrea? The girl who claimed she could travel back in time?"

"Yep," Tony said proudly. "That's my sister. And she did travel back in time. And so did I!"

Vance looked from Tony to the flashlight still lying on the ground. He looked as if he was studying the evidence, Tony thought, probably trying to decide if Tony was telling the truth or not. "It was Andrea who mentioned the flashlight last year. So this is what she meant." Vance picked it up, carefully studying it again. "I can see why she wanted one so badly. It sure works well, doesn't it? So this is how you get light in the future." Good thing it was a shock resistant flashlight, Tony thought, made for taking the bumps and knocks of camping. Otherwise the bulb would have been smashed by now.

Suddenly Tony realized that he felt tired. Apprehension caused sweat to pop out on his brow, and he slid down until he was resting on his heels, his back against the dirt wall. Maybe if he rested for a few minutes that feeling would disappear. How could he be a hero? How could he find adventure when he always had to be worried about taking care of himself? He hated being dependent on something like insulin. He hated having to time his shots and his meals. It felt too much like being a baby and he hated the idea that he was a baby. He hadn't waited to eat. That was the problem. He should have eaten right after he took his shot. He was in big trouble now.

"A flashlight," Vance muttered again, weighing it in his palm. "How do you light it? Where do you put the match?"

Tony laughed in spite of himself. "You don't light it with a match; you just push that button. Here." He took the flashlight. "Let me show you." He pushed the plastic button on and off a few times. "See, it's easy," he said, leaving the light on. He shone it at chest level on the boy. The light was bright enough to show surprise and pleasure mingling on his face and Tony felt a queer, uneasy excitement begin to build inside him. "I really am back in time," he crowed.

"It's been about a year since Andrea was here. How did you get back in time?" Vance asked. "And don't tell me you hit your head on a mirror and were knocked out, too. That's the story Andrea told Beanie, and I'm not sure I believe it."

"It's true," Tony declared. "My sister wouldn't lie about something like that. But that's not what happened to me. There's a tunnel in my Grandpa's house – in *your* house," Tony corrected, glancing in Vance's direction. "I was lying on the bed, staring at the armoire, trying to come up with a plan for moving it, and it just slid open! It was like magic! I went to investigate and here I am! It's my lucky day!"

"Well, it's not my lucky day. I just came to find my sister! She knows she's not supposed to be down here. Ma's going to skin her alive if I can find her!"

"I can help you look for her." Tony tried to sound eager, but he felt weighed down, as if fifty-pound weights were strapped to his limbs. He was sure that it wasn't by coincidence that Vance had found him. There was a reason for it and it must have something to do with the big adventure that he was looking for. Maybe this time he was the one who was being sent to help his relatives. He liked the sound of that! He had always dreamed of being a hero, and he wasn't going to let a few little symptoms stop him. He was tough. He could get by without eating, no matter what some silly old doctor said.

"I don't know," Vance rubbed his fingers over his forehead. "You'll probably be more trouble than you're worth, in the long run. What do you know about the tunnels, anyway?"

"Actually, I know quite a bit," Tony replied, importance ringing in his voice. "I went on a tunnel tour last fall with my class. We made a day trip to Moose Jaw. And, I have this!" Tony pulled out a folded piece of paper and handed it to Vance, pointing to the map of the tunnels he had copied from Andrea's diary.

Tilting the page toward the light so that he could see it better, Vance studied the hastily drawn map. "But these tunnels are supposed to be a secret."

"In your time, maybe, but not in mine. In my time, they've become the hit of the province – a real tourist spot. Everyone is coming to Moose Jaw to tour the tunnels. There have even been books written about them. The point is, I can help you look for Beanie. I know a lot about these tunnels. Come on, let's go back that way. She's definitely not down this way." Tony thought for a moment, studying the crumbling dirt walls of the tunnel. "Maybe she's back in that underground storage area where all the clothes are."

"Clothes? What clothes?"

"Come on." Tony eagerly jumped in front of Vance and hurried toward the forbidden tunnel. "I'll show you where it is."

Vance seemed reluctant, but he agreed. "All right, you can tag along with me for awhile. Just stay out of trouble. We need to be really quiet; we don't want to be heard. And if I say hide, you hide against the wall. Now, let's go find Beanie and get her out of here. I don't know how I managed to be a tunnel runner for so long. This place is pretty spooky." Vance turned around and followed Tony back up the tunnel.

Tony moved slower and slower. He was beginning to feel dizzy and slightly disoriented, and the bouncing beam of the flashlight didn't help any. Recognizing the symptoms, he knew that he had forgotten to eat after getting his insulin shot. Automatically, he reached for his backpack. His mother always made sure there were a couple of small juice boxes tucked in one pocket, for emergencies just like this. His hand reached up and grabbed air. His back pack! He had left it on the other side of the cave-in!

He was thirsty and he could feel himself sweating. He was in big trouble. "V-Vance," he called weakly just as his knees gave out. He sank to the floor in a heap.

Vance stood over him. "Come on, kid, quit fooling around. I don't have all day." He prodded Tony's shoulder with the toe of his shoe. "Come on." When Tony didn't move he stood looking down at him, a worried look on his face. "Are you all right, kid? You look a little peaked."

"Do you have sugar or something like that on you?" Tony asked weakly from his position on the gravelled floor. It was taking all of his strength just to ask the question.

"No," Vance said, feeling around in his pockets. "Are you hungry?" He had never seen a person looking so sickly. It was making him very nervous.

"I-I need some juice or something sweet, and I need it fast, before I pass out...." Tony's words drifted away and his eyes fluttered shut. He slumped farther onto the dirt floor, looking for all the world as if he had just died.

"Tony!" Vance yelled. He didn't know what to do. He slapped at Tony's face, as he had seen the doctor do when his Ma had fainted. It didn't help. He held his hand by Tony's mouth and felt shallow breath on his palm. Vance knew he couldn't leave Tony here. He bent down and picked up the limp body in his strong arms. Even though the kid looked small and scrawny, he was heavy. Vance wasn't sure that he'd be able to carry him far. Now what, he wondered, starting to panic. He forgot all about finding Beanie. His only thoughts were on getting Tony out of the tunnels and to the doctor as quickly as possible. But would he make it in time?

INTO THE TUNNELS

It took Andrea awhile to cool off. She stormed out of the house and headed down Ominica Street toward Main. Anger danced before her eyes as she relived, over and over, like a video stuck in her mind, the confrontation with Tony. How could he do that to her? He knew he wasn't supposed to read her diary! She felt betrayed and hurt. She felt like kicking something.

She crossed Main Street and found herself near the entrance to Crescent Park, the beautiful park area situated just east of Main Street. Stately trees dressed in summer greenery waved vibrant leaves in her direction, beckoning her. Crossing the footbridge, she suddenly realized that the last time she had been in the park more than seventy years ago she had had to jump the creek. The small bridge hadn't been built then.

Andrea thought terrible things about Tony as she marched through the park. Right now she felt as if she really did hate him and never wanted to see him again.

Reaching the other side of the park, she stood staring out across Third Avenue at the old, dilapidated houses. One house held her attention. It had a large screened-in area that leaned heavily to one side, as if it was sinking into the ground. An unkempt hedge with long straggling branches framed the property. A picture of a neat and trim house with a small fence jumped into Andrea's mind. A neatly painted sign had hung on the fence then. Viola's Boarding House, she remembered reading on the sign. This was her great-grandmother's house! This was where Vance and Beanie had lived as children, and where Andrea had slept for a few hours some seventy years before, just last year. The house was in bad shape now, barely recognizable. It made her sad to see it that way and she turned away from it and headed back into the park.

Andrea never stayed angry for long. Worries began to creep into her weary mind. She hadn't even told Tony that she was going out. Even though she still felt hurt and more than a little angry with him, she hoped he'd remembered to eat. Hurrying the three short blocks to the house, she climbed the wide stairs to the porch. The phone rang as she reached the door. Throwing it open, she dashed down the short hallway to the kitchen and grabbed the phone. "Hello?"

"Andrea, you sound out of breath, my dear." Her grandfather's voice greeted her and Andrea smiled.

"Hi Grandpa," she said. "How are you? How's Aunt Bea?"

"We're all fine here, Andrea. Don't worry about Aunt Bea. We only just arrived an hour ago and they've already whisked her away to be prepped for the operation. You know that she was on the waiting list, and when they phoned – well, we had to leave immediately. She's had her bag packed for weeks. She really wants this defibrillator so that her heart will settle down and beat more slowly. Things look really good for her, but we'll have to wait and see how the operation goes. We probably won't be gone for too long. Once Aunt Bea has this surgery, we can bring her home to recuperate.

"How are things going there? How are Vanessa and Tony?"

"We're fine, too," Andrea hedged, trying to put the absent Vanessa out of her mind. "Or mostly fine," she corrected.

"Oh, it sounds like trouble to me," Grandpa guessed. She had forgotten how well he knew her. "Tell me about it, my dear."

"Oh, Grandpa, Tony read my diary and I'm so angry with him." She could hear the annoyance in her voice. Tears prickled her nose. "I got mad at him, really mad, and now I'm upset with him and with me. I didn't handle it very well," she admitted, gripping the receiver. "I said some terrible things and then I ran out of the house."

"Hmmm," Grandpa Talbot murmured. He always did that when he was thinking. "Don't let your anger rule your own good judgement, Andrea. I know that in the past you could be a little hotheaded at times, but you usually snap out of it quickly."

Andrea snorted into the phone. "I wouldn't say that, Grandpa. I sure gave Tony heck today and I'm still mad at him!"

"Well, he did break a trust, and in doing that he hurt your feelings. I'm sure he's sorry for what he did. Tony can be impulsive, but he never means to hurt anyone. He just needs to grow up a bit and to think before he does something."

"He didn't seem very sorry."

There was a long silence on the end of the phone. "Do we need to be there, Andrea?" Her grandfather's voice was gentle.

"No!" Andrea realized that she had probably yelled in his ear. She pictured him pulling the phone away from his head and rubbing at his ear.

"Can you and Vanessa handle this?"

Andrea sighed, ignoring the little niggle of guilt that pulled at her conscience. She wasn't going to tell her

Grandfather about the absent Vanessa. "Yes, Grandpa. Even though I'm upset, I'll try to get a grip and handle it."

"Good, and I'm sure your parents will have something to say to Tony when they see him."

"Grandpa," Andrea questioned, suddenly remembering the Moose Jaw history book Tony had received for his birthday, "why did you give Tony that book about Moose Jaw's history?"

The telephone connection hummed in the silence. "Oh, I – uh – I need to get going, Andrea. Your Grandmother is waving at me to hurry up. Give everyone our love, and remember what I said. Don't let your anger at Tony overrule your love for him. It's your job to protect him, Andrea. That's why you're there, my dear. That's why you needed to be in Moose Jaw this summer."

"But what about the book?" Andrea sputtered, but Grandpa Talbot had already hung up. It seemed to her that the phone conversation had ended rather abruptly, as soon as she had asked about the book. She wondered what her grandfather was hiding. Why he was being so secretive? And what did he mean about her having to protect Tony this summer? Well, she wasn't going to get any answers listening to the dial tone.

She hung up the phone. She wondered again, if Tony had eaten since she'd given him his shot. If he hadn't he would be in trouble soon. Even though it took an effort, she pushed her anger aside and began to think about what she could make for supper. She rattled pots and pans around in the kitchen. She really wasn't a great cook, though she had to cook one meal a week at home. It was usually the easiest thing, spaghetti and a can of prepared meat sauce and a salad. Anyone could boil water and cook spaghetti.

Studying the sample menus that Mom had sent to Grandma, Andrea thought that everything looked and sounded so complicated, especially the evening meal. She didn't know how to cook chicken or anything like that. She wondered what Tony would like to eat. Perhaps as a peace offering, she could ask him what he wanted to have for supper tonight.

She opened the door at the top of the stairs and peered into the gloomy basement. "Tony?" There was no reply. Maybe he was sleeping. "Tony," she tried again, louder this time. Fear leaped into her limbs, making them heavy. "Tony, are you there?"

Suddenly she knew something was dreadfully wrong. She flew down the basement stairs, feeling again that strange pull wrapping fibres of the past around her body. They tugged at her, making her feel as if she was in a time-warped world.

"Tony?" Andrea called as she stepped around the furnace. She tried to ignore that strange feeling, but failed. Silence greeted her ears, except for a faint electrical hum that hung in the air. It seemed to be coming from inside the office. She flung open the door and peered inside. She gasped, leaning heavily against the door frame, her knees buckling. Tony was gone and the armoire had been moved from its place against the wall. A large gaping hole mocked her as she stood in the open doorway. Eerie, ghostlike shadows moved around the room. They seemed to dance and sway to an electrical current. Even from across the room she could see the tunnel entrance. It beckoned her, begging, willing her to enter its murky darkness.

So Tony had found one of the two tunnel entrances in this basement. Remembering how heavy the armoire had been, Andrea wondered how he had been able to move it. She and Vanessa had just managed to budge it last year with both of them shoving. Tony couldn't possibly have done it on his own. But who had helped him?

Andrea studied the gaping hole. The humming sound was growing louder. The air seemed to be alive. It crackled faintly and occasional wisps of colourful flashes were just barely visible. It must be magic, she decided, fear and dread flooding her numb limbs. So, had Tony actually been dragged back in time, or was he merely exploring the decaying tunnel system of present day Moose Jaw? Either way, she was worried. She didn't want Tony down there much longer. It was dangerous.

She moved closer to the tunnel's entrance. The air vibrated with electrical currents that grew more powerful the closer she stepped to the entrance. Was that how the time travel worked, she wondered. She wondered, too, what she should do. She glanced around the room, noticing that Tony's knapsack was gone, but his syringes, insulin and blood-testing supplies were still on the desk where she had left them. Didn't he realize how important they were to his well-being?

Quickly Andrea scanned the room. A large blue shopping bag was sitting prominently on the table near the armoire. Someone had wanted her to find it, she guessed. How had she missed it before, she wondered. Then she remembered how distracted she had been giving Tony his shot. Grandfather Talbot must have known that both she and Tony would be travelling back in time. Maybe that was why he had given Tony the book of Moose Jaw's history and why the blue bag had been left out. He might be trying to make things easier for her this time.

Andrea picked up the shopping bag. It was already packed with a few items. What was in here, she wondered. Maybe she was wrong about the bag and her Grandfather. Maybe he had just forgotten to take it with him when he left. She peered inside the bag. Peanut butter and digestive cookies? A thermos, a flashlight, and a note. She opened it to find a few words scrawled across the paper in her grandfather's messy writing. "Take ice, bread, bananas." Ice? Why ice? Frowning, she flipped the note over, looking for her name, or any clue that would tell her that it was really intended for her. Shaking her head, she decided to follow directions.

Grabbing the bag and thermos, she dashed upstairs and filled it with ice cubes from the freezer. She took a loaf of bread from the breadbox and grabbed the bananas, which sat on the counter. They were just beginning to ripen. She stuffed the items into the bag and picked it up. Racing downstairs and into the office, she spied Tony's medical supplies still on the desk. With a sigh she put them into the bag. It looked like she was going to be Tony's protector this summer, just as Grandpa had said. She hoped she would get better at giving him his shots.

There, she thought, stuffing the last items into the bag. She was as ready as she'd ever be, and much more prepared for time travel than she had been last year. She wondered briefly why her Grandfather hadn't warned her about this, but she thought she knew the answer. She had been so worried and afraid of getting stuck back in time that she had refused to talk to him or Aunt Bea about their memories of last year. Now she wished she had. Maybe they would have told her about this next time-travel journey that she was about to embark upon. Maybe he would have told her where to find Tony and why she needed to return to the past. All she knew for sure was that she needed to find Tony and find him fast. His insulin would be playing havoc with his body by now. She would find him and get them both back to the present as soon as possible. Nothing could make her stay in the past, not if she didn't want to. And she didn't. Period.

The tunnel entrance looked blacker and more sinister than ever. Andrea tried not to stare into its murky depths. She was sure the tunnel was magical. It seemed to have some kind of control over her.

The tunnel entrance leered at her. She could feel an electrical force surrounding her. She shone the flashlight on creaky, decaying wooden stairs that led downward. Shuddering, she took a deep breath and resolutely stepped into the hole. Her whole body began to tingle and vibrate. A noise seemed to roar in her ears, while flashes of light passed just behind her eyeballs.

I don't remember this, Andrea thought. It was like entering some kind of force field or energy field and she realized that she was probably being transported back in time by it. Something very bright flashed in front of her as she turned the first corner in the small tunnel and she had a vague sense of déjà vu. It was as if this very thing had happened to her before. She continued in the short twisting tunnel, recalling that it would hook up with the larger tunnel. It should only be a short walk after that and she would be at the underground storage area.

The tunnel was just as she remembered, dark and spooky, smelling old and stale, and feeling very cramped. She knew it was the short tunnel that led from Rosie's house and connected with the other tunnel that ran into the outside stairwell. It was claustrophobic, and she felt that old familiar sense of panic and fear knot into a mass in the pit of her stomach. Taking a deep breath, she walked on. She needed to find Tony, fast.

The powerful beam from her flashlight bounced against the dirt wall straight in front of her. Strange, she didn't remember that. She walked closer, trying to decide what it was. It wasn't until her toes touched a pile of dirt and a fallen timber that she realized what had happened. The small tunnel had suffered a cave-in. Was Tony trapped under it?

Frantically searching the pile of earth and wood, the bright beam of her flashlight bounced off a canvas bag sitting on the floor near the debris. Tony's knapsack! Tony had been here, but which way had he gone? And why had he left his backpack? Andrea picked it up, a sense of dread filled her stomach and she felt ill with worry. Suppose Tony needed the juice? She could feel the small containers pressing against the canvas. She had to find him fast. He had promised to never be without his backpack, but where was he? There didn't appear to be any way around the mess. She studied the ground, the beam of the flashlight coming to rest on smaller footprints and then scrap-

ing marks in the dirt and gravel. It looked as if someone had dragged two things through the dirt. Knees,
she guessed. Tony had had to crawl.

Bending down, Andrea felt a faint rush of air on
her cheeks. Had Tony really managed to get through
that? It reminded her of the horrible belly tunnels she
had had to crawl through during her last foray into
the tunnels. Worse, it was like the other cave-in she
had witnessed near the Imperial Hotel. Fear jumped
into her throat. She didn't want to crawl into the
unknown. What if the other tunnel had collapsed
too? What if Tony was lying unconscious out there,
buried in dirt and debris?

Realizing it would be a tight squeeze for her,
Andrea took a deep breath and resolutely got down on
all fours. Putting the heavy bag down in front of her
near the backpack, she grabbed Tony's sack by the
straps and pushed it into the hole along with the bag,
then crawled in after them. Finding Tony was her only
concern. She pushed the bags and then herself through
the small opening, sliding forward on her stomach.
Thoughts of strangling Tony flitted through her mind.
How could he do this to her? This was her worst
nightmare come true, this crawling through dirt and
cave-ins in the dark, damp earth. But she had to find
her brother. She wiggled her way through the small
opening, thinking about all of the delightfully tortur-
ous things she would do to Tony when she found him.

Suddenly she was out of the dirt and timbers and could stand upright. Scrambling quickly to her feet, she looked around. She recognized it as the tunnel that led to Rosie's. She knew that the storage area, where she had hidden in the barrel, was to the right. Nearby she saw a lantern hanging from a pole. It was lit. Everything looked the same as before down here and now she was certain that she had travelled back in time. Grunting with effort, she bent to pick up the bag, hoping she wouldn't have to carry it far. The knapsack she slung over one shoulder as she looked up and down the claustrophobic tunnel, wondering which way to search first.

Almost at once she began to hear strange noises. Someone else was down here. Was it Tony? Instinct took over and she began to move cautiously toward the sound. Holding her breath, she crept close to the tunnel wall, switching off the flashlight as she went. Its powerful beam would give her away in no time. She wondered exactly where the noises were coming from. Whoever it was was coming her way. She would have to find a place to hide. Keeping close to the wall, she hurried ahead, peering into inky blackness. She knew the large underground cavern was coming up soon.

The sounds grew louder and Andrea realized that they were coming from the storage area. The gangsters must be moving more liquor into the place. Or was Tony making that much noise? She hoped that he would be smart enough to keep quiet down here. Surely he realized how dangerous it was!

Andrea crept behind some boxes piled near the wall of the storage area. More sounds of shuffling and the dropping of wood on wood echoed loudly in the underground cavern. She heard the voices again, and this time they were close enough for her to understand the words. It was all coming back to her now and she felt her body begin to adapt, as it had that night last year, to the semi-lighted world of the underground. All of her senses were heightened, especially her senses of smell and hearing. She felt as if she was on full alert, ready to run or hide at the first sign of danger.

"Look at all this loot," a deep male voice said.

"Yeah," the second voice growled. "I wish the boss would get busy fencing this stuff. I don't like having it lying around like this. Someone could find it."

"Aw-w-w, you worry too much. Who would question us about it? Everyone knows we're the good guys. No one would ever suspect us." He laughed a deep hearty laugh that echoed wildly around the underground chamber.

"I don't know. I think some people are getting pretty suspicious. The business people just don't seem to trust us anymore."

"Hey, here's a nice dress. I'm gonna take it for my girl. She'll like it!"

"Just leave it here and let the boss get rid of it. He might find out and then you'll be in trouble."

There were more rustling noises and Andrea envisioned the man stuffing the dress into his coat. "He'll never find out. There's so much stuff down here one little dress won't make a difference. That's all the new loot. Come on, let's get out of here." The sound of a door opening and closing reverberated into the cavernous space, and then silence greeted her ears.

Andrea waited for a few minutes to be sure that she was alone, then she stepped away from the tunnel wall and into the storage area. She shone her flashlight around, expecting to see liquor bottles and cases piled high and strewn on the ground. She was shocked. The storage area appeared to be full of all kinds of merchandise, everything except liquor. Taking a step closer to the boxes, she peered inside. The first box contained ladies' clothes, hats and gloves. Others held pieces of expensive-looking jewellery, handkerchiefs and pocket watches. Some boxes contained small lamps, ornate hairbrush and mirror sets, and silverware. The items were all thrown together in the boxes, much of it spilling onto the ground. It was as if a giant hand had rummaged through a store, picked up a handful of things, and dropped them into the storage area.

Most of the boxes seemed to contain women's clothing. Andrea saw small pillbox hats with tiny pieces of veil hanging down the front. There were many pairs of white gloves. There were dresses of every size, shape, and colour. Andrea held up a gorgeous little blue dress with a pleated skirt to get a better look.

"You leave that dress right where you found it," a voice called out from the dark.

An Emergency!

Andrea jumped, letting the dress slip to the ground. Then she recognized the voice.

"Come on out," she said, biting back a laugh. "Come on, Beanie. I know it's you!"

The small figure emerged from behind a pile of boxes, a piece of broken casing held tightly in her hand. "Andrea Talbot," she asked uncertainly. "Is it really you?"

"Yes! It's me!" Andrea suddenly realized how good it was to hear young Beanie's voice again. When she had left the last time, she never dreamed that she would travel back in time again and that she would get to be with Beanie once more. It had been her one regret when she thought of her tunnel adventure. She really missed the younger versions of her grandfather and Aunt Bea. She really missed Vance and Beanie.

"Andrea Talbot!" Beanie sprang away from the boxes and dashed into Andrea's outstretched arms. "It's really you! It worked! I knew it would work! I've been calling you back, thinking about you and dreaming of you! And now you're here!"

They hugged tightly and then stood back to study one another. "I knew someone was calling me. I was having dreams, too, only most of mine were bad. I finally figured out that it was you in my dreams."

"You've grown," Andrea stated, looking Beanie up and down. She stood tall and thin at Andrea's shoulder, straight brown hair brushing her neck.

"So have you," Beanie agreed, blue eyes sparkling. "Your hair is longer now and – and you look like a girl!"

"I am a girl," Andrea reminded her with a laugh. She cast a glance around the storage area. "What's going on around here? This place used to be full of liquor bottles and cases and big barrels. Now it looks like someone's messy basement with clothes and junk all over the place. Besides that," Andrea commented, looking stern, "what are you doing down in the tunnels? I thought you promised me you'd never come down here again." She glared down at Beanie, hands on her hips.

"Something terrible has been happening," Beanie began. She waved her arms around, encompassing all of the merchandise surrounding them. "All of this belongs to the shopkeepers. There's a huge crime wave going on here. No one's business is safe. Almost every night someone else gets robbed, and no one is even sure how the robbers get into the stores. I know the police are involved, but no one believes me! That's why I'm down here. I'm trying to collect some proof. That's why I called you back here, Andrea. I knew that you could help!"

"The police aren't involved," Andrea said, shaking her head. "I don't believe they would be! That can't be true!"

Beanie nodded, excited to tell all. "Well, it is!"

"You're letting your imagination get away with you again, Beanie. You're wrong about the police."

"No, I'm not," Beanie said, stomping her foot in the gravel. It reminded Andrea of the night last year when Beanie had insisted on coming up with a plan to catch Ol' Scarface in the act of selling illegal liquor. Beanie had been right then; maybe she was right this time too. "I'm not wrong," Beanie repeated when Andrea didn't answer. "And you're here to help me prove that they're bad, Andrea. You have to help me!"

Andrea shook her head, refusing to admit that she had been summoned back. She didn't want to think that someone might have that kind of power over her. "Actually, I'm here looking for someone. He's a boy your age. My brother, Tony." She quickly described him and then explained, "That's why I came back. I need to find Tony."

"I'll help you look for him," Beanie promised, "but I need your help, too. You're the only one I could think of who would listen to me. No one else would believe that it's the cops. The police keep blaming the gangsters from Chicago. They call it a crime wave. But I know who's behind all of this. I just don't have any proof."

"It's probably Old Scarface." Andrea shuddered just saying the name.

Beanie snorted. "No. No one has seen him around since last year, not since that night you left empty liquor bottles on the steps of his hideout. We scared him off, or maybe he's in jail somewhere. But you would expect it to be the gangsters, wouldn't you?" Andrea nodded, still worrying about Tony. She had to find him soon.

"How long has this been going on?" she asked, trying to concentrate on what Beanie was saying.

"I don't know exactly," Beanie admitted. "But the shopkeepers in Moose Jaw have been hit by so many robberies that they're starting to talk about closing up their businesses and moving on to other towns."

"So, you think it's the police?" Andrea shook her head. The police officers were the good guys! "You've got to be mistaken, Beanie. The police are on our side, remember?"

"That's what I thought too, until I found out

about this theft ring."

"How do you know it's the police, Beanie?" Andrea studied her through narrowed eyes.

Beanie straightened her shoulders, proudly puffing out her chest. "I've been following the cops, tracking their movements, but I've never actually seen them doing anything illegal. I think they're getting suspicious of me though. They all know me by name."

Andrea bit back a laugh as she studied Beanie, serious and determined, a little paper notebook clutched in her grubby hand. She looked like a miniature Sherlock Holmes or Hercule Poirot. Andrea didn't want to hurt Beanie's feelings, but the idea was crazy! As if the police force was stealing from its own citizens! That was ridiculous. Only in the overactive mind of a ten-year-old child, Andrea thought.

"I'm not wrong." Beanie stomped her foot into the gravel again. "I just don't have any proof, and that's where you come in! You're going to help me!"

"How did you get involved in all of this anyway, Beanie? I thought we'd made an agreement before I helped you last year." Andrea glared down into Beanie's determined eyes. "You agreed to quit sticking your nose into dangerous places, especially these tunnels!"

"Honest, I did, for a long, long time. It's just that our neighbour owns a general store on Main Street. It's been broken into eight times in the past two months!"

"Eight times?" Andrea looked doubtful, her eyebrows drawing together in a frown.

"Eight times!" Beanie repeated. "Doesn't that seem odd to you?"

Andrea ignored the question. "Does your mother or Vance know about this?" she asked sternly, feeling like a parent. Between Beanie and Tony, she was growing up and acting more mature every day. She remembered with a twinge of guilt that she had left Tony alone and now he was missing. Maybe she wasn't so mature and responsible after all. "Well, do they?" she repeated when Beanie didn't answer.

Beanie had the good grace to look embarrassed, refusing to meet Andrea's eye. "No," she muttered, a sulky expression crossing her face. "They never listen to me."

Andrea sighed in defeat. Didn't Tony whine about that exact same thing? It must be something all kids thought. "How do you think I can help you, Beanie? I'm just a kid, too. I don't know how to catch thieves, especially if they're cops."

"Well, you sure came up with a good idea for catching the rum-runners last year," Beanie said. "I'll bet if we really think about it, we'll come up with a wonderful idea!"

"Look, help me find Tony first, so that I know that he's safe, and then we'll think about how we might be able to solve your problem."

"Promise?" Beanie asked.

"Sure," Andrea said. She wasn't sure at all. She just wanted to find Tony fast and get back to the present. She hated lying to Beanie, but surely Beanie was mistaken. This must just be her playful imagination. The whole police force couldn't be corrupt, could it? This being in the past was too dangerous and scary for Andrea. Her first instinct was to grab Tony, return to the future, somehow bolt that tunnel entrance closed and forget all about Beanie, Vance, and the fact that she had ever travelled back in time. She shook her head, trying to clear her conflicting thoughts. It was happening again. She had only been in the tunnel a few minutes and already she was confused about where her loyalties should lie, just like last year.

"Okay —" The word was just coming out of Beanie's mouth when they heard loud noises moving closer and closer. "Hide!" Beanie whispered as she dived behind a large box of household items.

Andrea took refuge behind a huge pile of clothes, squatting down to stay out of sight. Whoever was in the tunnel was in an awful hurry. The person didn't seem to care how much noise he made. Andrea was afraid to think who it might be. Only the bad guys, the gangsters would walk though the tunnels with such confidence. Her heart had jumped into her throat.

A distorted shadowy figure came around the corner of the tunnel and entered the storage area. The grotesque shadow bounced off the walls, large and ugly.

Andrea ducked further into her hiding place, only her eyes peering out.

The figure entered the main part of the cavern and stood for a moment under the weak light of the lantern. She recognized the shape of his head. "Vance?"

"Vance!" Beanie scooted around the boxes and ran toward her brother. "Look who I found! It's Andrea! She came back!"

Vance shifted the heavy body in his arms and Andrea recognized it. "Tony!" She jumped the boxes and sprinted to his side. A feeling of apprehension churned in her stomach as she gently touched Tony's forehead. "What happened?"

"I don't know, exactly. We were on our way to find Beanie and he got really tired and then fell to the ground like a ton of bricks."

"He hasn't eaten for a long time. He needs sugar." Andrea quickly set the shopping bag down and rifled through it. Her fingers touched the grainy surface of a sugar cube and she pulled it out and gently pushed it into Tony's slack mouth. Panic clawed at her insides, threatening to spill over, but she held it firmly in check. It would do them no good to have her hysterical.

"Why give him sugar?" Vance questioned as she pushed the cube under Tony's tongue and then pressed his teeth together with shaky fingers. "I'd give him something to put some meat on his bones. He's as skinny as a sparrow."

"He needs the sugar," Andrea said. "I hope this works." Waves of panic made her knees weak. Please work, she prayed silently. "Let's get him to the house quickly."

Andrea led the way down the tunnel. I'm sorry, Tony, she thought, trying to keep tears at bay. I'm so sorry. I never meant to leave you alone for so long. Please be okay, she prayed. Please be okay.

She walked beside Vance, keeping her hand firmly around Tony's jaw. She wasn't sure she was doing the right thing, but she didn't know what else to do. She had seen her mother do this a few times, in the very beginning, when they were still in the experimental stage with Tony's insulin amounts and he had gone into insulin shock. It had worked then. She hoped that it would work now.

She led the way, practically dragging poor Vance down the tunnel, keeping one hand gripped around Tony's jaw. She hurried along toward Grandpa Talbot's house, her only thoughts on getting Tony back into the office, back to civilization where medical help was only three short numbers away on the phone, if she needed it.

"How did you get here?" Vance asked as he shifted Tony's heavy body in his arms.

"I came through the short tunnel that leads right

into Rosie's basement," Andrea said. "There was a cave-in, but I managed to crawl through it and get into the wider tunnel. The entrance is right around here somewhere." She found the flashlight and switched it on, searching the area for something familiar.

"Where's that smaller tunnel entrance?" she demanded, dropping to her knees, shining the flashlight along the dirt floor. "Where is it?" Genuine fear gripped her stomach as she dug at the loose dirt with her hands.

"There's been a cave-in here. It must have gotten worse," Vance said gently. "You were lucky not to have been trapped in there." He prodded her with his foot. "Don't worry about it, I'll help you dig it out later when we have more time. Let's just take Tony up to Ol' Doc Anderson's place. He'll know what to do."

Andrea refused to budge. She clawed at the tunnel wall. "It's got to be here! Where is it? I have to get us back to the future," she wailed, tears mingling in her voice. "He needs modern medicine. I don't even know if diabetes and insulin have been discovered yet in your time!"

Beanie touched her tenderly on the shoulder. "Come on, Andrea. Let's get Tony some place safe and comfortable."

"B-but," Andrea stammered in defeat. She couldn't find an opening and that was the only way she knew to get back to the future. Her worst nightmare was coming true. She was stuck in the past with a sick brother. How would they ever get to the future?

AT ROSIE'S

Wiping away her tears, Andrea allowed herself to be pulled to her feet by Beanie. She followed Vance down the tunnel, every footstep planting her more firmly in the past. She wondered if she would ever see her parents again. The thought was a scary one and she pushed it away, concentrating on Vance's back.

"I think we should take him to Rosie's house." Beanie skipped a few steps to catch up to Vance. "That way you wouldn't have to carry Tony too far, and if he needs a doctor, we can run and get one."

Vance snorted. "I'm not going there." His voice was firm and flat.

"Take him to Rosie's, Vance," Andrea ordered. Rosie's house belonged to Grandpa Talbot, in the present. Maybe the tunnel entrance that they were about to use would whisk them into the future. With hope clutched tightly in her heart, Andrea felt her spirits lift. The beam of the flashlight shone ahead onto a dirt wall and she felt panic rise. Then she remembered that the tunnel was concealed behind a door, camouflaged, she thought, so that others wouldn't be able to find it too easily. Skirting around Vance, she searched for the doorknob. "I'll figure out what I need to do at Rosie's."

Slowly she pushed open the first door and awkwardly stepped through, encumbered by Tony's backpack, which swung from one shoulder, and the heavy blue bag. She remembered this tunnel and the doorway well. With a slight grin, she recalled how she had tried to run like the wind, limping with the weight of the coins bulging in her pocket, through both doors last year, with gangsters hot on her tail. It had been a challenge remembering to slam the doors shut as she went along, hoping to slow the men down. She closed this door while Beanie skipped ahead toward the next one. There were two doors in this passageway, if you counted the heavy one that slanted over the outside stairwell. "I'll get that heavy trap door up on top." Andrea pushed carefully past Vance and climbed the wooden steps. She looked up to see the door set at an angle above her. She had been down here today to get the key to Grandfather's house. What would she find when she opened that door?

As she mounted the wooden steps, she prayed to be magically transported back to the present. Holding her breath, she concentrated on modern things, hoping this would do the trick. Her hands touched the rough door, but she felt no electrical energy field. None of her limbs had tingled. Her heart heavy with disappointment, she was certain of what she would see when she pushed open the heavy door above her, and she was correct. The tall white fence was gone, as were the garage and carport. The backyard was open and full of dry prairie grass. With an overwhelming sense of dread she realized that she was still back in the 1920s with a comatose brother and no modern medicine. What would she do?

The slanted door fell open heavily on its hinges and she climbed out of the stairwell. She glanced up at the house, noticing that it was the same white, wood frame building that she had been in last year. The three windows, one on each floor of the large house, overlooked the backyard. The windows were open and curtains rustled in the warm breeze. Looking down the street toward Main, she noticed a couple of horse-drawn carts heading toward the train station. A Model T car rumbled by, its large spoked wheels crunching loudly. She sighed audibly as she glanced down at her blue jeans, colourful T-shirt, and thick white running shoes. In her rush to get to Tony, she had forgotten that she might end up in the past.

She hadn't dressed for the occasion, she thought with chagrin. She would stick out around here like a sore thumb.

Vance struggled up the outside steps under the weight of Tony's body. "I'm not going to Rosie's," he panted. "You can't make me, Beanie."

Beanie stared at her older brother, her arms akimbo. "Everytime you refuse to visit her, Vance, you're hurting her. Don't be like this!"

Andrea shifted concerned eyes between Beanie and Vance. "What's going on?"

Vance continued as if he hadn't heard. "I won't go in that house. If you want Tony to go there so badly, then you carry him."

"Vance," Beanie pleaded. "It's an emergency. Tony needs help! No one is going to fault you for turning to Rosie at a time like this!"

"What's going on?" Andrea asked again. She wished they would just quit arguing and get Tony up to Rosie's place. This was no time to be fighting, not with Tony hanging limply in Vance's arms.

Andrea stepped closer to Vance. Dropping the bags at her feet, she reached to feel Tony's forehead again. "Here, you take him," he ordered as he plunked Tony roughly into her arms. She staggered under his weight, nearly losing her balance.

"You're rude and mean." Beanie glared at Vance. "Rosie was your friend!"

"Well, not anymore," Vance declared hotly. He turned his back on the three and walked toward Main Street.

Andrea watched Vance walk away, stiff and unforgiving. She wondered what was with him, but let the questions die on her lips. Getting Tony someplace safe was her first priority. She struggled under Tony's weight, nearly dropping him. Vance was back in a second. "Never mind," he said. "I'll carry him into the house and up the stairs, but I'm not staying." As he took Tony, he glared at Beanie. His eyes looked hot enough to burn holes into her head.

"Okay," Beanie and Andrea both agreed at once. Andrea didn't know what was going on. She would ask questions later. She quickly shut the slanted door; then picking up the bags, she followed Beanie and Vance out of the backyard, around the side of the house. A weird sense of déjà vu filled Andrea as soon as she pushed open the front door. This was her grandparents' house all right. She had only just used this door an hour ago. Yet here she was, back in time, and the house was a rooming house, and Rosie one of its tenants. Everything was very confusing.

Beanie hurried up the stairs where Andrea remembered Rosie's small apartment to be. A baby was crying somewhere in the house. When Beanie knocked on the door Andrea heard a harsh voice call out. "Who's there?"

"It's me, Beanie, and – and Andrea," Beanie said

against the wooden door. "Please let us in, Rosie. We need help."

It seemed to Andrea that the door opened with reluctance. She glanced up the last three steps to see Rosie peeking out of a narrow crack between the door and the wall, staring down the steps toward her. "What do you want?" she asked rudely.

"But," Andrea sputtered, surprised at the less than friendly greeting. What was with everyone around here? Hadn't she been the one who had helped save Beanie last year? Rosie's eyes moved past her to Vance and Tony. "That's my brother, Tony," Andrea explained. "He needs help."

"I'm not a doctor." Rosie clutched the door in clenched fists, the colour draining from her face as she studied Vance.

"Don't worry," Vance muttered as he pushed past Rosie and into the kitchen with Tony in his arms. "I'm not staying." He carried Tony across the hardwood floor towards one of the tiny bedrooms just off the kitchen.

"Rosie, please," Beanie said. "You're being almost as pigheaded as Vance. Won't you invite us in?"

Rosie stepped back. Andrea and Beanie bolted into the tidy kitchen. It was just as Andrea had remembered it from her last visit, neat and small with a wooden table pushed under the window. Vance carried Tony into the front bedroom and dumped him onto the bed. "I've done my duty." He turned and marched out of the bedroom and through the kitchen. Andrea heard his feet pounding down the stairs and then the clap of the front door banging closed.

"What's wrong with him?" She asked the question, but her mind was really on Tony. The other two remained pale and silent. She didn't have time for this right now. She heard a low moan mingling with the sound of a baby's angry wails. "Shouldn't somebody do something about that baby?" she asked over her shoulder as she hurried into the bedroom.

Tony lay on the bed, tossing his head, his eyes still closed. She set her bags down on the floor with a thump. "Do you have a cool cloth and some water in a basin?" she called.

"What about ice?"

Andrea turned to stare at Rosie. Had Rosie really asked that? Was this her way of making a joke? The beginnings of a smile peeked out from the depths of her somber eyes.

"I brought ice with me," Andrea replied, watching Rosie's eyes grow wide. "Actually, water would be fine, Rosie; we'll get to the ice, later. And Tony'll need something to eat."

"I just made soup this afternoon," Rosie told her, "and I have buns, just warm from the oven. Would that do?"

Andrea nodded. "That'd be fine. What about milk

and some kind of vegetable to go with it?"

"Just let me know when he's ready to eat." Rosie backed toward the door. "And Andrea, I'm sorry if I sounded rude and uninviting when I met you at the doorway. I've been having a bad time and I just don't trust a lot of people to be civilized to me these days." She closed the door on Andrea's surprised face.

Tucking Rosie's troubling words in her mind to be examined later, Andrea turned her full attention to Tony, a sense of panic threatening to spill over. Her heart was beating a mile a minute. She would hyperventilate soon if she didn't calm down. "Tony?" His eyes fluttered open for half a second and then closed again. Was she doing the right thing, bringing him here? Was he really going to be okay?

Rosie hurried back into the room with the basin of water and a clean cloth. "What's ailing the boy?" she asked.

"Thanks," Andrea said as Rosie set the basin on the floor near her feet. She wondered how she could answer Rosie's question. Taking the wet cloth, she wrung it out over the basin and laid it on Tony's forehead. How could she explain diabetes? Had they even heard of it? She knew that it had been around for centuries. Wasn't it the ancient Egyptians who accurately described the symptoms in their records? Still, insulin hadn't been invented until some time during the 1920s. Would it have reached the Canadian prairies yet? "He gets these fainting spells if he doesn't eat properly," she explained. It wasn't really accurate, but it would have to do for now.

The wails of the baby grew even louder. "Someone should really get that baby. She's probably wet or hungry." Andrea glanced up to see both Beanie and Rosie standing like statues, faces frozen. "Can't you hear that poor baby?"

"Well, you'll find out sooner or later," Rosie said resolutely. "Just you remember, girl, I helped you out. Don't you go snubbing me!" She turned from the room, walking across the kitchen to another doorway as Andrea's bewildered eyes followed. The crying grew even louder for a second and then cut off entirely, leaving the house with an eerie silence. In less than a minute Rosie was back, a cute, chubby baby perched on her arm, its thumb tucked neatly into its mouth. Rosie turned the baby to face Andrea, her own face guarded and expressionless. "This is my son," she announced, "This is –"

"This is baby Alan!" A smile split Andrea's features and she reached for the baby.

Rosie beamed as she eagerly handed the baby over to Andrea. "You like him?" she asked.

"Of course I like him," Andrea replied. "What's not to like about a baby, and what a sweetie he is!" She nestled him on her lap on the bed and stared into his big blue eyes. He grinned at her around his thumb, a toothless grin that stole her heart in an instant. The bed moved and she glanced behind her.

Tony had his eyes open. "Wh-where am I?" he mumbled, looking around.

"You're still back in time. You're at Rosie's house."

Tony grabbed at the cloth on his forehead, dragging it slowly across his face. "I'm sorry, Andrea," he said weakly, his arm falling to the bed beside him. "I'm really sorry about reading your diary. I shouldn't have done that."

She knew that she would forgive him anything, if he would only wake up and be his own self again. "It's okay, Tony," she soothed, smoothing his short hair back from his forehead. "I shouldn't have flown off the handle either. Rosie's going to get you something to eat. You need to eat."

With a concerned glance at her baby, Rosie hurried from the room. "I'll get that soup now. It's hot and ready, and so are the buns." Rosie brought in a tray with the food on it and set it on a wooden chair near the bed. Then she picked baby Alan off Andrea's lap and left the room with Beanie in tow.

"Who's that girl?" Tony asked weakly.

"I'm Beanie," Beanie answered with a big grin. "You look about my age. I think you and I will be great friends, but you need to eat first. Rosie makes good soup!" She made slurping noises as Rosie dragged her out of the room, quietly shutting the door behind them.

Andrea spoon-fed Tony until he gained a bit of strength and could sit up and eat on his own. "I'm so tired," he mumbled between sips of soup.

She was just glad to hear him speaking and looking better, though he was still pale. "That's normal, after what you've been through," she remembered. "Just rest."

Tony fell right to sleep as soon as he had finished eating. She knew that that wasn't unusual after such a traumatic experience. She wrestled the blanket out from under his body and covered him before joining the others in the kitchen.

"Thanks, Rosie," she said as she set the tray down beside the sink. "I hope you don't mind that he's sleeping right now."

"Poor little guy. Here, you have some soup, too. I have a big pot full." Rosie placed a bowl on the table and gestured for her to sit down.

"Where's Beanie?"

"I sent her home. I knew her mother would be getting worried about her, it being suppertime and all." Rosie sat across the table from Andrea, jiggling the baby up and down on her knee. "She said she'd be back right after supper. She wants to make sure your brother is okay. Does that happen to him often?"

"Not if he takes his – uh – his medicine on time." It was on the tip of her tongue to say insulin shots, but she didn't want to have to explain that. She ate enthusiastically. "This is so good," she said. "I didn't realize I was so hungry!" She reached for a bun and took a large bite. "How old is he?" She waved the bun in the baby's direction. His father must be Big Al, alias, Ol' Scarface. It all seemed to fit, since Rosie had been his girlfriend.

Rosie pulled the baby close, kissing the top of his tiny bald head. "He's four months old. I love him, but I sure didn't realize that babies would be so much work."

Andrea studied Rosie across the table. Her face looked haggard and drawn, as if a huge weight of worry lay on her slender shoulders. "Don't you have anyone to help you out with him?"

Rosie shook her head, tears glistening in her eyes. "I'm not considered acceptable company since I was in the family way."

"You mean –" Andrea's mouth fell open in disgust. Were people really that mean seventy years ago? "Well, it's not the crime of the century to be a single parent, you know."

"A single parent?" Rosie thought about it. "Is that what you call it in your time?"

Andrea nodded. "I know for a fact that Big Al never came back to Moose Jaw. You told me so yourself at the restaurant last year."

Rosie looked puzzled. "I never said anything about that!"

Andrea smiled and stood, gathering her dishes up and putting them beside the sink along with Tony's. That was the thing about time travel. She could recall a conversation that she had had last year with a ninety-year-old Rosie, when in Rosie's world, that conversation wouldn't happen for more than seventy years. It sure gave a person a lot to think about.

"No, you didn't tell me anything last year, but you did when – never mind." Andrea sighed in defeat. It was sure hard explaining to someone that you had travelled back in time only to meet again in the present. "I just can't believe that people are so nasty."

"They are," Rosie answered shortly, rubbing the tears away. "The only ones who visit me regularly are Viola, that's Mrs. Talbot, and Beanie. Vance won't even speak to me and neither will most of the people in town."

Andrea scooped baby Alan off his mother's knee and twirled around with him. "How could someone be angry and upset with this cute face? He's adorable." The baby chortled in agreement, reaching out to grasp a lock of her hair.

"Well, they are." Rosie's voice broke and she folded her arms on the table, dropping her head into them. Her shoulders shook with quiet sobs. "You're the first person to really rejoice and celebrate my baby Alan. Even Viola, with her kind heart, tends to look at him as a – a burden."

Andrea clumsily patted Rosie's shoulder. She had

heard about how tough society could be on unmarried women who got pregnant in the old days. Some were actually banished; most were shunned. "I'm really sorry that's happening to you, Rosie. That's terrible and mean and unkind. How can they be like that?"

"People I thought were my friends won't even talk to me anymore. They sail by me in the street as if I'm a disease. I don't even go out much anymore. I get Beanie or Viola to buy my groceries and to do errands for me. So does my neighbour downstairs. He's been very helpful."

Baby Alan leaned out of Andrea's arms, reaching for his mother. "He's a smart baby," Andrea commented, placing him on Rosie's lap. "See, he knows you're sad and he wants to comfort you."

Rosie gathered her baby close to her breast, tears spilling down her cheeks. "I love him so much, but I'm so tired. I almost can't cope with everything anymore."

"You need to sleep," Andrea decided. "Let me take care of the baby for awhile; you go take a nap. Do you have another bed?" Andrea remembered that Tony was sprawled out across the narrow bed just now.

Rosie nodded, pointing at the other door. "I'm lucky to have gotten this place at a good rent, and with two bedrooms. It's nice and roomy for two people. Although when I first rented it, there was only me. You'll take good care of him?" She stood hovering in the doorway, her body swaying with fatigue.

"You know I will," Andrea replied, holding baby Alan close. "I won't let anything happen to him, Rosie. You have my word."

Rosie studied her and then gave a tired nod. "Thanks, Andrea. I knew you were a good person when you went back into that underground cavern and found all those coins of Vance's and didn't steal one of them. I trust you." Her mouth smiled, but the smile never reached her tear-filled eyes. She turned around and entered the other bedroom, quietly closing the door behind her.

How long she spent cooing and cuddling Baby Alan, Andrea didn't know. She bounced him on her knee, listening to him chortle with delight, waving his fists in the air. "Your father was a mean man," she told the baby. "He had Vance beat up in the tunnels, and he threatened me. Somehow he managed to fool your mother into thinking that he was a really great guy, and then he took off for Chicago and never came back. I hope you're not like him. What am I saying?" Andrea laughed. "I know you're not like him. I've met you in the present and you're this friendly old man with a scar on this cheek." Andrea touched the baby's soft cheeks, examining each one. A faint line, almost like a birthmark ran down one cheek. "So, you were born with that scar, just like the old Rosie told me last year. That's so weird."

THE CONFRONTATION

The baby grew tired and fell asleep in Andrea's arms. She rocked him for awhile, listening to the stillness around her. She thought she would go stir-crazy in the quiet kitchen, with no radio or television to turn on. She paced quietly around the room, wondering what people did for entertainment in this day and age.

Soon the baby awoke, whimpering and waving his fists. Andrea perched him in her arms and began to pace the floor. He chewed on his fingers as he cried.

"You're teething, Alan," she said. That was probably why Grandpa had sent the ice. It was a Talbot family tradition and cure-all to tie a piece of ice into the corner of a washcloth and let the baby chew on it. She held the squirming baby in one hand while she knelt and opened the blue bag. She opened the thermos, picked out a piece of ice and put the lid back on. Searching Rosie's drawers, she found a clean washcloth and tied the ice cube into the corner. She stopped at one of the wooden kitchen chairs and sat down, turning the baby around on her lap so that they were looking at one another, and gently held the cold spot to his mouth. Baby Alan grimaced and pushed the ice away. She dabbed his lips with it and he opened his mouth. "Good boy," she said quietly. The baby's hand came up to grasp the cloth and hold it in his mouth as he gnawed at the ice.

It was only a matter of minutes before she heard footsteps running up the stairs. Beanie must be back. Andrea quickly opened the door and pressed a finger to her lips as Beanie came up the last few stairs. "Shh-h-h. The others are asleep."

Beanie dropped down on the steps and Andrea perched just inside the kitchen door with baby Alan on her lap. "I came back as soon as I could."

Silence filled the room. A breeze blew in from the open windows and Andrea could hear voices calling below. "I wish there was something we could do. I'd kind of like to go out and explore a little bit. When I was here in the past, last year, I didn't get to spend much time out of the tunnels. This time I'd like to see Moose Jaw in the 1920s." It actually felt good being back in the past again with her friends. Maybe they didn't need to hurry back to the present as quickly as she had thought they should. She decided to hang around for awhile to enjoy her friends and have a small taste of an old-fashioned life. It was like being at one of the old villages where the workers dressed and played the part of old-timers. Today Andrea would play the part of a 1920s young girl. It would be fun.

"There is something we could do," Beanie said excitedly. "We could take the baby for a walk! Rosie has a pram! She doesn't use it at all, but I do. I get to take baby Alan for walks."

"What's a pram?" Andrea wondered.

"You know, a perambulator."

"What?" It sounded like something from outer space.

"Well, how do you take babies for walks in modern times? We put them in a perambulator – a pram." She gestured wildly. "With wheels – you push it –"

"Oh, you mean a baby stroller."

"Stroller?" Beanie questioned, shaking her head. "You sure talk funny."

"It's a stroller because you stroll down the street with your baby, I guess."

"Well, pram or stroller, let's take baby Alan for a walk."

"Good idea. Let's go." Andrea stood up and started down the stairs; then she remembered Tony. "Maybe I shouldn't leave him."

"He'll be fine," Beanie assured her. "He's really tired. Besides, we'll leave them a note so that they know where we are. We won't be gone long."

"Okay." Andrea quickly scribbled a note, leaving it propped on the kitchen table. "Let's go."

"Aren't you forgetting something?" Beanie grinned, looking Andrea up and down. She was wearing her thin T-shirt and tattered jeans. "You'd better put on something decent. You could get arrested for dressing like that in this town."

"But I don't have anything to wear."

"Well, you do now." She pulled something out from behind her back and held it toward Andrea. It was a cute blue dress not unlike the one Andrea had been admiring in the tunnels. "I got it for my birthday this year, but it's very big on me. Mother says I'll grow into it. She's always making my clothes way too big and then expecting me to wear them for years and years. I almost drown in some of them. You can borrow it, Andrea. Come on, get changed and let's go."

Andrea grabbed the dress and pulled it over her T-shirt and jeans. It fit well enough, even with her own clothes underneath. Wiggling out of her jeans, she slung them over a kitchen chair. "How do I look?" she asked, whirling in a wide circle, the skirt flaring out around her.

"You look like you belong here," Beanie replied. "But you need to do something with your hair."

Beanie expertly gathered up the wispy strands into a bun at the back of Andrea's neck and pinned it into place. Then she found an old black hat of Rosie's and put it on Andrea's head. "There. Now you really look as if you belong!"

They walked quietly down the stairs and out to the wide front porch. The pram sat in the corner, looking heavy and awkward to Andrea's modern eye. "Here, you hold the baby and I'll get the baby carriage." She wheeled it to the steps and tried to lift it down. "It's heavy, Beanie. How do you ever get it down the steps on your own?"

"I usually get someone to help me."

"Well, I don't see anyone volunteering around here, do you?" Andrea grabbed the huge pram by the base and tried to lift it. "Come on and help me, Beanie. We're strong. Remember that I managed to carry those wooden liquor cases last year, and we moved that huge armoire, too. We can move this baby carriage."

Beanie gently laid the baby down on the porch, making sure that he was well back from the edge and in no danger of rolling off. She grabbed her end of the pram and together they wrestled it down the stairs. "There." They settled Baby Alan into the baby carriage. "Where do you want to go?" Beanie asked Andrea.

Andrea thought about the park. She had been

there just this afternoon. How much had it changed over the years, she wondered. "I want to see the park."

"Good." Beanie grasped the handle with both hands and began to push. "That's my favourite walk."

The girls ambled down Ominica Street in the evening air, past stately houses where people sat on the porches, visiting and calling back and forth to one another. The pace of life seemed slower here. Andrea couldn't remember a time when she had ever seen so many neighbours sitting outside, chatting to one another. It was nice, she thought, to have the time to do that sort of thing. She couldn't remember the last time she had seen her parents sitting on the step, visiting with the neighbours. The blue dress swayed as she pushed the bulky baby carriage over the uneven ground and she felt like an extra in a movie production. After all, she was only playing a part in these olden times, wasn't she?

At Main Street a few ancient-looking automobiles chugged past. Andrea looked down toward the train station four blocks away. She could see it standing prominently at the end of the street. Even at dusk it looked busy with people coming and going. Andrea loved the atmosphere of old time Moose Jaw. People strolled leisurely down the street. She glanced around at the buildings nearby. They were made of brick from the factory just out of town, ornate and charming, with wood frame windows and trim. Each looked unique. Some had pillars and columns reaching up into the big prairie sky. Some had wooden arches and fancy carvings. The buildings were very attractive, she thought. They helped to make Moose Jaw a pretty city.

"This is where the underground cavern is," Beanie whispered. She gestured toward the brown brick building on the corner of Main and Ominica. Beanie leaned closer, whispering in Andrea's ear. "The forbidden tunnel must run right along here, under this part of Main Street. I've seen lots of cops hanging around here lately. At night it's been like Grand Central Station with all the action. I'm sure they're up to no good."

"You don't know that for sure, and besides that," Andrea grinned, trying to change the subject, "the front part of the business is a bookstore now, in my time. You go there a lot, Aunt Bea. You like to read."

"Really? I like to read?" Beanie wrinkled her nose, then she thought about what Andrea had said. "Aunt Bea?" she questioned.

Grinning, Andrea nodded. "We're related! You're my Great-Aunt Bea and Vance is my Grandfather."

Beanie flung her arms around Andrea. "I'm glad."

"Me, too," Andrea smiled.

She turned around, studying Rosie's house, just up Ominica Street. She looked back at the warehouse. A big sign on the side of it read Jackson's Furniture. It looked like a factory, store and warehouse all in one. "You're right, Beanie. I've never thought of it, but you're right. The underground cavern would have to be right under this building."

"And the door that leads from the underground storage area would have to lead right into it," Beanie added. "I've seen cops carrying boxes of stuff in and out of that warehouse. I'd sure like to know what's going on there."

Andrea didn't like the speculating look she saw creeping into Beanie's eyes. "All we're doing right now is taking this baby for a walk. Forget anything else, Beanie." Andrea wrestled the baby carriage from her and pushed it across Main Street.

"I didn't mean we'd do something now, but we might want to do something later...."

Andrea sighed. That child had a one-track mind. "I'm going to the park." She could see it, one block ahead, looking green and inviting, but very different. There were very few trees, and they were small, not the majestic giants she had seen only this afternoon. The bridge didn't exist. The park was just an open area of grassland, except for the impressive stone library, which stood in the park on the corner of Athabasca and Langdon. It was one of her favourite buildings in Moose Jaw. She admired it for a moment, wondering how it had been built without all of the modern technology, especially the huge domed ceiling inside.

"Look," Beanie pointed across the park. "There's Vance heading this way. Vance!" She waved her hands trying to get his attention.

Vance looked up, saw who it was and made an abrupt turn, heading in the other direction. "What's he doing?" Andrea asked.

"He's being a rude boor." Beanie bit the words off between clenched teeth. "He doesn't go near Rosie or the baby. He treats them so terribly."

Andrea watched Vance's stiff back walking away from her. Anger pumped through her veins. "You look after the baby. Don't leave the park! I'm going to have a word or two with Vance. He's acting like a jerk!"

Andrea lifted the blue dress to her knees in a most undignified fashion and sprinted across the grass. She was tempted to call Vance's name, but thought she should use the element of surprise. It would be just her luck to have him spot her rushing toward him, and run away from her. She jumped the creek at the narrowest place and ran up the short bank, gaining on Vance.

Huffing and puffing, she grabbed his arm and held on. "I-I need to talk to y-you," she panted. "Y-you're avoiding me."

"I'm not avoiding you, I'm avoiding –" Vance glared over her shoulder at Beanie and the baby carriage. The top of baby Alan's head was just visible.

"You're being silly, Vance," Andrea admonished. "Rosie is your friend. She needs your help. You're condemning her because – why? Because you think she made a mistake, or – or committed a crime in your eyes?"

"She should have left town." Vance's blue eyes were stormy.

"You mean she should have gone into hiding?"

"I don't care what she does!"

"Well, I think you do, Vance. Look, you're hurting Rosie and you're hurting yourself." Andrea saw something flicker in his face for a brief moment and knew that she had guessed right.

"She should have done the right thing."

"What's the 'right' thing, Vance?" Andrea's voice was quiet yet commanding. "Would you have had her traipsing after Ol' Scarface, following him down to Chicago and what, marrying the jerk? That would have been the stupidest thing she could have done!"

"I don't know." Vance wrenched his arm away. "I told you, I don't care. She was stupid and foolish."

"Yeah," Andrea agreed softly. "She made a mistake. Should she be condemned for the rest of her life because of it? Should we punish both her and that adorable little baby because of it?" Vance snorted, dragging his hand through thick hair. "How can you resist that sweet little baby, Vance?"

"Babies are nothing but trouble," he replied flatly.

"They just cry and need lots of attention. He'll be big trouble, too, just like his father, Ol' Scarface!"

"Why?" Andrea cried. She was losing her patience. "Did he have any choice about who his father is? None of this had anything to do with him, Vance. None of it is Baby Alan's fault."

"Go back to your modern times, Andrea Talbot," Vance yelled, backing away from her. "Leave the past alone! You're just stirring up trouble! You're making me think about things I don't want to think about. Leave me alone!" He turned on his heel and stormed away, leaving Andrea standing alone in the middle of the park.

"I would go home if I could," she yelled after him, her voice tight with unshed tears. "I hate it here!" She thought she saw him hesitate for a moment before he broke into a run, disappearing from sight, but she couldn't be sure.

The rest of the walk was quiet and moody. Beanie tried to cheer her up, but she was still seething over Vance's rude remarks. How could he be so heartless? He was her grandfather, or he would be, but at that moment, she was ready to punch some sense into him. He was being stubborn and hurtful.

They returned from their walk as the evening shadows began to lengthen across the prairie town. Rosie stood at the upstairs window, watching for their return. She waved tentatively to get their attention, and then came down the stairs to stand in the shadow of the doorway to take the baby. He was getting fussy and Andrea guessed that it was probably his supper-time. She and Beanie struggled to get the pram back up onto the porch and then quietly followed Rosie up the stairs.

"There's a police officer, Constable Paterson, who lives right there," Beanie pointed to the suite just below Rosie's. "He's too nice to be crooked."

"Help yourself to some milk," Rosie called from the bedroom. "I'll be out soon."

"I'd better get home, Rosie," Beanie replied. "My ma will be looking for me soon." She turned to Andrea and flung her arms around her. "It's wonderful having you here again, Andrea. I don't feel like an aunt. In a way, I feel like I have a big sister. Big sisters help little sisters out with their problems, you know," Beanie said, a cunning expression on her face. "Have you thought of a plan to help me prove that the police are the ones breaking into the stores and stealing things? That's what big sisters do, you know."

"What about Vance?" Andrea hedged.

Beanie sighed, shrugging her shoulders in defeat. "You saw how he acted in the park."

Andrea nodded. "He may be my grandfather, but at this point, I'm ready to wring his scrawny neck! He's being so pigheaded! Why is he being like that?"

"The whole town is like that, Andrea. Everyone

shuns Rosie. I've been with her walking down Main Street, and people who used to be her friends turn away and ignore her. It's so sad."

Andrea had a lot to think about. She had watched movies like that and read books. She had thought it had been exaggerated, but maybe it hadn't been.

"I wonder how long Tony will stay sleeping." She silently pushed the door to the bedroom open and peeked inside, wondering what to do. She shouldn't be worrying about helping Beanie get rid of corrupt cops; she should be thinking about how to get Tony safely back to the future.

"Do you think that small tunnel Tony and I came through is totally blocked by the cave-in? We did have to crawl, but there was enough space for us to get through." She thought for a minute. "I want to go look for a way through to that tunnel. It has to be there! We have to get home soon. Tony will run out of medication and then I don't know what'll happen."

"So that means you won't stay here in the past and help me with my problem?" Beanie asked.

Andrea shook her head, her eyes avoiding the disappointment on Beanie's face. "I can't Beanie. I have to get Tony back to the future. I'm going to leave him here for now while I investigate." She searched for a flashlight in the bag. "I'll be back for him as soon as I find out how to get into that tunnel again."

Beanie sighed. "I understand." She gave her a

quick hug. "Good luck, Andrea," she whispered. "I really do hope you can get through that cave-in, but I'll miss you."

"Me, too." Andrea waved goodbye and walked cautiously down the stairs, the bright blue dress brushing her knees as she moved. She stepped out on the wide porch pulling the heavy outer door shut behind her. "Oh-h-h, I didn't see you there." A man had just come up the walk, startling her.

"Sorry, Miss." He tipped his hat in her direction. "I was just out taking a stroll. It's a lovely evening, don't you think?"

"Yes, Sir." Andrea smiled uncertainly up at him. He was tall with broad shoulders and an open friendly face.

"I don't think we've been introduced," he said, extending a large hand, palm up. "I'm Constable Paterson, newly of the Moose Jaw Police Force."

Andrea put her own tiny hand in his large paw. "I'm Andrea Talbot. I'm a – a shirt-tail relative –"

"Of the Talbot family?" Mr. Paterson asked. He smiled down at her as she nodded. "Fine family," he commented, releasing her hand. "A very fine family. Well, I must be going."

Andrea watched as he climbed the stairs. "Bye," she called over her shoulder. She scurried around the side of the house to the slanted door and quickly heaved it open. It wouldn't do for a member of the police force to see her entering the cellar. He might follow her. She carefully lowered the heavy door using her back and shoulders. She waited for a moment for her eyes to adjust to the dim light. She wouldn't use the flashlight until she was absolutely certain that she was alone in the tunnels.

She carefully pushed open the door and stood listening for a moment. All was quiet. When her eyes had adjusted, she moved into the suffocating tunnel, hoping that she would be able to find the place where the cave-in had occurred. Walking slowly through the tunnel, she once again felt terror flood into her body. The ceiling seemed to descend, ready to crush her. Dead air hung about her face, putrid and stale. Scurrying sounds could be heard nearby and Andrea's heart kicked into overdrive. She shone the flashlight on the wall, searching for a clue – any small sign that the entrance was nearby.

In the darkness, even with the help of the flashlight's powerful beam, Andrea couldn't find the place where the tunnel entrance should have been. She walked rapidly up and down the length of the tunnel, searching for evidence of its existence. She couldn't even find the cave-in, but it had to be here! Where was it? She kicked at a small stone, hoping that it would reveal even the tiniest hole behind it. In several places she even bent down and put her cheek against the dirt wall, hoping to feel a tiny breeze, but the tunnel entrance did not reveal itself. It was almost as if it had disappeared into thin air.

Terror grabbed hold of her heart and shook it, making her dizzy. Where was the opening? It should be right here! The realization that she and Tony might be forever stuck in the past finally hit, and she sank to the tunnel floor, the blue dress pooling around her legs. They had been wrong to think they could escape. Oh, what would become of them? How would Tony manage without modern medicine? She refused to think of the likely outcome.

Frantic now, she crawled on her hands and knees, the flashlight bouncing brightly against the dirt floor. Nothing looked as if it had been disturbed. It was almost as if the cave-in and the other tunnel entrance had never existed. Tony and Beanie had been mistaken. There was no way home! They were truly stuck in the past with a limited supply of insulin. What would happen to Tony when that ran out?

Andrea sat in a miserable heap on the tunnel floor, oblivious to the fact that the dress was getting dirtier by the minute. She tried to calm her pounding heart and keep her tears at bay. Being stuck in the past wasn't that bad, she tried to convince herself. There were a lot of good things about it like, like.... She couldn't think of one positive thing. Pictures of her parents, heartbroken over the loss of their two children, filled her head. But surely there was some way back to the future! Grandpa Talbot wouldn't have let them come if he had known they wouldn't get back. But maybe he didn't know this would happen....

Andrea's thoughts scattered like the prairie wind when she heard noises coming from the underground storage area. Quickly switching off the flashlight, she huddled against the wall of the tunnel, listening. Sounds of busy activity echoed toward her, and curiosity got the best of her. She moved cautiously toward the sounds, ready to turn and run if anyone should come bursting into the tunnel. She would worry about Tony's predicament later; right now she had to protect herself in the past.

At the place where the tunnel widened into the cavern, she slipped silently along the dirt wall, as far back in the shadows as she could get. About a dozen men were bringing more clothes and items into the storage area. They used the warehouse door against the far wall, the one where she had found the coins last year and had nearly been caught by the gangsters when the door had unexpectedly swung open. These men spoke in loud and jovial voices, which, she was sure, would carry a long way through the tunnels. Didn't they care? Weren't they concerned about being caught?

She watched carefully as they carried box after box into the already crowded storage area. After awhile, the men stopped and stood in a group near the doorway. "It looks like we're done for tonight," one of them announced.

"Doesn't the boss need to have a look at all this stuff?"

"He's just outside the door. He'll be coming soon." The men leaned back against the boxes, waiting.

Suddenly the men all snapped to attention as another man filled the doorway. Andrea squinted in concentration. He was a tall, thin man with a little black moustache, chiselled features, and a big nose. She couldn't see his eyes clearly, but she bet that they were small and beady. As he stepped down the stairs, Andrea gasped in surprise. The light filtering from the warehouse had caught him just right, shining on two rows of shiny buttons, and she realized that he was wearing a uniform! Was he a police officer? Squinting, she tried to get a better look, for the man seemed very familiar.

"Good evening, men," he greeted as he walked around the boxes. With the men snapped to attention, it seemed to her that it was an inspection of sorts. "It looks as if you've done another good job of relieving the upstanding citizens of Moose Jaw of their possessions." The men laughed. "Keep up the good work, men! I'm counting on you."

The boss returned to the warehouse with the men slowly following him. As each man passed through that beam of light, Andrea watched. Her stomach churned as she saw that all of them were wearing uniforms. Was Beanie right? It sure looked like it. It looked like the whole Moose Jaw Police Force was corrupt. I'd better get out of here fast, she thought, before someone finds me down here. She gathered the dress to her knees and slipped silently into the tunnel, and then headed at a run back to Rosie's place.

STAKEOUT AT MIDNIGHT

Tony felt much better. He stretched lazily in the strange bed and his foot brushed something soft and warm. Lifting his head from the pillow, he saw Andrea sprawled out beside him on top of the blankets. She was sleeping in a dress he had never seen before. Where were they, he wondered. Studying the dark room, Tony noticed a tall narrow dresser in the corner and one wooden chair. His memory came flooding back. He was back in time! He was at Rosie's house.

He tried to concentrate, wanting to remember everything that had happened. Little snippets of memory teased him, flitting through his mind on the wings of a hummingbird, keeping the facts just out of grasp. He thought he could remember a girl about his age, but he couldn't be sure. Why was everything so fuzzy? He knew something important and exciting had happened; he could feel it. He wished he could remember what it was.

He heard small scraping noises outside the bedroom window. Who could that be at this time of night, he wondered. He hopped carefully out of bed, leaving Andrea to sleep in peace. Creeping to the window, he drew back the shade and peered into the moonless night. He could just make out the darker shadows of the houses nearby. He heard a cat meow in the distance and smelled the cool night air. The whole world seemed to have shut down for the night. The absolute silence was almost deafening to his modern ears.

The scraping sounds came again, from the kitchen, Tony realized, and he turned in time to see the bedroom door swing silently open on oiled hinges. A young girl stood gesturing excitedly for him to follow her. He studied her for a moment. She looked a lot like…"Beanie," he whispered, surprise making his voice louder than he had intended. "I read about you in – I mean, Andrea told me all about you and I finally get to meet you!"

Beanie placed a warning finger over her lips and motioned for him to follow her. He slid out into the kitchen on sock feet, noticing that his shoes and knapsack sat on the floor near the door. He grabbed his shoes in one hand and his knapsack in the other and quietly followed Beanie down the wooden stairs. They crept past Constable Paterson's place and out through the big front door, pulling it closed behind them. "Why were you sneaking around in Rosie's apartment?" he asked.

"I came to see if you were still here. Where's Andrea?"

Tony gestured toward the second floor of the house. "Upstairs sleeping."

"I guess that means that she didn't find a way back to the future," Beanie said. "I'm glad for me, and I'm glad to see you're awake and recovered," Beanie observed quietly, plunking herself down on the top step of the wide porch while Tony put his shoes on. "I need your help."

"What for?" Tony shouldered his backpack and sat looking at her expectantly, his eyes shining with excitement. He was fully recovered and ready to tackle anything.

"No one's helping me with my plan. We need to catch the culprits who are breaking into the stores on Main Street. It's the cops, I'm sure of it. Can you help me, Tony? Can you help me prove it's the policemen?"

"Sure!" Tony stuck his chest out, proud to be asked for his assistance. Most of the time he was treated like a pesky little brother. It felt good to be called upon. He'd been wanting to have an adventure since he first went into the tunnels and he had had to be carried out because of his own forgetfulness. Now was his chance to redeem himself, to be a hero. "I don't think I really know the problem, though." He thought it would be a good idea to understand everything before he went into action. His parents and Andrea were always accusing him of jumping into something without really understanding what was involved. This time he wouldn't make that mistake.

"Remember all those clothes and things in the storage area down in the tunnels?"

He thought back. His brain was a little foggy still and he sure hadn't paid much attention to that part of his journey. He remembered glancing at the boxes and then hurrying past, figuring that more exciting things awaited him farther down the tunnels. "Sure, I remember."

Beanie went on to explain how the clothes and things were being stolen from the stores at night and no one could catch the thieves. She told him about her friend's parents losing so much merchandise that they might need to leave Moose Jaw. "I know it's the cops," she repeated with conviction. "We even heard them in the tunnels that day."

"Are you sure?" Tony was dubious. "Maybe it's not them and they're just getting blamed for it."

"I think it's them, but there's only one way to find out."

"What's that, Beanie?"

"We'd have to spy on them. That's why I'm here this late at night! That's why I came to get you! It's midnight, you know," she said importantly. "My Ma will sure have something to say about it if she finds out I've snuck out at this time of night! I'm hardly ever up this late."

"Me either," Tony admitted, "I never get to stay up late, but what a neat idea you have, to spy on the bad guys!" His eyes lit up. "That reminds me of a movie I saw! They followed the bad guys around until they caught them in the act! Maybe we should try it!"

"I don't get to see too many movies," Beanie sighed. "I wish I did. I go to the Saturday Matinee sometimes, if Ma has enough money. Sometimes Vance gives me money and I go to the movie theatre." She beamed, changing the subject. "I knew you'd have a good idea! Let's do it! I know where we could hide to watch for them!"

"Good." Tony began to root around in his bag. He pulled out two square items.

Beanie stared at the shiny black boxes in Tony's hands. "What are they?"

"Oh, I forgot, you're from the past. These probably weren't even invented yet in your time." He put a walkie-talkie into Beanie's hand and showed her how to operate it. "See, press this button and talk. We can talk to one another from far away."

"I don't believe you," Beanie said, shoving the

walkie-talkie back into his hands.

"Here, I'll prove it to you. I'll stay here. You go around behind the house and listen and see what happens. You turn it on, like this." He showed her where the on/off switch was. "Now, I'll talk to you. When you want to talk back to me, you press this button."

He waited impatiently while she dashed around the side of the house. He waited for a few seconds more to make sure that she was out of hearing distance, then he switched on his walkie-talkie. "Beanie," he said softly into the box. He didn't want to be overheard, even though he was positive that no one was around. "Beanie, do you read me? Beanie?"

There was the sound of static and then a squawk. "Wow! This thing actually works! How can I read you, Tony? You're not a book!"

He laughed out loud and then quickly covered his mouth with his hand to stifle the sound. "It's an expression, Beanie," he whispered into the walkie-talkie. "I'm coming back there now, over and out."

She was waiting for him behind the house.

"That is so wonderful! It'll really help us out! What else do you have in there?"

"Well," he thought for a moment, remembering the toy gun and the remote control car. "I have some neat toys. I'll show you them later."

"Come on then," Beanie demanded impatiently. "Are you coming or not?"

"Of course I'm coming! We're going to catch those bad guys, no matter who they are!" He fell into step with her as she led the way toward Main Street.

"Oh," she suddenly remembered, "I forgot to ask. How are you feeling?"

"I'm fine now, I've recovered, and as long as I don't do anything stupid I should be okay."

Beanie accepted that answer and stopped as they neared Main Street. "Now what?" Tony wanted to know. He glanced around, curiously. Nothing moved and the only light source was from the street lamps high above their heads. It was so quiet. He strained his ears, listening. Tall brick buildings marched in two straight rows toward the train station, one row on each side of Main Street. He could see a majestic-looking building one block south. It had a clock tower and its lighted face shone clearly in the night.

Nothing moved. Only crickets chirped in safe dark places. "Wow! This is so neat! So this is what olden day Moose Jaw looks like," he marvelled, scanning the scene stretched out before him. They stood in the shadow of a large brick building.

"This is the warehouse," Beanie told him.

"The warehouse?"

"Yes, you know, that storage area is under this building."

"How did you figure that out?" he asked.

She shrugged her shoulders. "It just makes sense. Besides, everyone knows that strange trucks and cars come by here during the day and at night. What do you think they're carrying away with them?"

"Are you sure that this is Main Street?" It didn't look like the busy, brightly lit thoroughfare he was used to. Where were the cars, the motorcycles, the roller bladers, and the people? Something else seemed to be missing, too. "Noise!" he realized. "Where's all the noise?"

"What noise?" Beanie asked.

Tony listened intently. "There's no noise of traffic driving by, no horns or sirens in the distance. I've never heard it so quiet before."

She shrugged her shoulders. "I guess it's all what you're used to."

"Yeah," he agreed, wondering what she would think of modern-day Moose Jaw. He pushed that thought aside. He had more important things to think about. "Now what do we do?" he asked again. He didn't want to spend the whole night standing in the dark, doing nothing.

"We wait, watch, and listen," Beanie said, pulling him back into the shadows again. "But first, let's get closer to the train station. It's the businesses on that end of Main Street, the clothing shops and the general stores, that have been hit the hardest. Those are the ones losing the most merchandise."

Scanning the deserted street, Tony and Beanie dashed like frantic gophers across High Street. They slipped from building to building along Main Street, careful to stay in the darkest shadows. An old car or two was angle-parked, nose in. The businesses had closed up long ago and no one seemed to be about. The most difficult and dangerous part was crossing the side streets. That was when they put themselves the most at risk. They would mould themselves to the shadows of the corner building, watch and listen for foot traffic, and then run across the road as quickly and quietly as foxes on the hunt. Soon they came to River Street.

"See that store across the street?" Beanie pointed to a general store that carried everything from food to clothes. "That shop belongs to my friend's family. That's one of the stores that's been robbed so much."

They were within a block of the train station. It stood proudly at the end of Main Street, the white brick of the clock tower reflecting small amounts of light. Beanie tapped Tony on the shoulder and pointed to a business with a long, tapered entranceway, its door deep in the shadows. She settled into the darkest corner, pulling him down with her. They had a clear view of the general store across the street. "This is the perfect place to hide. No one will see us here, but we can see everything that happens."

"So now we wait," Tony said, settling down beside

her. Something crumpled under him. Gingerly he sat up and pulled out a thick piece of paper. "What's this?" Smoothing it out, he leaned toward the light to get a better look. "It's an advertisement for something."

Beanie quickly scanned the paper. "It's a poster advertising the big parade the day after tomorrow. It must have fallen down from somewhere."

Tony carefully folded the paper into squares. "I'm going to save this for a souvenir," he said, tucking it safely into his pocket. "It's probably worth something back home in my time."

Beanie nodded absently, her mind on the job at hand. "I have a feeling it won't be too long before something happens."

After thirty minutes of waiting and watching from the doorway, Tony was ready to call it quits. His behind was numb from sitting on the cement and his back was sore. He wasn't used to sitting in one place for long. "Let's go, Bean —" he said, but Beanie nudged him with her elbow. He held his breath. The sound of heavy footsteps filled the air.

Tony and Beanie squeezed farther back into the shadows, then froze. The footsteps were coming toward them! Tony felt his heart speed up, its thumping sound reverberating in his chest. What am I doing here, he wondered frantically.

The heavy steps moved slowly past them. He

watched from the shadows as the big person walked by. It was a man in a uniform. He continued up the street at a leisurely pace, whistling a tuneless melody. "Did you get a good look at him?" Beanie wanted to know.

"Not really," Tony admitted, "but he looked like a police officer. He was wearing a uniform."

"Exactly." Beanie confirmed. "He was wearing the police uniform and boots. It's those boots that make so much noise." From the same direction, came the sound of another pair of footsteps, but these were different somehow. They hurried along the sidewalk and didn't seem quite so loud. Beanie pushed back into the corner again. "Here comes someone else."

It wasn't until the footsteps were almost upon them that Beanie realized that they were coming from across the street. The sound stopped abruptly. She nudged Tony in the ribs and pointed excitedly as another person slithered along in the shadows. Obviously that person didn't want to be seen.

They watched as the second person came to a stop right in front of the general store. He was also wearing a police uniform. He seemed to be waiting for something. Beanie wondered what it could be. She moved quietly, but quickly, squeezing her head out around the corner, motioning Tony to do the same. They both looked just in time to see a faint flash of light. It seemed to be coming from the police officer on their side of the street. The second officer, near the general store, lit a cigarette, the match flaring for a brief moment. Then the man stepped into the shadows of the general store where the door was located.

In the deep silence of the night, they heard the unmistakable sound of the door being forced open. The shadow of the man appeared briefly through the window of the store and then disappeared. "He's inside," Beanie said needlessly. "Let's get closer."

"You're nuts," Tony said, refusing to budge. "This is close enough. Don't forget that other cop is out there somewhere. He's the lookout. He'd spot us in a second."

"You're probably right," Beanie admitted reluctantly. "Let's just wait and see what happens."

They didn't have long to wait. The second police officer reappeared at the door. He slipped silently through it, closing it carefully behind him. Stepping out onto the sidewalk again, he lit a cigarette, letting the match burn for several seconds before he dropped it and crushed it beneath the heel of his boot. "Look," Beanie whispered, pointing at him. There, under his arm, as he walked back up the street, was a small box and several pieces of folded material. "See," she hissed in Tony's ear. "He's stolen something! Now we know how it's done. Come on, let's follow him."

She dragged Tony by the shirt out onto Main Street. He worried briefly about the other officer, until they heard the heavy sound of his feet heading away from them and toward the train station. Staying in the shadows, they crouched close to the ground and moved quickly along the edge of the buildings, following at a distance. "I want to get closer," Beanie whispered. "We need to make sure we don't lose him in the dark."

"This is close enough for me. We could get hurt if we get caught."

"You stay here then," Beanie said as she ran to keep up with the quickly retreating police officer. She left Tony lagging behind, wondering what he should do. By the time he had made up his mind to stick with her, it was too late. The cop and Beanie were both too far ahead. Jogging along in the shadows, he squinted ahead through the darkness looking for any sign of movement. Where had Beanie disappeared?

Tony kept a sharp lookout, making sure that no one else was about. He slipped from shadow to shadow against the buildings. He was halfway up the next block when he spotted her crossing Fairford Street. Then it happened. She must have kicked something lying in the road. It clanged loudly and she froze in her tracks. Tony saw the police officer whirl around. He stood staring at her, caught in the lighted street lamp. "Halt!" the man yelled, drawing his billy club. Beanie didn't wait a second longer. She whirled away and whipped around the corner, running down Fairford Street toward the darkened park, the cop in hot pursuit a few metres behind her.

Tony ran after her. The cop had his billy club raised above his head. "Hide, Beanie!" Tony yelled. Instantly he realized his mistake and froze.

The police officer must have heard him, for he halted and swung around. Tony dived toward the wall of the nearest building, burrowing between two immense columns of cement, hiding in the dark shadows. He stood stone still, trying not to pant too loudly even though his heart thundered in his ears. Senses straining, he waited until he heard the sound of heavy footsteps moving away from him; then he cautiously poked his head around the base of the white pillar. Seeing the police officer's back, he followed, keeping back a safe distance.

The cop hesitated at the corner of the park, as if not sure where to go. A tall darkened building that looked like a school stood on the opposite corner. Tony hadn't seen where Beanie had gone, but neither had the cop. He seemed to be peering into the darkness of the park. He took a step or two onto the grass as Tony sidled closer. A clump of bushes stood nearby. Tony heard a small scurrying sound and then a yelp of surprise. "I got ya," the cop yelled.

Tony stood statue still, a few metres away, in the shadow of a tree, watching as Beanie squirmed, trying to get out of the cop's grasp. How could he save her, he wondered, fear paralyzing his limbs. He watched in horror as the cop began to drag Beanie out of the bushes, yelling bad words at her. Suddenly anger replaced fear. With swift and sure movements, Tony wiggled out of his backpack, unzipped it and grabbed the toy gun. He would be the hero, the good guy in the movie. Confidence surged into his body, making all of his actions sure and precise. The gun was a toy, but at that moment it looked and felt real. Holding it in his hands, he was sure that he could do anything. Taking a deep breath, he yelled, "Stop or I'll shoot!"

The cop froze for a moment, then laughed. "Says who?" he sneered. "You sound like a young punk looking for trouble."

He'd show that cop who was boss, Tony decided. He pointed the toy at the cop and pulled the trigger and held on. Three sharp blasts pierced the night as the gun fired. Bursts of colour flashed from the barrel, making the black plastic gleam like metal. The gun looked convincingly real, even to Tony. The cop must have thought so too, for he dropped his hold on Beanie and took off running toward Main Street. Beanie cheered and raced to Tony. "You did it," she yelled, kissing him on the cheek. "You're my hero."

Tony beamed. "Whew! That was close. Come on," he said, grabbing her by the arm. "I don't think we have much time to lose. I think he'll be back looking for us with more police. We need a safe place to hide."

"It's too late," Beanie answered, looking toward the far end of the park, near the library. "See those lanterns? They're coming this way. Quick! Follow me!"

She crouched down and ran across Fairford Street and into the schoolyard. The building was engulfed by its own huge black shadow. "We'll be safe here," she said, dragging Tony back into the blackest shadows near the wall where the steps led up into the building.

"Are you sure?" he asked, trying to keep the quiver out of his voice. "Those lanterns are pretty bright."

"Sure," she answered confidently. "This is Victoria School – it's my school. We can hide in here." She pushed against the side of the staircase, and a small opening appeared. "Only the kids know about this. We use it all the time for hiding in."

They sat hunched beside the stairs and against the wall, watching as the lanterns advanced through the park. About halfway across, they seemed to stop, becoming stationary. "What's going on?" Tony asked.

"I don't know, but I think it'll help us. Come on. Let's go while we can."

"Where will we go?" Tony wanted to know.

"Back to Main Street. They won't look there. They think we're hiding in the park, see?"

Beanie was right. The cops seemed to have spread out through the park, heading toward her house. She was really glad that cop hadn't gotten a good look at her face. He would have recognized her for sure. "Come on, Tony. Let's go."

Carefully, stealthily, they flattened themselves against the schoolhouse and crept down the length of the building. At the corner of the building they turned to go behind it and were lost from sight to anyone in the park. They ran across the schoolyard and over to High Street, only slowing as they neared Main Street. Watching for any movement, they stayed in the shadows and then dashed across the street. "Where are we going?" Tony asked.

"Let's see if we can get into the tunnels," Beanie said. "They won't look for us there!"

"The tunnels?" He was both shocked and excited about entering the tunnels again. "Should we do that?" he asked, common sense winning over.

"Should we even be out here this late at night, pretending to be Sherlock Holmes?" she answered.

"Okay." Tony gave in without a fight. He really did want to see the tunnels again, even if they scared him. "Which way do we go?" He was totally disoriented.

"Just follow me," Beanie replied with confidence. "I know what I'm doing."

DREAMS DO COME TRUE

Vance stormed through the park, seething, think-ing vicious thoughts about Beanie. It was after midnight and she wasn't home! Their Ma had just made the discovery and sent him out to look for her, and he had to get up early to sell newspapers. "Girls," he muttered as he marched through the dark. First Andrea had lectured him about his treatment of Rosie, and now Beanie! He had to admit though, that he did feel badly about fighting with Andrea. He could see how upset she was about being stuck in the past. He couldn't imagine trying to live somewhere that was foreign and strange. The farthest he had ever been away from home was to Regina for the Exhibition one year. What would it be like to wonder if you would ever see your family or home again?

He was so engrossed in his own thoughts and anger about having to go look for Beanie that he didn't pay any attention to the lights swaying in the distance. It wasn't until they were upon him that a sense of alarm registered in his tired brain. By then it was too late to flee. "Halt!" a voice called. Strong arms grabbed him, pinning his hands behind his back.

"Wh-what's going on?" he sputtered. "I didn't do anything."

"What are you doing in the park?" a voice demanded. With bright lights shining in his eyes, Vance couldn't see who held him captive. Fear clogged his throat, making breathing difficult. Was it gangsters? Had Ol' Scarface finally come back to settle that old score? What did these men want with him?

"I'm just passing through," he answered lamely. He wasn't about to tell them he was out this late looking for his little sister. Let them draw their own conclusions.

"It was him all right," a voice declared, pushing a lantern into his face.

"I tell you, I didn't do anything," he said. "I just got into the park myself!" He squirmed, trying to free himself, but the men who held him were stronger than he was. He realized with alarm that these men weren't mobsters at all; they were policemen.

"Take him to the station," the voice commanded. "We'll get better answers from him there. We have our ways." Sharp laughter filled the air and Vance shivered. It sounded just like Ol' Scarface.

As if to prove they meant business, a rough hand grabbed his hair. "We do have our ways," a voice sneered.

"I didn't do anything." Vance protested more loudly this time. "I didn't do anything I tell you! Leave me alone!"

"Leave the boy alone." A loud commanding voice caused the others to whirl around.

"Why, Paterson," one of the men jeered. "What are you doing out at this time of night? I thought you were on the day shift."

Officer Paterson stepped into the circle of light. "I know this boy, and I'll vouch for him. He wouldn't do anything wrong." When the officers made no move to release Vance, Paterson took a decisive step forward. "I said, unhand him."

"All right, all right," the men grumbled, but did as Paterson requested. "But if it wasn't him, who was it? Did you hear those gunshots? Someone has one powerful weapon, I tell you. Those bullets went whizzing by my head! It's a miracle I wasn't killed!"

"Well, it seems to me that you're wasting your time looking here. You can see that this boy is unarmed. And besides that, where would he get such a weapon? Go try elsewhere." Mr. Paterson put a protective arm around Vance's shoulders and prepared to walk away.

One of the men stepped close to Mr. Paterson, a

sneer on his face. "Better watch your back, Paterson."

"Is that a threat?"

"You take it whatever way you want."

Officer Paterson studied him for a moment and then turned away from the group, taking Vance with him. "Now what was that all about?" he said under his breath as the last of the men disappeared into the dark, grumbling as they went.

"I don't know, sir," Vance replied. "But thank you. You didn't have to do that for me."

Officer Paterson let his hand rest upon Vance's shoulder. "You're a good kid, Vance, and I know you're innocent of whatever they're accusing you of. I don't know what they were up to, but it looked more like a lynching mob than any kind of police work I've ever seen. There are strange things going on around here. The more time I spend in Moose Jaw, the more my gut instincts tell me that something is not quite right, but I haven't been able to put my finger on what it is yet. Oh well," he sighed. "I'm just glad I got here in time. There's no telling what that gang would have done to you, and that worries me. They looked like a bunch of mobsters."

Vance jumped at the word *mobsters,* wondering if Officer Paterson knew of the tunnels and the rum-running that had gone on in Moose Jaw. "Thank you again, sir," Vance muttered.

"You're welcome," Officer Paterson nodded at him.

"Now, just where are you off to this late at night?"

Vance sighed audibly. "I'm out looking for Beanie, again!"

"She must keep you hopping, with all her antics."

"She sure does," Vance agreed. There was no doubt in his mind where Beanie was. It had something to do with the tunnels. All she seemed to do these days was get herself into trouble. She really didn't seem to understand how dangerous it was to play in the tunnels, even if she thought she could stop the robberies from happening. Realistically, what could she do? She was just a kid. For a brief moment, he wondered if the cops had been looking for her! "Naw," he said aloud, totally dismissing the idea. Where would she have gotten a powerful gun like the policemen had mentioned? Anyway, she wouldn't even know how to use it. What kind of trouble could one little girl get into that would make that many cops want to catch her?

He waved a hand at Officer Paterson and turned to sprint toward Main Street. "Vance," Officer Paterson called him and he turned back.

"Yes, sir?"

"If you or Beanie are in any kind of trouble, you will come to me, won't you?" When his request was met with silence, the police officer continued. "I mean it, Vance. I might be able to help."

Vance nodded, pressing his lips together to keep from smiling. It wouldn't do to get too attached to this man, he reminded himself. Hadn't his own father abandoned them, leaving them to fend for themselves? Why would a stranger care about what was happening in his life? Vance had to admit though, it felt good to have someone concerned about his welfare. It was almost as nice as having a father to worry about him. "Thank you, sir," he said gruffly. "I'll keep it in mind."

As he continued toward Main Street, his instincts from being a tunnel runner took over. He slid into the shadows of the building at the corner and stopped, listening for sounds. All was quiet. No automobiles chugged down the street, and it was too late for people to be out. Hesitating in the doorway, he felt his heart speed up. Something didn't feel right. The hairs on the back of his neck prickled and stood up. It was almost as if he was being watched!

Standing in the shadows, he held his breath, waiting. He wasn't sure what he was looking for until he heard the sound of footsteps travelling toward him. He slid along the building a few metres away from the corner. He didn't want to be too close. If the person turned at the corner he would at least have a chance to escape.

Suddenly the footsteps got faster. They sounded different somehow, more solid, perhaps. As if the person had stepped off the sidewalk and into the street. The steps were headed away from him. He cautiously moved back to the corner, staring into the dark street. There he thought he saw the shadow of a man step onto the sidewalk on the other side of the road. The shadow merged with the shadow of the large warehouse on the corner of Ominica Street and Main, and the man was lost to Vance.

His movements had been suspicious and Vance's curiosity was aroused. He slid farther along the building, and then, gaining courage, stepped onto Main Street, quickly crossing. The man had disappeared. Straining his ears for any sound, Vance melted into the shadow of Jackson's Furniture Factory. Where had the man gone so quickly? Vance hadn't even heard the sound of a door opening. The tunnels, he realized, remembering that the storage area was just below this building. There must be a tunnel entrance close by, and knowing Beanie, he would have to look for her in the tunnels. Since he couldn't waste time searching for another entrance, he did the only thing he could. He took off for Rosie's place, just up the street. He could enter the tunnels through that outside stairwell. Positive that he would find Beanie somewhere underground, he hoped that he could get to her before she got herself into trouble.

It was only a minute or two before he stood under Rosie's window. He had thought that Beanie might be here, trying to convince Andrea to help her with some bizarre scheme, but the darkened kitchen window told him he would be wasting his time looking for her there. Catching his breath, he descended into the back stairwell and slipped quietly through the doors, carefully closing them behind him.

Andrea awoke with a start, sitting up straight in the strange bed, her breath coming in sharp gasps. She'd had that nightmare again, and this time she had seen the faces clearly. She had been running and running through a long tunnel which had no hiding places, a man breathing down her neck as he chased her. It was like being on a conveyor belt; she ran fast but didn't seem to be getting anywhere, and the man kept gaining on her! Then ahead of her, another man materialized out of the dirt wall and grabbed her. Together they pulled her to a stop; rough hands reached for her neck....

She shook her head, dislodging the dream from her weary brain, and prepared to get comfortable in the bed again, wondering if she would be able to go back to sleep. She stretched her legs. Feeling that they were caught in the blankets, she looked down at them. In the darkness of the room she realized that her legs were caught in the long dress she was wearing. Of course, this was Rosie's spare bedroom and she was back in time. Where was Tony, she wondered with alarm. He had been asleep when she had stretched out beside him. Now he was gone.

She was positive that he had gone back to the tunnels. Where else would he go at this time of night? Quickly searching their belongings on the floor confirmed that he was gone. Tony's backpack was nowhere to be seen. She had no choice; she had to find Tony. He had no idea the kind of trouble he could get into in the tunnels, but she did. With a long sigh, anger and worry making her forget to be quiet, she pulled on her running shoes, grabbed a flashlight and headed for the door.

It took every ounce of courage she had to slip out of the silent house and around to the backyard. The very last thing she wanted to do was go back into the tunnels alone, especially at this time of night. But Tony was there – he had to be, and it was up to her to take care of him. Hadn't Grandpa Talbot told her that on the phone? With a sigh of resignation, she pulled the heavy door open and clumped down the stairs. Why did Tony insist on being so foolhardy? She seethed as she pushed her way through the doors. Even in her anger she remembered to shut them. It wouldn't do to announce to anyone her presence in the tunnels.

In her sleep-fogged brain, reality and fantasy collided as she moved into the tunnel. Panic nipped at her mind. Was this reality, or her horrible dream? She slipped through the tunnel, willing herself not to run.

She couldn't shake the feeling that something terrible was about to happen. Trying to calm herself, she took a long deep breath and slowly exhaled. Just let me find Tony fast and get out of here, she willed silently, wishing that she could let him fend for himself.

She reached the storage area and stopped to listen. Hearing nothing, she continued, using the lanterns as her only guide. The walls seemed to close in on her as soon as she entered the forbidden tunnel. The lanterns were much farther apart than she remembered and it was almost pitch dark. She strained to listen, her scalp tingling in fear. Stumbling over a small object on the dirt floor, she instinctively reached out toward the narrow walls to catch herself. Her hand encountered soft material as a voice rasped, "Now I've got ya! You've been following me!"

She screamed, a loud piercing sound that reverberated through the tunnel. A hand clamped itself over her mouth. "You can't get away!" The words were whispered in the darkness as warm moist breath fanned her cheek. Just like in her dream, instinct took over. She kicked the man hard in the shin. Hearing him grunt in pain, she wrenched herself free and whirled around, fleeing toward the storage area. Suddenly she was lost in the dream again. Reality blurred and she wasn't sure what was real anymore.

The forbidden tunnel was so black she felt as if she was suspended in space. Hiking her dress up to her knees, she ran. Her heart had already kicked into triple time and it was hard to catch her breath. Just as she neared the storage area a man seemed to material- ize from the tunnel wall. He grabbed her as she ran past. "I've got her, Boss," he called out.

"Good, hang on to her," the voice called from behind. Andrea heard footsteps coming closer, then felt her arm being grabbed. She was whirled roughly around by the arm and found herself face to face with the sinister-looking man in her dreams. Her heart stopped as she felt hands on her throat once again. "I want to watch you die."

Fingers tightened around her neck, making breath- ing difficult and her nightmare real. She began to see stars. Visions of her parents and grandparents flashed before her eyes and she knew that this was the end. Just like in the dream, she was about to die....

Tony Takes Charge

"What was that?" Beanie asked from her hiding place in the storage area.

"It sounded like Andrea," Tony whispered. They could hear the sounds of feet scraping on gravel and some grunts and groans coming from the forbidden tunnel and then a weak call for help. "It is Andrea!" Tony stared at Beanie with owl eyes of fear. "What are we going to do?"

"I don't know," Beanie said, jumping up from behind the boxes, "but we better do something fast! It sounds as if they're hurting her!" She dodged around boxes and heaps of clothing and turned toward the forbidden tunnel, colliding with someone bigger. "Oh!" Beanie looked up into a familiar face.

"Sh-h-h," Vance warned, his finger to his lips. "We

don't want to be found out."

"That's Andrea!" Tony called, running toward them. "We've got to save my sister!"

The shuffling noises grew louder. It sounded as if the men were moving through the forbidden tunnel toward the storage area, dragging something with them. "We'd better hide for now," Vance said. "Let's see what they're going to do with her."

"They might beat her up," Tony whimpered, "or even kill her."

"No," Vance reassured, although he wasn't sure himself. If they started to hurt her, he decided, he'd rush them. He had the element of surprise on his side and he might be able to save her. "We're not even sure it's Andrea."

"It has to be Andrea," Beanie said. "Who else would it be? She was probably out looking for Tony and ran into those men. One of them is the guy that chased me. He stole something from the store! We saw him do it!"

"Yeah," Vance said grimly. "So what? What do you think you can do about it, Beanie? All of your running around in these tunnels has caused nothing but problems, and now one of us is in real trouble."

"I know," Beanie agreed, a look of chagrin on her face. "But that man stole something, Vance! I know he did! It's the same guy that chased me into the park! We didn't know Andrea would get into trouble!"

"Sh-h-h," Vance warned, leading the way toward a large stack of boxes. "We'll worry about him later. Right now, let's hide and see if this is Andrea. You know, even if it isn't, we'll have to rescue her. Whoever it is, we can't leave her in the hands of these creeps."

Suddenly three figures emerged from the forbidden tunnel, moving toward the far wall of the storage area. The two taller figures walked, one on either side of a smaller person, whom they held under the armpits. "Ya knocked her unconscious, Boss," the taller one complained.

"I didn't neither. She turned around so fast, she smacked into the wall."

"You had your hands around her throat, Boss. I thought you were gonna strangle her."

"Well, we can't have her wandering around these tunnels anymore. She's seen and heard too much. We sure don't need women down here taking a Sunday stroll. You'll have to get rid of her somehow."

"Me?" the tall man squeaked, halting in midstep. "You want me to do her in?"

"Yeah."

"How? I ain't never killed anyone before."

"I don't care how you do it, just get the job done! And, I don't want anyone to find the body, you got that? Nobody!"

"What would I do with the body?"

The boss sighed loudly. "Dump it in the creek.

177

Better yet, throw it onto one of the empty railway cars heading south. They wouldn't find the body until the train hits Chicago. I'll help you get her into the warehouse, but after that, you're on your own. I can't be seen around here. Get rid of her quickly and report back to me!"

"Sure, boss," the man sputtered. The men dragged Andrea through the maze of boxes, up the three crudely built stairs and through the door. It closed with a loud thump, leaving the three friends shaking with fear.

"They're going to kill her and it's all my fault," Beanie wailed.

"It's my fault more than yours," Tony sniffed. "I was the one who wanted to travel back in time in the first place! I thought this would all be fun – like a game or something...I didn't think it'd be so dangerous."

"Cut it out, you two," Vance said sharply. He was as worried as they were, but he couldn't let it show. He was the oldest; he needed to think of a plan. "I can't think when you're whining, and that's not going to help Andrea. We need to get into that warehouse. They're not going to waste a lot of time. We need to think fast. I still can't believe it's cops talking like that!" Vance shook his head. "What's this world coming to?"

They moved closer to the door, trying to stay behind boxes just in case the cops suddenly reappeared. Once there, Vance motioned the other two to hide. Creeping closer to the door, he pressed his ear against it, listening. Hearing nothing, he reached for the knob and gently turned it. The door swung open and Vance peered inside.

The warehouse was full of furniture and huge wooden crates. In the centre a room had been built. It looked like an office. The door had been left open and a beam of light slashed across the floor. Vance could hear the murmur of voices.

"What's going on?" Beanie whispered.

Vance waved her silent and then motioned for them to follow him. The trio crept up the stairs and into the warehouse, making sure to close the door behind them. They made their way across the gloomy warehouse, until they were just outside the office door. Vance, who was closest to the door, strained his ears, but he couldn't hear what was being said. He inched forward until he could see into the room. It was a small office with a large wooden desk, a table and a few chairs. Andrea was tied to one of the chairs, her arms secured to her chest, a gag in her mouth. Two men were in the room with her. One paced back and forth as he ran agitated fingers through his hair. The other sat back in a chair, balancing on its two hind legs, his arms folded at his chest. On the opposite side of the room another door to the office stood slightly ajar. Afraid of being spotted, Vance slipped back a few metres, the younger two following him. "I wish I could hear their plans. Then we'd have an idea of how we could rescue her."

The three huddled together in the shadows, each wracking his brain. No plan emerged. "Maybe one of us could sneak into the office," Beanie offered, looking dubious.

"We'd get caught for sure." Vance sighed. "If only I could be a fly on the wall."

"A fly on the wall?" Tony questioned, then he smiled. "You still use that expression, Grandpa. Now I know what it means...if only we could find a way to get inside the office –" Tony's head popped up. "I think I just might have an idea!" Whipping his backpack off, Tony undid the zipper. It rasped in the silence, sounding like thunder in their nervous minds. He paused, but no one heard. Reaching inside, he pulled out his walkie-talkies and the remote control car.

Beanie picked up first a walkie-talkie and then the toy car. Turning it over in her hand, she asked, "What kind of car is this?" as she examined its black and white paint job. "What's this red bump on top?"

"It's a police car," Tony said. Rummaging around in a side pocket, he came up with several elastic bands and some string. "I got it for Christmas last year. It's my favourite toy!"

"Now isn't the time to play," Vance said. "Put that stuff away! We might have to run fast and I don't want to be tripping over your toys!"

"But Vance, this just might work!" Tony explained as he fiddled with the car. "That's a walkie-talkie. Beanie will tell you how it works." Beanie quickly explained while Tony searched his backpack for a few more things. "If I put this elastic band around like this, it'll hold this button down," he said as he worked. "That means that if the cops in there talk, we'll hear what they say through the walkie-talkie we have out here."

"But how are you going to get that thing close enough to the bad guys for us to hear what they're saying?"

Tony grinned. "That's the easy part." He placed the walkie-talkie on top of the remote control car and then wrapped the string around both the car body and the walkie-talkie. "Help me tie this on really tight. We don't want it to fall off in the office."

Vance shook his head. "What are you going to do? Sit by the door and push that car into the room? We'll be spotted for sure."

"No," Tony answered, holding up the remote control box. "I'm going to steer it into the office using this. I'll show you how it works." He switched on the power button and pressed forward. The car made a whirring noise and moved ahead a few centimetres. He turned a tiny steering wheel on the control box and the car curved around in a figure eight. "See how it works?"

Beanie and Vance stared at the car, their eyes popping. They had never seen anything like this toy in their lives. "It's a miracle!" Beanie said. "It's magic!"

Tony giggled. "Not in my time, it's not. It's just a simple remote control toy. The thing is, I'll have to get close enough to see where it's going." He left the car where it was on the floor and handed Beanie the other walkie-talkie. "You just listen here. We should be able to make out what's being said." He scooted toward the door.

"Be careful," Beanie whispered, huddling farther into the shadows, clutching the walkie-talkie in sweaty hands.

"Be quiet," Vance warned. "We don't want to get caught."

Tony nodded and carefully positioned himself near the open door. He sat back in the shadows, his head just sticking into the light, hoping that no one in the room would notice. He pressed the button and the toy car whirred toward him. He steered it around the open door, trying to keep it in the shadows, hoping that it wouldn't be seen. Waiting until both men were looking away from the door, he quickly steered the car into the room. He watched as it zipped around a large wooden filing cabinet. Moisture popped out on his forehead and he felt a slight tremor in his fingers. He hoped this was from fear and worry and not from his medical condition. He couldn't have problems now.

Manoeuvring the car under the table, he pulled back into the shadows and gestured toward Vance and Beanie. They shook their heads, motioning toward the other walkie-talkie, and he knew that they still couldn't hear anything. He'd have to get the car closer to the men.

Positioning himself back near the doorway, he scanned the room, wondering where to place the car. He watched for a few minutes as the one man continued to pace, his route always taking him within centimetres of Andrea's chair. The other man sat in his chair near Andrea. His best bet would be to get the car under Andrea's chair! Could he do it without being caught?

Wiping sweat from his forehead, he decided that he would have to take a risk. They would never hear anything unless he could get the car and the walkie-talkie close enough. Waiting until the pacing man was at the far end of the office, his back toward the room, Tony held his breath and pressed the button. The car moved slowly under the table and through the legs of a chair. Steering it around the desk, he managed to get it under Andrea's chair just as the pacing man turned on his heel and started back across the room.

Tony ducked out of the light, leaning his back against the wall, trying to calm his pounding heart. That was probably the scariest and the bravest thing he had ever done in his life. He peered into the darkness and watched as Beanie and Vance put their ears toward the walkie-talkie. Their smiles and waves of triumph told him everything he needed to know. They could hear!

As soon as Tony had made his way back, Vance started whispering excitedly. "We need to get her out of there now! They're just waiting for a car to come for them. That man they call the boss is sending a car and those two men are going to kill Andrea and dump her body on the train. It leaves the station in twenty minutes!"

"What can we do?" Tony asked, suddenly numb with fear. "We can't let them kill Andrea!"

"We're just kids," Vance reminded them grimly. "These guys are adults, and they have weapons!"

Beanie's grin almost lit up the dark warehouse. "So do we!" She pointed to Tony's backpack on the floor between them. "We have a really powerful weapon, one that they're afraid of. Isn't there a way we could use it again?"

Vance shook his head. "What kind of 'powerful' weapon do you two think you have?" Tony drew the toy gun out of his knapsack.

Vance took it gingerly, turning it over and over as he examined it. "This isn't real," he said, doubt in his voice.

Tony smiled. "No, it's just a toy, but they don't know that!"

"There are only two of them," Beanie pointed out,

"and we managed to scare one of them off once before with this toy."

Tony smiled. "Maybe there's a way to use the gun and the walkie-talkie to make it seem like there are more of us, but first, I have to get the car and that other walkie-talkie back."

"Just do it quickly," Vance muttered, worry etched on his face. "We don't have much time."

"Don't you want to know the plan?" Tony asked.

Vance shook his head. "We don't have time for you to explain it all. Just tell me what you want me to do. This is going to be a one-shot deal; it's all or nothing. We won't have time for Plan B if this one fails."

"It won't fail," Beanie said, crossing her fingers and making a wish. "It can't fail. We have to save Andrea."

Tony took up his position by the office door and waited for the chance to move the car again. What was making him so brave, he wondered. He should be a mess of nerves, considering the grave danger Andrea was in. Pushing worrisome thoughts away, he concentrated on the job at hand. When the pacing man turned his back, Tony pressed the button. The car shot ahead, bumping into a leg of Andrea's chair. Quickly he tried to steer around it. The car moved backward, bumping into another leg. He was losing his touch! Fingers suddenly nervous, he couldn't get the hand-eye coordination right!

Feeling eyes on him, he looked across the room.

Andrea was staring at him, her eyes wide and questioning. Holding up the remote, he gestured wildly on the floor near her feet. Andrea understood. Blindly she stretched her legs, pushing the car out from between her feet and under the table as the man turned back toward her.

"Stop squirming around, Girlie," the man said loudly, stopping before her chair, roughly punching her shoulder. "You ain't going anywhere, except for a long train ride south." He laughed. "Kiss this world goodbye, you're done with it."

Tony took advantage of the man's preoccupation. Pressing the buttons, he steered the car under the table. It skirted the filing cabinet, zipping through the door and out into the dark warehouse. Picking it up, he hurried back to Vance and Beanie. "Okay," he whispered, pulling the elastic band off the speaking button. "This is ready to go now."

"You'd better tell us how this is going to work," Vance decided, looking scornfully at the toys on the floor between them. He didn't seem to put much faith in the plan.

Tony sighed. "Well, I was thinking that you could yell into this walkie-talkie, once I get this one positioned in the room. I'll operate the remote control car. This car has a siren, too! If I press this button, it'll make a loud wailing sound. It'll really scare those guys, especially with you yelling, 'This is a raid,' and

186

with the gun firing." He picked up the car and turned it over. "You know, I think this plan is really going to work! Beanie, you're going to have to fire the toy gun." He showed her how it worked. "Don't stop firing it, and once the bad guys have cleared the room, you need to get in there and untie Andrea. I just hope they're scared enough to run first." He took a deep breath. "Can we do this?"

"Of course we can!" Beanie said.

"We don't have a choice," Vance reminded them. "And once we get Andrea, we'll hit the tunnels, through the door we came in, and we don't look back until we're all safely at Rosie's place, got it? Don't stop, no matter what's happening behind us."

Tony and Beanie nodded. "Okay, let's put this plan into action."

"Yell into that walkie-talkie," Tony advised. "We want to make sure that those guys hear you and are really afraid. Make a lot of noise." He handed Beanie the gun to carry, and, grabbing the car with the walkie-talkie still tied securely to the roof, Tony moved toward the door. Beanie followed along behind, being careful not to bang the gun against anything. Once near the doorway, Tony put the car on the floor and stuck his head around the door jamb. Everything was as it had been before. The pacing man still paced. The other man had picked up a knife and sat cleaning his fingernails with its sharp tip.

Tony knew that the siren button would have to be switched on while the car was still in his hands. He would have to work fast, pressing the button, putting the car down and getting it into the room. He sent a quick prayer heavenward, that his plan would work, and then he pressed the button.

A piercing wail rent the air as gunshots filled the room. A commanding voice called that this was a raid and the men froze. The man balancing on the chair fell over backwards with a loud thump. He lay dazed in a heap for a second, then scrambling to his feet, he dashed out the far door and into the warehouse. The pacing man stared at Andrea as if deciding what to do; then he too took off as if dogs were hot on his trail. Through the noisy confusion, Beanie shoved the gun at Tony and ran into the room. She struggled with the knots that held Andrea prisoner while Andrea sent garbled messages through the gag. Finally Beanie understood and pulled the gag from her mouth. "Get the knife, on the floor," Andrea gasped.

Knife in hand, Beanie quickly sliced through the ropes. "Come on, let's get out of here." Hand in hand, the girls ran from the office. Tony dropped the remote, but kept the gun, running along behind. He didn't have time to stop and collect his toys. It was a small sacrifice to pay for Andrea's safety.

Vance brought up the rear. Bursting through the warehouse door and into the storage area, the kids ran. Vance shut the door and followed behind, Tony's backpack bouncing on his back.

They ran along, the only sounds uneven breathing and their feet crunching on the gravel. Vance was terrified that they would encounter someone using the tunnels, but luck was with them. They pushed through the doors, coming at last to the outside steps that led into Rosie's backyard. "Sh-h-h," Vance warned, as he shut the last door. "We can't stay here long, but we have to make sure no one's out there." Pushing past the girls, he carefully opened the slanted door a crack. Cool air rushed in as he peered out into the silent world. "It's all clear," he said, pushing the door farther open. "Come on, let's get out of here. Beanie, you're coming home with me." He grabbed her arm, clamping strong fingers around her wrist. "I don't want to lose you!"

Andrea shook out her dress. "Th-thanks for rescuing me," she said, trying to keep tears away. Her voice shook. "I thought I was – I was –"

"I know," Vance replied, patting her clumsily on the shoulder. "I'm just glad that we were there and that we made it in time."

"I've never been so scared in all my life," Andrea continued. "Not even last year, when Ol' Scarface was so mean to me."

Beanie wriggled out of Vance's grasp. Throwing her arms around Andrea's waist, she hugged her tightly. "I'm glad you're safe."

"Yeah," Andrea sniffed. "Thanks for saving me, Beanie, and Tony, and Vance." She smiled, grabbing Tony too. "You're a hero, Squirt!"

"We can do this in the morning," Vance said, his eyes scanning the dark. "Someone's going to come looking for us, soon. We'd better get going."

They whispered quick goodbyes, Vance and Beanie sliding into the shadows to hurry home, while Andrea and Tony crept upstairs to Rosie's place. "I feel a little weak and shaky," Tony said as they slipped quietly into Rosie's kitchen.

"We can check your blood, if you think we should, Tony. It might be out of whack because of all of the excitement, but you shouldn't need insulin until morning. Remember. You only get it twice a day and never this late at night. I think it was just all of the excitement and stress we've just been through."

Tony nodded, "You're right. I'm just really tired right now."

Andrea nodded. "I'm going to bed. I'm beat."

ARRESTED!

Andrea hadn't been in bed for more than a few minutes when a thundering noise pounded into her brain. She sat up at the sound of a door crashing against the wall with a loud bang.

She stumbled out of the bedroom. "What's going on?" Her hair was sleep-tousled and stuck out in every direction. Tony tagged along after her.

"Sh-h-h," Vance directed, gesturing wildly for her to be quiet. Pulling a wide-eyed Beanie into the room behind him, he shut the door and crept over to the table. "Keep the lights off."

Baby Alan had woken up with all the noise and was screaming at the top of his lungs. "We were almost caught. There's something going on out there." They stood frozen around the table and the open window, and Andrea had that familiar sense of déjà vu. It was only last year that she, Vance, and Rosie had sat beside the darkened window, watching the gangsters look for a limping man on the loose.

Andrea, Vance, Beanie, and Tony drew near to the window, hidden behind the white curtains. "We just barely managed to escape those guys," he said, indicating the group of uniformed men who stood in a cluster beside the cellar entrance. "They're up to no good. They're carrying clothes and things from the warehouse. I think we really scared them with our rescue plan. They're up to something."

Andrea studied the men closely. "That one is the boss!" She shuddered. "He's the one in my dreams! He's the one who grabbed me by the throat in the tunnel. He wanted me dead!"

"I don't like this." Vance leaned closer to the window. "I wish that baby would be quiet, I can't hear a thing!" Sounds of murmuring and strains of a lullaby came from the closed bedroom door.

The boss appeared to be giving the men orders. He pointed up to Rosie's rooming house and then at the cellar. "– we can blame it on him." The words floated on wind currents into the open window. "We'll come out smelling like a rose and we'll have caught the criminal. No one will suspect that it was us! They'll all think he's the real crook."

"We'll get him, Boss," one of the men replied.

"Give me five minutes to get home first. I can't be seen anywhere near here at this time of night. Then go and arrest him. Jeffreys, you run and get that pesky newspaper reporter, Hamilton. He can capture the whole thing. Get him to bring one of those cameras, too. They can splash his picture across the front page! He'll never work in our town again. That'll teach him to meddle in our business! Even if he is a cop!"

The boss strode around the side of the house and out of sight. "I don't like this," Vance whispered as they watched the cops milling around in the backyard, checking their pocket watches. "They're trying to frame Mr. Paterson!"

Baby Alan had quit crying and Rosie suddenly appeared in the kitchen. "What's going on here? Is this a party in my own house? Someone forgot to invite me," she said wryly. "And I thought you weren't ever going to step foot in my house again." She pinned Vance with a glare.

He had the good grace to look embarrassed. "Sorry, Rosie. I –"

"Never mind." Rosie juggled the baby to her other arm. "What's going on?"

Vance quickly filled her in on Andrea's rescue and their quick escape from the tunnels, and then his and Beanie's need to return. "This was the best place to come."

Rosie looked stricken, a sick look crossing her face.

"I heard you say that they're out to get someone? Oh no! I'll bet they mean –" But it was too late. The five minutes was up. The police barged into the front door of the rooming house, almost breaking it off the hinges. It banged against the wall behind it as heavy footsteps trampled up the stairs. Baby Alan began to scream again and Rosie patted his back.

"They're coming here," Tony guessed, clutching Andrea's arm. "They're going to arrest us all!"

"No." Rosie thrust the wailing baby into Andrea's arms and pulled her housecoat tightly around her waist. "They're after Constable Paterson." She flung open her own door and headed down the stairs as the police banged on the door a floor below.

Rosie pounded down the stairs, followed closely by Beanie and Tony. Andrea hovered inside the doorway, clutching the screaming baby to her chest. Vance stood near the top of the steps in shadows where the police couldn't see him, a stricken look on his face. "You're under arrest," vibrated through the house.

A very disgruntled and sleepy-looking Paterson was dragged from his bed, handcuffed, and pushed roughly out into the small hallway. He stumbled and fell to his knees. "You can't arrest him," Rosie yelled, pulling at one of the officer's arms. "He's innocent, I tell you! He's innocent."

"Shut your mouth, Rosie." One of the police officers made a threatening gesture in her direction. "We might have to do a little more investigation and discover that Paterson here had an accomplice, a female accomplice, if you get my drift." He laughed, a grating sound echoing in the darkened hallway.

"Go back to your apartment, Miss Rosie," Paterson pleaded. "Don't get yourself in trouble because of me. I'll get out of this somehow. I will. Don't worry, Miss Rosie."

"What do you think he did?" Beanie demanded. "I want to know what he did." Rosie put a restraining arm on Beanie's shoulder, but Beanie shrugged it off. "What did he do?"

"It's not your business, kid, but he's been stealing from many Main Street businesses. We've been watching him for months and we've finally got enough evidence to nail him. Go get dressed, Paterson, unless you want us to parade you through downtown Moose Jaw in your pajamas!"

"That's all a lie," Beanie shouted. "I know that's a lie be –" Rosie slapped a hand over Beanie's lips.

"The child is distraught," she explained in a controlled voice. "She's never seen anyone get arrested before."

"You don't have proof," Tony added. "Where's your proof?"

An officer pulled a woman's dress out from under his jacket. "We found this in his room. It's one of the items missing from Campbell's Department store. We also found boxes of stuff in the outside stairwell behind this house. He's the culprit and he's going to jail!"

Paterson shrugged his arms in defeat. "I'll go get dressed and come with you, but you haven't heard the end of this from me."

AFTER A SLEEPLESS NIGHT of anger and worry, everyone met at Rosie's apartment. Beanie arrived first, having woken at the crack of dawn. She had finally managed to evade her mother's watchful presence and slip out the side door, arriving at Rosie's door within minutes. Knocking quietly, she tried the knob and found the door locked.

Footsteps sounded across the wooden floor and the door swung open, revealing Tony's anxious face. "You might as well come in," he said with reluctance. "I'm just about to get my insulin shot for the morning." He screwed up his face, tears already glistening in his eyes. "I hate having diabetes."

"What exactly is it?" Beanie wanted to know. "I don't think I've ever heard of it before. What does it do to you?"

"I hate it!" Tony repeated, his voice hoarse with emotion. "It's a condition that happens to some people, like me. I don't know if I can explain it exactly, but being diabetic means that my body doesn't produce insulin. You need insulin so glucose or sugar gets absorbed into your cells and used for energy. A person can die without insulin. So I have to get insulin by taking shots and I have to watch what I eat and when I eat. It's a real pain. I hate it!"

Beanie thought it all through. It didn't make much sense to her. "So, do you have to go see the doctor every day to get a shot?"

Tony smiled. "No, my family learned how to do it for me. Usually my mom does it, but since we got to Moose Jaw, Andrea's been doing it."

"That sounds horrible. I wouldn't want to give anyone a needle!"

"Me either." Tony winced. "They tried to teach me how to do it myself in the hospital. Actually, they made me do it once. I tried to refuse, but they still made me. I never want to do it on myself again!"

"Is Andrea going to help you with it now?" Beanie asked, noticing Andrea hovering near the bedroom door. "Can I watch?"

"No way!" Tony shook his head.

"Come on, Tony," Andrea urged from the doorway. "Let's get this over with so we can all eat. Everyone else is going to arrive soon, and you don't want to be the last one eating, do you?"

"No," Tony agreed. He heaved a big sigh and turned toward the door. "I'm coming." He dragged his feet across the room. "I hate this!"

"I know," Andrea said, sympathy making her voice soft. She shut the door, leaving Beanie standing alone in the deserted kitchen.

VANCE ARRIVED AT ROSIE's out of breath, after selling his newspapers. An early edition of the paper was tucked under his arm. He had managed to save the last copy for himself, which had been difficult. Everyone wanted to read the news about Constable Paterson's arrest. Vance's mother, Mrs. Talbot, came rushing up the steps behind him. Breathlessly she pulled the *Times Morning Herald* out from under his arm and laid it down on the kitchen table. Everyone crowded around.

A picture of Hugh Paterson, looking angry and bewildered, jumped off the front page while the headline screamed, *City Police Crack Theft Ring – Arrest One Of Their Own.* "Read it, Rosie," Beanie urged.

"I can't," Rosie replied, turning away from the table. "I'm too upset. He's innocent! We all know that! What are we going to do about it?"

The room was silent except for the gurgles of a contented baby Alan, who sat perched on Tony's lap. Rosie glared around the room at the blank faces. "We have to help him!"

Mrs. Talbot reached out to pat Rosie's arm. "There's nothing we can do, dear." Her brown hair was tucked up into a bun, revealing a slender neck. Brown eyes cast worried looks in Rosie's direction. "I don't want you doing anything foolish, my dear. You have this baby to worry about."

Rosie shrugged her arm away and began to pace the length of the small room. "I don't believe that there's nothing we can do!"

"Listen to reason, Rosie," Vance urged. "Remember what those cops said to you last night – it was a threat! If you try something, they'll get you, too. Paterson can take care of himself."

"How?" Rosie demanded. She whirled around to confront Vance. "How is he going to take care of himself? It'll be a quick trial! The other officers will say he's guilty! He doesn't have a chance!"

"What do you care, Rosie?" Vance shot back, frustration making his voice harsh. "He's nothing to you."

Rosie grabbed Vance's arm, looking as if she wanted to punch him. "He's my friend," she said, her nose mere centimetres from Vance's surprised face. "That's more than I can say about some people in this room – like you, Vance."

"He's my friend, too." Mrs. Talbot stepped between Vance and Rosie. "I just don't see how we can help. We're just two women and a few children, with not even one husband between us – not a man to help us. Who's going to listen to us?"

"That's not a good attitude to take," Andrea piped

up as she finished reading the article. "This is a democratic country, isn't it? Don't we have the right to voice our concerns and opinions? Besides, we all know Mr. Paterson is innocent! There's got to be something we can do!"

Vance ran his fingers through his hair in frustration. "Ma's right, though. Who'd listen to some kids and a couple of women, especially one who's – who's –"

Rosie turned steel eyes in Vance's direction. "Well, say it, Vance," she spat. "We all know what you're thinking. Who's going to listen to a woman who's shunned in her community? Who's going to listen to a fallen woman? That's what you were going to say!"

Vance blushed and turned away, then whirled back again. "Well, it's true," he burst out angrily. "It's true! There's no denying it! Who would listen to you? All they would do is make you the laughingstock of the town and talk about you behind your back!"

"Well, they already do that," Rosie said, "so what's the difference?"

"Vance," Mrs. Talbot stepped in, pulling his arm to drag him away. "That's enough! Don't be so rude!"

"I don't see what any of this has to do with Mr. Paterson," Andrea said. "So, Rosie had a baby and she isn't married. And you don't have a husband, Mrs. Talbot. It isn't the end of the world. People don't really hold that kind of thing against anyone, do they?"

Mrs. Talbot stared at Andrea as if she had suddenly

grown two heads. "You must lead a very sheltered life, young lady."

Rosie took Andrea by the arm and sat her down in a chair. "Let me give you the facts of life, Andrea. Ever since I was in the family way, people have ignored me. Friends, former friends, have passed me by in the street. No one talks to me. Shopkeepers will take my money, but they're rude to me. That's the way it is here. It may be different in your time, but this is what I'm up against."

"So, you want people to hate and despise you even more, Rosie?" Vance directed his question from across the room.

Rosie sighed and squared her shoulders. "What else could they do to hurt me, Vance? They already shun me. It's not as if I'm going to lose friends by trying to help Mr. Paterson. Actually, I'm trying to save a friendship." She smiled a bright smile, light filling her eyes. "Constable Paterson is one of the only people who treats me like a normal person. He's kind and friendly to me. He treats me like I wish my own father would. He's been wonderful." Rosie cleared her throat. The light in her eyes shone out and a smile of determination touched her lips. "I'm going to find a way to help Mr. Paterson. He needs help and I'm going to do it, no matter what you think."

"Andrea," Rosie turned to her, the light of determination still glittering in her eyes. "Could you watch baby Alan for awhile? I have things to do."

"Sure," Andrea agreed, "but where are you going? What are you going to do?"

Rosie peered into a mirror above the kitchen sink, smoothing back her hair and placing a hat on her head. She pulled crisp white gloves out of her handbag and pulled them on. "I don't know, but the first thing I'm going to do is go visit my friend. He needs to know someone is on his side."

Mrs. Talbot moved from her chair. "I'm coming with you."

"Ma-a-a-a," Vance complained. "You don't know what you're getting yourself into. It could mean big trouble."

Mrs. Talbot pierced him with a threatening gaze. "Mr. Paterson has been my friend – our friend too, Vance. I'm going with Rosie."

"Thank you, Viola." They hugged briefly and then broke apart.

"Well, I'm going back to work," Vance announced rudely. He clapped a soft-brimmed hat on his head and pushed his way out of the crowded kitchen. "I can't seem to talk sense into anyone here anyway."

"I'm going with you, Ma," Beanie called out, jumping from her chair by the window.

"Me too," Tony replied, looking at Andrea, who nodded.

Suddenly the room felt deserted. Andrea paced,

holding baby Alan in her arms. He reached up to grab a strand of her hair, trying to put it into his mouth.

"What's going to happen, Alan?" Andrea whispered against his bald head. "I'm frightened."

ROSIE GETS MAD

Tony practically had to run to keep up with Rosie and Mrs. Talbot. He stretched his short legs even farther, wondering how Beanie could manage it so easily. They had come down the front steps of Rosie's house and turned west, heading away from Main Street. "Where are we going?" Tony wheezed, finally catching up to Beanie.

"To the courthouse." She pointed to the stately brick building that stood at the end of the block.

"Come on," Beanie urged Tony. She climbed the steps behind the women. "I don't want to miss anything."

"Someone must have warned the police we were coming. Look." Mrs. Talbot and Rosie were met halfway up the steps by a contingent of uniformed men. They blocked the women's way into the court-house.

Beanie dragged Tony to one side and whispered frantically, "Do you see who that is?" She stared pointedly over her shoulder at the officer who seemed to be in charge. "That's the man who wanted to kill Andrea! He's the one they call the boss!"

Tony stared hard at the man with the beady eyes and a moustache. "You're right! It is him! He seems to be pretty important around here." Tony noticed the sergeant's stripes on his shoulder.

"We demand to see Constable Paterson." Rosie's voice could be heard loudly in the morning air. There was a low rumbling reply. "Every prisoner has rights. We demand to see him."

There were more rumblings and then the Sergeant spoke. "Now, ladies," he said, "what seems to be the problem?" He listened, teasing his moustache with one finger as Rosie and one of the officers debated the matter. "I don't see why these ladies can't have a few minutes with our guilty colleague. He might even confess to them. That would save us the time and expense of a trial."

Tony watched Rosie's back grow stiff. She put white-knuckled hands behind her back and squeezed hard. "Th-thank you," he heard her mutter, and he knew that it had taken great restraint for her to keep her comments to herself.

The women were escorted into the courthouse. "The jail cells are in the basement," Beanie offered. She sat down on one of the cement steps to wait. "This may take awhile." When the police officers had disappeared back inside the brick building, she said, "What are we going to do? We have to catch that Sergeant! He seems to be in charge of everything around here."

"We're not going to do anything until we find out what's happening with Mr. Paterson," Tony said wisely. "We don't want to put him in more danger, do we?"

Beanie shook her head. "No, but we have to nab that guy somehow. We can't let him get away scot-free."

It seemed like an eternity before the women emerged from the building. "I was never so mad," Rosie said, pausing beside the children. "That Sergeant is so patronizing and sure of himself! He took great pleasure in belittling me! I'd love to be the one to knock him off his high horse!"

"How's Constable Paterson?" Beanie asked, jumping up beside her mother.

"Well, he seems fine under the circumstances. He was surprised to see us."

"Surprised, but happy, I should think." Rosie squeezed Mrs. Talbot's arm, smiling at her.

"He told us to go home and forget about helping him." Mrs. Talbot patted Beanie's shoulder. "I don't know what else we can do at this point."

"I do." Rosie flounced down the stairs, pulling the offending newspaper article out of her pocket. She shook it under their noses. "I'm going over to have a good long talk with Isaac Hamilton. He wrote this piece of garbage. We have to tell him the truth! Are you coming with me?"

"Do you think we should?" Mrs. Talbot questioned. "I wouldn't want Hugh – Constable Paterson to be upset with us." Colour invaded her cheeks.

"I think he'd be really happy to know there's someone on his side, Viola, even if it is one fallen woman and a few excitable children! He needs us now!"

"You're right." Mrs. Talbot squared her shoulders and followed Rosie down the steps. "I'm with you. Let's go see what we can do to get him out of jail!"

They marched a few blocks over to the newspaper office, which was housed in another brick building just off Main Street. "Builders sure liked to use a lot of bricks around here." Tony commented, looking around.

"I like brick," Beanie replied. "Besides, Moose Jaw has always had a lot of fires, so they passed a law that buildings had to be built out of brick."

All four visitors crowded into the newspaper office. A wooden counter ran the length of the room and the sound of noisy presses could be heard running in the backrooms. "Afternoon." The man at the desk greeted them. He wore a black visor and a long white apron smeared with black ink. "What can I do for you?"

"We want to see Isaac Hamilton, the author of this article." Rosie shoved the newspaper under his nose.

"Isaac," the man called out. "People to see you. They don't look too friendly," he added under his breath. He shuffled some papers together and then walked away from the counter, toward a desk, where he sat down within earshot. Like all newspaper people, he seemed nosy, Tony thought.

An office door opened and a young man about Rosie's age walked to the counter. He nodded in greeting, his eyes just barely lighting on Rosie. "Afternoon, Mrs. Talbot, what can I do for you?"

Mrs. Talbot glanced at Rosie, who shook her head as if to say, ignore his rudeness. "We're interested in this article you wrote, Mr. Hamilton," Mrs. Talbot said.

The thin man puffed out his chest. "I did a good job, didn't I? If I do say so myself."

"You didn't tell the truth," Rosie burst out, rattling the paper under his nose. "These are all lies! I thought newspaper people checked their facts before publishing anything! Did you even talk to Constable Paterson? Did you try to get his side of the story?"

Mr. Hamilton turned his shoulders away from Rosie, addressing Mrs. Talbot. "Tell your companion that those are the facts that were given to me! I just reported them!"

"Those are the lies given to you, Isaac!" Rosie slammed the paper down on the counter. "I thought you were an honest newspaper reporter! Why didn't you go out and do some investigating – find the truth?"

Mr. Hamilton gave up ignoring Rosie, since she refused to play along with his silly game. "Look, Rosie. Keep your nose out of this! I printed the facts, the information that the police gave me. You've got to accept what they say; after all, they are the police!"

Rosie snorted. "In this town you can't trust the police! Why didn't you try to get facts from someone else? There are always two sides to every issue."

Mr. Hamilton looked extremely uncomfortable. "Well, I –"

"You were just lazy, Isaac, just like when we were youngsters in school and you'd beg me to write your essays. You didn't bother to track down another opinion because you were too lazy."

"Perhaps," Isaac bristled, "but there won't be anyone to talk to. It's Paterson's word against the police. Who are most people going to believe, especially since Constable Paterson has only been in Moose Jaw for such a short time? There's no one to talk to, Rosie."

"What about the shopkeepers? What do they believe? What about Mr. Paterson, himself? What could he tell you?"

"Look, if it'll make you feel any better, I'll go interview him, but I can tell you what he's going to say. He'll profess his innocence! That's what any man in that situation would do."

"And you think he's guilty?" Rosie's precisely clipped words dropped like chunks of ice onto the counter.

"No, no," Mr. Hamilton said, sliding back from the counter. "I'm just saying that it wouldn't make an interesting story, that's all. I'm not talking about being innocent or guilty here. I'm talking about what sells newspapers! And an article about a corrupt cop definitely sells papers."

"Look, Isaac, if you're not interested in doing some investigating, I am. Lend me one of those newfangled cameras."

"What? Not on your life, Rosie. I don't care if we have known each other for years. I'm not lending you an expensive camera."

The older man strode purposely toward the desk, looking intently at Rosie. "I'm Thomas Smith, the newspaper editor," he said, extending his hand first to Rosie and then to Mrs. Talbot. "Did I hear you say that you're a writer of sorts?" he asked Rosie, smiling kindly. "I'm always on the look out for new writers." His greying hair bounced on his head as he rubbed his stubbled chin. "You think you have a different perspective on this story?"

Rosie nodded. "Yes, sir. I'm positive that Mr. Paterson is innocent."

"Don't listen to her. Don't you know who she is, Mr. Smith?"

Rosie's face lost all colour, her stricken eyes glaring at Isaac. Mr. Smith patted Rosie's clenched fist as it lay motionless on the counter. "I don't care who she is, Hamilton," he said. "In this office, people are guests. Always. And you'll learn to treat them with respect." He paused for a minute. "Or perhaps this isn't the place for you, Hamilton. Do I make myself clear? Now, go work on that other article."

"Yes, sir," Isaac Hamilton muttered, backing toward his office. "I'm sorry, Rosie."

Rosie nodded, unable to speak, while Mr. Smith cleared his throat. "It doesn't matter who you are," he said to the group in general, as he fumbled wire-rimmed glasses onto his face. "You deserve to be treated with respect here."

"Thank you, sir." Rosie's voice was low and rough. Tony could tell that she was fighting back tears.

"Nonsense, that's just common courtesy. Everyone deserves that. Now then," he cleared his throat, glad to be back on a safer topic. "You say you want to do some investigating into this case?" Rosie nodded. "What makes you think that Hugh Paterson is innocent?"

"Well, sir. I know him. He lives in the apartment below mine. The police claimed the basement and the back stairwell of the rooming house were full of stolen goods, but we know they're lying. These children were down there only moments before the police arrived and they didn't see a thing. The police must have planted the evidence and then a few minutes later they arrested Constable Paterson as the thief. I think I can prove that Hugh Paterson is innocent, but I'll need a camera to do it."

Mr. Smith rubbed his chin. "If I lend you a camera, young lady, I want a guarantee from you."

"Oh, I'd take good care of it, sir. Don't you worry about that."

Mr. Smith chuckled. "No, I'm sure you would. But, what I want is a full report, an article on your findings. We might be able to use some of it in a follow-up story."

Rosie's eyes grew wide, a smile creasing her lips. "Yes, sir!"

"Now, I'll go get the camera. You wait right here."

Rosie clapped her hands together. "We did it! We did it!"

"You did it, my dear," Mrs. Talbot said. "You did it all on your own, Rosie. I'm proud of you." She patted Rosie's shoulder and then pulled her close for a brief hug. "Tell me though, Rosie, do you know how to operate a camera?"

Rosie shook her head, grinning widely. "I've never touched a camera in my life!"

"Well," Tony blustered. "It can't be that difficult! All you do is point and shoot." He demonstrated the method, a palm-size, imaginary Instamatic camera between his hands. "Like this."

All three females threw puzzled looks at Tony. "I think you're mistaken, Tony." Beanie pointed to the huge black camera Mr. Smith was hefting onto the front counter.

Tony's eyes widened at the sight of this old-fashioned camera. It looked like something straight out of the Western Development Museum! It was a big black box with a strap on top, probably used for carrying the thing. It had a large glass lens on the front and funny-looking accordion-style folds in the body of the camera. It looked heavy too, Tony thought, judging by the way Mr. Smith heaved it onto the counter. Tony slapped a hand against his forehead. He had forgotten for a moment what era he was in! He wondered what everyone would think of a camera small enough to fit into a pocket, one that took colour pictures, too!

"This is how you use this camera," Mr. Smith said. He told Rosie how to slide the film holder into the camera, as he demonstrated. "Now, pull out this baffle and the camera is ready to go. You just press this button right here," he said, indicating the shutter. "Once the picture is taken, you have to replace this baffle and then the film holder can be removed.

Understand?" Rosie nodded, but Tony could tell by the confused look on her face, she wasn't too sure.

"And, you'll be needing this as well." Mr. Smith placed a tin pan and a small bottle on the counter beside the camera.

"What's that for?" Tony wanted to know.

"This is a flash pan," Mr. Smith informed them, "and this is flash powder. This will provide the light needed to take the photograph. Just before you take it, you'll need to spread some of this powder onto the flash pan. You'll have to time the snapping of the shutter on the camera with the flash of light from the flash powder; otherwise your picture will be too dark. And," he added, staring pointedly at Beanie and Tony, "that flash powder is dangerous. It can cause burns if you're too close. It makes a loud explosion of sound and the bright light can cause temporary blindness. Be careful with it." Rosie nodded and began to gather the paraphernalia from the counter. "You'll need this, too," he added, lifting a wooden tripod and laying it beside the camera. "Since the camera is too heavy to hold steady, you'll need to secure it onto the tripod like so. This'll help you get a clear picture.

"Make sure you get a good shot," Mr. Smith added. "Everything is expensive and I can only spare one film sheet for you. One shot is all you're going to get, so make sure it's one we can use." Rosie gulped and nodded, handing Tony the flash pan and Mrs.

Talbot the gangly tripod. Grabbing the heavy camera by the strap, she lifted it down from the counter.

"What's the plan, Rosie?" Beanie asked, squinting at the jar of flash powder in her hand. She held the door open as everyone passed through it and out into the street.

"I don't know, yet," Rosie admitted, "but it had better be a good one."

THE PLAN

Andrea was pacing up and down the narrow kitchen, her white runners squeaking on the hardwood floor. The cranky baby was held tightly in her arms and she wished that she could be anywhere but where she was right now. It wasn't that she didn't like baby Alan; it was just that she didn't care much for babysitting. Babies scared her when they cried for no reason. She would rather have been out with the others where all the action was taking place, and they had been gone for hours.

She paced toward the window and looked out. Evening was approaching. She whirled around again, the blue dress slapping at her calves. It was getting dirty and dingy-looking already. She felt as if she'd been wearing it for weeks.

Footsteps pounded up the steps. She ran to fling open the door. "Hi Vance!"

Vance tossed a look in the baby's direction and headed straight for a chair, ignoring her greeting. "Wow! What a busy day! We sold every copy of the paper! You should see it out on Main Street! Everyone's still standing around, reading the paper and talking about it! I even saw four people reading the same paper at once! It's incredible!

"Have you heard from anyone yet about how Mr. Paterson is doing?" Vance cast a worried look in Andrea's direction. "Has anyone thought of a way to get him out of jail yet?"

"I haven't seen anyone in hours! I'd sure like to know what's going on, too. This is when a cellphone would come in handy."

"A what?" Vance asked, his voice puzzled.

"Never mind," Andrea sighed. Some modern inventions were just too complicated to explain. "Tell me, what are people saying about Mr. Paterson and the robberies?" She jostled the baby up and down. He was probably getting hungry. Rosie and the others had been gone for a long time.

"Most seem glad. They think the culprit has been captured. They can't wait for it to go to trial. Some of the shopkeepers though," Vance said, "they aren't totally convinced. Thank the Lord for that. I heard a few of them talking together on the corner. They think Paterson is innocent. A couple of men got into a really heated argument about it! I was sure there would be fisticuffs! Someone mentioned that Mr. Paterson might be getting beaten up in jail. That scares me. Would cops beat up on other cops?"

"You know they would," Andrea said, thinking about her own world.

Baby Alan continued to whine and cry, chewing on one small fist. "What's the matter with him?" Vance finally asked.

Andrea shrugged her shoulders. "I don't really know. He might be hungry or something." The baby squirmed, trying to pull away from her hold. "I think he's getting tired of me. He acts like he wants down, but when I put him down he cries even louder than before! I sure don't understand babies."

She continued to pace, studying Vance under lowered lashes. For someone who said he could care less about the baby, he sure didn't act like it. Whenever he thought she wasn't looking, he would watch the baby, an unreadable expression on his face. She suddenly had an idea. She stopped pacing and held the baby away from her body. "I'm tired of holding this kid!" She made her lips droopy and sagged her shoulders, trying to look exhausted. "I need a break."

"I guess I could hold him," Vance muttered. The words seemed to be trapped in his throat. They came out high and squeaky. He gingerly took the baby and propped him up on his knee.

"Thanks," Andrea beamed. "Mind if I go and lie down for a minute? I'm really beat."

"Go ahead." Vance bounced the baby awkwardly on his knee.

Andrea walked purposefully into the bedroom and pushed the door almost shut; then she stood looking through the narrow crack. She wanted to see what Vance would do next.

He studied the baby, bouncing him up and down on his knee. "Hello there, young fellow," he said softly. "You seem to be doing a little better." The baby grinned a big toothless grin, waving his fists in the air. "Are you happy with your new friend?"

Baby Alan gurgled happily and grabbed a fistful of Vance's shirt and stuck it into his mouth. "Hey," Vance complained. "This is my last clean shirt." He tried to release the baby's fist from his clothing. "Gee, you're strong! Let go of my shirt!"

He bent his head closer, and Baby Alan found something more fascinating to play with. He grabbed a lock of Vance's hair and hung on. "Ouch," Vance yelped. "You brute! You're pulling my hair."

The baby chortled as Vance fought to free his hair. "There. Now I'm going to turn you around the other way. That way you can't grab anything." As Vance turned the baby around, he touched his cheek. There, the small scar was visible in the afternoon light. "How did that happen?" he wondered aloud. "Your father had a scar from a knife fight right here." Vance ran a light finger down the baby's cheek. "You have a birth-mark, or a wrinkle or something, right there, too. That's amazing!"

Sounds as loud as elephant feet reverberated up the stairs. Vance looked wildly around. "Andrea, come and take this kid." Andrea drew back from the door-way. Let Rosie see Vance with the baby. She needed to know that he didn't hate her as much as she thought he did.

Stuck holding the baby, Vance could only watch the look on Rosie's face as she entered her apartment. She smiled a huge, happy smile, her eyes becoming teary. She bent over Vance to get the baby, but kissed Vance's cheek first. No words were spoken, but the look that passed between Vance and Rosie said it all. They were friends again, and Andrea knew that they would be for a long time to come.

"We got a camera to use," Tony cried, as he and Beanie carefully leaned the heavy tripod into the cor-ner.

"What's the plan?" Andrea had hurried out of the bedroom to have a good look at what she considered an ancient camera. Did the thing even work?

"We don't have a plan." Beanie plunked herself down in one of the chairs and sat swinging her legs back and forth.

"I thought the camera might come in handy. I'd like to take a photograph for evidence, but I'm not quite sure what to do."

"I saw a movie once where –" Tony began.

"Never mind, Tony." Andrea tapped her brother on the back to keep him quiet. "You're always talking about what happened in some movie. This is real life!"

"Yeah, but in this movie –"

"Forget it. It's probably not even worth talking about."

"But it is, Andrea. See, the detective hides a camera where he knows the bad guys will be, and then he waits and takes pictures!"

Rosie stopped playing with the baby and turned to stare at Tony, a look of joy spreading over her face. "What a great idea! Tony! You've saved the day!"

"What are you thinking?" Mrs. Talbot eyed Rosie suspiciously. "I don't like the sound of this."

Rosie was excited, her voice loud and exuberant. "We could hide the camera in that storage area you all talked about. The one with all the stolen goods. The corrupt cops are sure to come there sooner or later. After all, they're going to want to get rid of that merchandise soon – very soon. I'd be there to snap the photograph! What a perfect idea, Tony!"

Tony felt like he was walking on clouds. "Yes!" he emphasized, making a fist in the air. While Rosie continued to talk about the plan, his thoughts turned inward as he evaluated his physical condition. Did he really feel like he was walking on clouds, or was it a problem with his diabetes? He wanted to ignore it. This was the most exciting event that had happened so far and he didn't want to miss it. He tried to ignore his feeling, but he remembered what had happened the last time he had ignored it. Sighing in defeat, he made up his mind, tapping Andrea on the shoulder. "I need you," he whispered, pointing to the bedroom. Andrea didn't make a move. She was too engrossed in Rosie's dangerous plan. "Come on, Andrea," he repeated. "I need you, quickly."

She reluctantly got to her feet and followed him into the bedroom. He was already lying on the bed. "Quick," he ordered. "Leave the door open a bit," he said as she began to shut it. "I don't want to miss anything."

While she got the supplies ready, he listened, his eyes closed. "Hurry, Andrea," he pleaded. "Please."

Andrea was getting more relaxed at taking care of Tony's needs. It hardly bothered her to poke his finger and squeeze the blood out. She tested it and then filled the syringe with the correct amount of insulin and gave him the shot. "Hurry, Andrea," he begged again, as she got up to clear away the supplies.

"You're all done, Squirt."

He popped up on the bed. "I am? Already? I didn't even feel it!" He looked down at his leg. "Are you sure you did it?"

"Cross my heart and hope to die." Andrea made a cross over her heart, grinning from ear to ear. "You know what this means, Tony, don't you?"

"No, what?"

"It means you're getting used to it! It's not bothering you nearly so much now! Way to go, Brother! I'm proud of you!" She dragged him into her arms and planted a sloppy kiss on his cheek.

"Yuck!" He wiped at his face. "Girl germs!"

She laughed. "Come on, let's go see if we've missed anything important." She grabbed his hand. "I am proud of you, Tony!"

He laughed. "Me too!"

Mrs. Talbot was just gathering up her things. "I'm going home to get supper. I've had a stew simmering on the stove all day. I'll bring it back here for all of us to eat. I'm sure Rosie won't mind, and we do have some planning to do."

"But how will you get it back here?" Andrea asked, certain that the family didn't own an automobile.

"We have an old wagon. I'll use it to pull the stew in. I also made buns yesterday. They'll still be fresh."

"Why don't we all just go home and eat, Ma?" Vance suggested. "That would save you dragging the soup all the way over here."

Mrs. Talbot blushed prettily and looked away. "Well, I – uh, I thought I'd take some fresh stew over to

Constable Paterson, too. I've heard that the prisoners aren't fed too well. And I want to bring him up to date on all that's been happening. I'll be back in a minute." She waved a dainty hand and quickly left the apartment before Vance could question her further, but his eyes followed her, a worried expression creasing his forehead.

"What's going on there?" he asked, focusing his eyes on the door through which his mother had just disappeared.

Rosie gently pushed him down into one of the straight-backed kitchen chairs. "I love your Ma as if she was my own, Vance. She deserves a little happiness in life. Let her have it," Rosie pleaded, tears in her eyes. "She deserves it."

"You mean she likes Mr. Paterson?" Vance frowned, shaking his head.

"You're thinking about your Pa," Rosie guessed. "All men aren't like him, Vance. They don't abandon their wife and children and take off to Chicago to live the fast life."

"How do you know, Rosie?" Vance sounded belligerent and angry. When she didn't answer he sighed, then pressed his lips together. "I'll try to be understanding, Rosie, but I can't promise anything. I feel all confused inside."

Rosie rubbed his shoulder as she passed by. "Just think about it, Vance. You're a reasonable person." She scooped the baby out of Andrea's arms. "Come to

Mama, Baby Alan. You must be hungry by now."

"Rosie's right," Andrea confirmed from her chair near the window. "Life is too short to complicate it by being angry and upset with people."

"Yeah," Vance grumbled. "Just let me think for awhile. Things are happening too fast around here."

THE STEW WAS SERVED and everyone came to the table to eat. "Okay, what's this plan?" Mrs. Talbot asked as she spread butter on a warm bun.

The room was silent, everyone eyeing one another. Tony finally spoke up. "If you'd just let me tell you about this movie I saw," he pleaded. "I think we could make it work."

"Okay," Andrea sighed. "Tell us about the movie."

Tony took a deep breath. "Well, I saw this movie once where the detective camouflaged the camera. The bad guys didn't know it was there."

"That's easy to do, Tony, when the camera is twelve centimetres by eight centimetres, but this camera is huge! How could we ever hide it?" She stared at the camera sitting on the floor in the corner of the room, the huge flash pan beside it. "That'd be like trying to hide an elephant!"

"We could hide it behind some boxes," Beanie said, "with just the lens part sticking out for taking photographs."

"And cover it with something like –" Tony scratched his head.

"Like a stolen dress," Rosie decided.

"Yeah, a dress would work," Tony continued, excitement ringing in his voice.

"Does anyone know how to work this thing?" Andrea pulled the camera out of the corner, dragging the tripod behind her. "And what's this for?" She held up the flash pan.

"That makes the extra light needed for the photograph to turn out," Rosie informed her.

"So, we need someone to snap the picture and someone to hold this thing?" Andrea held it above her head. "It's heavy. Once this thing flashes, those cops will be onto us in a second. I don't think we'll have a chance to get the camera out of the tunnel safely. Anyway, where does the film go?"

Rosie showed Andrea how the film holder slid into the camera. "We'll only get one shot, so it had better be a good one."

Mrs. Talbot put her spoon down, frowning. "This is more complicated and dangerous than I thought. I don't think it can be done. It's not worth getting anyone else arrested, or hurt over, is it?"

"Yes, it is, Viola." Rosie exclaimed. "One photograph might be all we need to get rid of these corrupt cops! We just have to make it the *right* photograph!"

"How are you thinking of getting the camera and

all this other stuff out of the tunnel once the photo has been taken?" Andrea asked.

"We'd need a decoy," Rosie said, softly. "Something to draw their attention away from the camera."

"I could be the decoy," Vance volunteered. "I know the tunnels better than anyone and I can run fast. I could do something to get the cops to chase me and you two could grab the camera and equipment and hustle it over to the newspaper office."

Andrea felt excitement begin to bubble in her stomach; either that or she was beginning to feel sick with fear and worry. "I wonder if we really need to use that heavy flash pan. Would our flashlights work well enough?"

Tony thought about it. "I think we'd better use the flash pan. The light will be blinding, and that's good. We can't risk having a dark photograph, so the more light, the better. But, after the photo's been taken, we could both turn on the flashlights. That'd keep the cops confused and blinded for at least a few more seconds. That'd give us all a chance to get away."

"We'd have to time it just right," Vance said. "The flash pan needs to be lit just as the photo is being taken." He thought for a minute. "Maybe Rosie could say, 'Now', and then –"

"I could light the flash pan," Andrea volunteered. She didn't want either Beanie or Tony having that job. "But I'm a little afraid of it."

"And you have every right to be," Mrs. Talbot said, patting her arm. "Use a long candle. Do you have one, Rosie?" Rosie nodded and Mrs. Talbot continued. "It would be wise for you to put that flash pan on something. Don't try to hold it up. Perhaps you could prop it up on something, then you'd be out of danger."

"That's perfect," Rosie exclaimed, clapping her hands excitedly. "Let's do it!"

Supper done, Mrs. Talbot got up from her chair. "I'm going to go take Mr. Paterson some stew and buns. Don't go anywhere until I get back. Tony and Beanie, you are far too young to be involved in such a dangerous scheme. You'll stay with me."

"Aw-w-w, Ma!" Beanie wailed, but Mrs. Talbot stood firm.

"You, Beatrice, and Tony, will help me with the baby until Rosie gets back. This may take all night. We're only guessing these men will return to that storage area tonight. This plan may be all for naught."

DOUBLE-CROSSED

Andrea thought of Mrs. Talbot's words many times as she crouched against the dirt wall of the storage area, waiting for the cops to come. As soon as Mrs. Talbot had returned, Rosie, Andrea, and Vance had gathered up the equipment and snuck into the storage area, via the tunnel that started in the back stairwell. They had moved quickly through the tunnel, afraid that the policemen might return to gather up the few articles of clothing they had framed Constable Paterson with. The cops had left the 'evidence' strewn all over the outside steps.

Once in the storage area, Andrea had breathed a sigh of relief. They had set up the camera close enough to the wooden doorway to get a good photograph of whatever action was taking place. The camera was hidden behind a stack of boxes; only the big box and camera lens was visible. It blended into the dark underground cavern very well, but they had placed a black dress over it, just in case.

Rosie and Andrea sat crouched behind the camera, against the dirt wall. Andrea had left the soiled blue dress at Rosie's, knowing that she would need to move quickly and confidently and her jeans would work best for that. Vance was farther away, hiding, but close enough to shine his flashlight when it was needed. Andrea had the other flashlight. The flash pan, she had propped on a pile of boxes, facing the warehouse door. She had carefully poured the flash powder into it and covered the whole thing with a dark dress. The plan was for Rosie to say, "Now," loudly enough for Vance to hear. Andrea would light the flash pan and stand back. Vance would switch on his flashlight. Rosie would snap the picture. Vance would leave his light on, making sure to attract as much attention as possible, while Andrea and Rosie stayed perfectly still. Hopefully all of the cops would follow Vance into the forbidden tunnel while Andrea and Rosie quickly gathered the photographic equipment and got out of the storage area, into the tunnel and back to the surface.

Andrea felt her stomach lurch. She knew that the plan wasn't perfect. There were too many things that could go wrong, but they had no other choice. This had to work, it just had to!

Andrea's bottom had fallen asleep along with her feet. Pins and needles pricked at her toes and she wiggled them to get the circulation moving in them. "Sh-h-h," Rosie suddenly warned. "Do you hear voices? Get ready, Vance, I think they're coming," she called softly.

"Ready," Vance replied.

The voices grew louder and Andrea felt her heart jump into her throat. It was time to light the candle! With fingers trembling, she fumbled with the match, managing to strike it against the rough side of the matchbox. It flared to life with a hiss that she was sure could be heard for miles around. Holding the flame to the wick, she watched it catch fire and then tamped the candle into the earth floor behind a huge stack of boxes. Its light was very weak and Andrea prayed the cops wouldn't notice it. She hadn't been in this much danger since last year. She hoped that she would remember what to do. The metal latch on the door clanged and the door burst open.

"Okay, men, let's clear this stuff out. Paterson may be our scapegoat, but I don't think everyone believes us. We need to get this out of here tonight."

Rosie nudged Andrea sharply in the ribs. "There's the Sergeant," she whispered, peering around the boxes.

"That fence better get here soon," the Sergeant was

saying. "We won't wait all night for him. We need the cash for these goods now. I'm going to go check for him once more. You men get these boxes into the warehouse." Andrea could see him suddenly bend over a box. "Hmm-m-m," he murmured. "Here's a pretty trinket." She watched as he slipped it into his pocket and then walked nonchalantly into the warehouse.

"Why does he always get to take stuff and we don't?" a thin man whined.

"What do you mean?" his companion asked.

"Did you see him just pick up that bracelet? I'll bet it was worth a fortune. I'm getting tired of doing his dirty work and getting a few cents in return, while he gets rich. We deserve something, too. After all, we're the ones taking all the risks."

"Yeah," a few voices murmured in agreement. "Let's grab something."

They rifled through the boxes closest to the warehouse door. Andrea could see a lot of women's clothing being flung about. "There's not much left," the whiner complained, dropping a colourful dress on the floor.

"Oh, I don't know," one of the men commented. "I think my wife would really like a pretty dress like this."

"And a hat," another man added.

"I'm going to get my wife a new hat and dress. She'll love it."

"Won't she wonder where it came from?"

"Naw. I'll just say I got a bonus for solving a case. She won't question it. But, men, we'd better hurry up. The Boss is bound to be back soon. We don't want to be caught stealing his stuff. He'd really have our necks!"

"It's not his stuff," one of the men reminded the others. He stuffed a woman's dress under his navy blue uniform jacket and buttoned it up. "Hurry up," he warned the others.

"What are you men doing?" the Boss demanded from the interior of the warehouse. "Let's get a move on it!" The men scrambled to conceal their stolen property under their uniforms, then quickly picked up boxes and began to cart them out of the storage area and into the warehouse.

"What are you waiting for?" Andrea demanded when the men were gone. "We're in danger here! Just take the picture!" She was sweating with worry.

"I want a picture of the Sergeant," Rosie declared. "The only way to put a stop to all of this is to catch him in the photograph. Otherwise a few of these beat cops will be arrested and the Sergeant will get off scot-free!"

"Rosie!" Andrea wanted to scream with frustration. "You're nuts!"

"Maybe," she agreed as the men shuffled back for more boxes. "Now get down and be quiet."

As more and more boxes disappeared, the risk of being discovered grew greater. Every time the men returned to the storage area, Andrea cringed. She was desperately worried that one of them would wander over and begin taking the boxes behind which they were hiding.

"Come on, Sarge," Rosie muttered each time a figure stepped from the warehouse and down the three steps into the storage area. "Come on, Sarge. Come and get your photograph taken." She kept her finger on the shutter button and her eyes peeled on the doorway. She didn't want to miss her one chance of taking the perfect photograph.

Suddenly, when Andrea was certain that their hiding spot would be next, the Boss stepped through the doorway. He paused on the top step, looking straight at the camera, and she was sure that they had been spotted. Her breath caught in her throat as she fought the urge to run. Then he turned. Andrea could see the flash of white teeth as he smiled in profile. "Come in and see how much is left. I want you to get it all out of here tonight."

The Boss turned around and stepped quickly down the last two steps. Behind him came a weaselly-looking man in a black trench coat. Rosie squeezed Andrea's arm in a death grip and pulled her close. "That's the fence," she whispered into Andrea's ear. "That's the man who's buying the stolen goods."

"Just say, 'now,'" Andrea pleaded, staring at the lit candle in her hand. Could she really light the flash pan at the exact moment Rosie needed it? She could feel sweat running down the back of her neck. Had she ever been this frightened before? Only in her dreams, she realized, and this was like one of her worst nightmares. Her heart felt as if it was going to beat its way out of her chest.

"I want to get them both in the photograph," Rosie murmured, keeping her eye glued to the lens. "I want to get them shaking hands!"

"Wh-" Andrea half sputtered, but Rosie nudged her in the ribs and she shut her mouth. Rosie was nuts – certifiable! How had she ever talked her into this crazy scheme?

The Boss and the fence walked closer to the camera. Andrea felt her hair stand up on end. If they didn't stop soon, they would be nose to lens! They might see the light from her candle! Rosie was endangering all of them! How would they ever escape? "Can you get rid of this stuff tonight?" the Sergeant was asking. His voice sounded desperate to Andrea.

The fence must have realized this, for he took his time answering. He carefully took out a cigar, held it under his nose and sniffed. "Hm-m-m," he said. "I love the smell of a good cigar."

The Sergeant stood tensely beside the fence as he lit the cigar and took a deep drag, blowing smoke rings toward the low earth ceiling. "Now," he turned lazily to the Sergeant. "What did you say?"

"I said," the Boss was obviously trying to stay in control. "I said, can you get rid of the goods tonight? I need them out of here!"

"Well," the fence gazed around. "There's a lot here. I might need to hire extra men. I don't think I'll be able to give you the kind of price you were hoping for...." He let the thought hang in the air as he took another drag on the cigar. "If you'd only come down in price, I might be able to help you out."

The Sergeant clenched his fists, turned away, then changed his mind and turned back again. He grabbed the fence by the lapels of his coat and pushed him roughly up against a stack of boxes. "I don't *deal* with a fence," he spat. "You pay me what it's worth or else."

The fence laughed and stuck his cigar close to the Boss's nose. "It seems to me that you're in a bit of hot water, Mr. Po-lice Sergeant." The fence made the words sound dirty. "You do deal with fences, and you'll deal with me at the price I want to pay, or this stuff doesn't move."

"You do as I say," the Sergeant returned, stepping away from the cigar, "or I'll have you arrested." He turned to see his men hovering just inside the doorway, watching as the drama unfolded.

The fence laughed again, a nasty sound that sent shivers down Andrea's spine. "You won't arrest me," he said confidently. "I have too many secrets to tell — too many of *your* secrets to tell. I'm sure many people in this town would love to hear all about you and your corrupt band of coppers over there." He jerked a thumb toward the cluster of men. "So, the tables are turned, Sergeant. I'll pay you what I think I can get, considering that it's been stored in these terrible conditions. Some of it's dirty, mice have nested in it, and it's high volume over a short period of time, meaning I'm more at risk for taking it all. Let me see, I'll pay you...." He scratched his chin lazily and then named a price that sent the Sergeant into spasms.

"You can't be serious," the Sergeant sputtered, his fists clenching and unclenching.

"I am serious, man, dead serious. Remember, your job, your reputation is on the line, not mine. You need me." He smiled and brushed patronizingly at the Sergeant's shoulder. "You need me to protect your so-called innocence. Take it or leave it. I haven't got all night."

The Sergeant spat a few nasty words into the air and then reached for his gun.

"I wouldn't do that if I were you," the fence warned. "Turn around and take a good long look before you start shooting."

The Sergeant turned around, seeing what Andrea saw, three burly men in fancy suits and hats, carrying Tommy guns. Two guns were aimed at the constables standing near the door. One was trained on the Sergeant himself. Gesturing in defeat, the Sergeant put his gun away. He could see that he had been double-crossed by the fence and by the gangsters. He waved at his men to continue to haul the boxes away. "If I ever catch you in a dark alley – you'd better watch out. I'll be out to get you, you slimy snake."

The fence tsked. "Sticks and stones, Sergeant," he sneered. "Be careful. You might find yourself at the wrong end of a gun one day soon." He laughed and then signalled, and the men with the Tommy guns disappeared into the warehouse.

Andrea felt like she was having a heart attack. She gestured wildly at Rosie, mouthing the words: "Say now! Say now!" Still Rosie waited.

The Sergeant had turned and begun to stalk toward the door. Say now, Andrea willed. Let me light this thing and get it over with. Her hand shook badly, sprinkling candle wax over a wide area.

"Hey, Sarge," the fence called. "I always shake on my deals, don't you?"

The Sergeant hesitated and then flung a few choice words over his shoulder and continued on.

"No deal, Sarge, without a handshake." He's really rubbing it in, Andrea thought. She almost felt sorry for the Sergeant, until she remembered how he had terrorized her and would have killed her if she hadn't been rescued.

Rosie stiffened up and got ready. Andrea stood up, peering over the edge of the box. She could just make out the top of Vance's head across the way. Carefully, she moved the candle closer to the flash pan with one hand, and pulled the dress away with the other. She was ready.

The Sergeant slowly turned and waited for the fence to get within handshaking distance. Hand out-stretched, the fence stepped forward. With great reluctance, the Sergeant lifted his hand.

"Now!" Rosie yelled.

Say Cheese!

Andrea sprang into action, extending the lighted candle toward the powder in the flash pan. Brilliant light suddenly flooded the cavern as a loud boom shook the ground. Rosie snapped the photograph. Tiny bits of dirt rained down around Andrea and she wondered if they had started a cave-in. This was something no one had even considered! Everyone froze for a moment; then pandemonium broke loose. "I've got it," Rosie yelled, making a fist in the air. She and Andrea quickly gathered up the equipment and edged toward the tunnel as Vance waved his flashlight around in a wide arc.

"Hey! Over here!" Vance called loudly, gesturing toward the forbidden tunnel.

"He's heading that way! Get him!" They saw the

men surge toward Vance, knocking over boxes in their haste to reach him. He shone the light full in their faces for a second and then whirled around and sped into the tunnel, the light suddenly disappearing altogether.

Andrea held her breath as she edged quickly along the wall behind Rosie. There was no one left in the underground cavern. Every man had followed Vance, but there was no saying how far into the forbidden tunnel they would go. "Hurry, Rosie," Andrea pleaded, almost stepping on her feet. "Let's get out of here."

"I'm moving as fast as I can." Rosie grunted from the effort of carrying the heavy tripod and camera. "This thing weighs a ton!"

Once they reached the tunnel, Andrea shifted the still warm flash pan into her other hand. "Here, let me help you with that thing." She let Rosie take the camera part, while she carried the legs. They walked one behind the other, Rosie going first. They quickly reached the first door and Rosie pushed it open and then waited while Andrea paused to close it behind her. They half fell into the tiny stairwell, the scattered clothes on the ground getting caught in their feet.

"I think I've got the best shot of all! Let's get this over to the newspaper office right away!" They moved up the cellar stairs. Heaving open the heavy outside door, Rosie listened intently. Cool night air rushed in to greet them. Hearing only crickets, they stepped out onto the grass and let the lid down. A movement in the third window above caught their attention. Mrs. Talbot stood, holding Baby Alan and waving at them.

"Boy, this sure brings back memories," Andrea said. "Remember, Rosie? You were the one standing in that very window last year, making me go back into those horrid tunnels to find Vance's coins."

Rosie chuckled. "I know. I felt bad about that afterward, but you were a hero. And you were brave. You really saved his neck."

"Yeah," Andrea agreed, smiling. Then she remembered he was still in danger. "I sure hope Vance is okay. What if they catch him, Rosie?"

"They won't," Rosie said, trying to sound confident. "He's too smart for that."

Pushing worrisome thoughts of Vance aside, Andrea pulled at Rosie's arm. "Come on. We're not finished yet. We have to get this camera and the film sheet over to the newspaper office right away. I hope Mr. Smith is still waiting for us."

"Oh, he'll be there," Rosie said confidently. "They work at night to get the paper out. Let's go, but be quiet. If we see even one moving shadow, we'd better hide. It looks suspicious, two women out this late at night."

Once inside the forbidden tunnel, Vance slowed a bit. He wanted to stay visible to the cops who were chasing him, keeping their attention focused on him and away from Rosie and Andrea. He let the beam from the flashlight bounce off the walls and the ceiling as he ran, knowing that the men behind him would keep following it.

Moving quickly out of the forbidden tunnel, into the brighter tunnel, he switched off the flashlight. Clutching it tightly, he picked up speed, running straight down the tunnel toward the train station.

He could hear thundering footsteps coming after him. Thank goodness he had a bit of a lead; otherwise he might have trouble staying ahead of the cops. He ran past the flickering lanterns and the centre pole, which stood just outside the tunnel door into the Four Star Café. How well did the cops know the tunnels, he wondered. Did they know about the small entrance that led from the tunnel into the janitor's room at the train station? He had hoped that he could rest there awhile and catch his breath. Figuring that might not be the safest thing to do, he quickly slipped through the tiny opening into the dark janitor's room. He paused briefly, just to make sure he was alone, then skirted the cleaning supplies and headed for the door. Listening intently, he heard footsteps on the stairs outside the door. He also heard the pounding feet of the police behind him. With no time to waste, he slipped out of the door and into the brightly lit stairs of the train station, closing the door firmly behind him. Scanning the area, he saw two cops stop their conversation and look his way.

Thinking quickly, he approached the first person he saw. "Carry your bags, Ma'am?" he asked, politely tipping his cap.

The woman smiled. "What good manners you have, young man." She handed her luggage to him and started toward the doors with him following closely behind. The cops would never catch him now.

THE QUICK WALK to the newspaper office was accomplished without incident. The town was dead quiet. It was almost as if all of the action in Moose Jaw that night was taking place underground. As soon as Rosie and Andrea entered the office, Mr. Smith grabbed the film holder out of Rosie's hands. He headed for the back of the shop. "Go ahead and write down everything you saw. I'm going to see what we have here."

Rosie skirted the long wooden counter, looking for something to write on. She came upon a large wooden desk with an old fashioned typewriter sitting on it. "I can type!" She beamed, pulling open a desk drawer looking for paper. "I'll type up my report."

Andrea sat in a chair nearby while Rosie hunched over, pounding away on the typewriter. She wanted to tell Rosie about the ease of computers in her world, but decided against it. Computers wouldn't be around for many decades yet. There was no sense in getting her hopes up about them. She thought about Vance, wondering what had become of him. She was beginning to get worried. They had been in the newspaper office for almost fifteen minutes. How long did it take to outrun the cops?

As if he had heard his name, Vance suddenly blew into the office, slamming the door behind him. "Hey, I made it!" He flung his arms into the air and twirled around.

Andrea jumped up and hugged him, dancing. "Hurray! How did you do it?"

Vance clapped her on the back. "I'll tell you all about it later, but first I want to know what that photograph looks like."

"I d-" The words died on Andrea's lips, for Mr. Smith was suddenly back in the office, doing a little dance of his own.

"Young lady! What a wonderful photograph you've taken!" He waved it in the air over Rosie's head. "Have a look!"

Rosie grabbed it out of his hand and held it steady while Andrea and Vance crowded around for a look. The picture was grainy and not of very good quality. It had caught two men reaching to shake hands, the fingers just connecting. Only the fence was recognizable, for his face was toward the camera. The other man, the Sergeant, had turned slightly away, his features blurring. The buttons on his uniform shone out though, as did the crest.

"Wow," Vance breathed. "Rosie! You did it!" He gave her shoulders a quick squeeze.

"No," Rosie sighed, disappointment in her voice. "I wanted to get the Sergeant and I didn't! Look at this!" She shook the photograph. "All we know for sure is that a cop is involved. You can't identify the person from this! It could have been anyone!"

"Let me see what you've written, young lady." Rosie quickly pulled the crisp white paper out of the machine and handed it to Mr. Smith. He scanned it, his smile of excitement growing by the second. "What is your name?"

"Rosie. Actually, Rosalind Saunders, but most people call me Rosie."

"Well, Rosie, I think you've done a fine job. I'm going to use your story and your wonderful photo of the two men. This will really set this town on its ear!" He scanned her article again. "I'm going to have to cut the parts about other officers being involved."

Rosie made noises of protest, causing Mr. Smith to speak more loudly. "We can't use it if we don't have proof. And I wouldn't talk about this to anyone. You realize that you three could be in some danger. You've got the cops suspicious and scared. And there's the fence to consider, too. Remember he's most likely a gangster. It's a dangerous situation." He looked at them, a worried expression on his face. "Go straight home and stick together. I do hope we catch these men soon. The town won't be safe until we do."

"I just hope it helps to get Constable Paterson set free." Rosie stood up, stretching sore shoulders. "We'd better get going. Your mother will be starting to worry, and Baby Alan will be getting hungry."

"Come back and see me tomorrow afternoon," Mr. Smith directed. He didn't even stand around to say goodbye. He had turned back toward the back of the shop. "Stop the press," they heard as they headed for the door. "We've got the story of a lifetime to get out by tomorrow morning! Let's get working on it! When this hits the streets, things are going to blow sky-high."

EXTRA! EXTRA!
READ ALL ABOUT IT!

Tony awoke with a start to find Andrea sprawled beside him, asleep on top of the blankets, still fully dressed. She was against the wall and he wondered how she had managed to climb over him without waking him. It must have been very late when she and Rosie got back last night. The morning light was just beginning to shine into the window and he knew that it was very early. He slipped out of bed and pulled his clothes on. Hearing soft sounds coming from the kitchen, he eased open the door and found himself face to face with a wide-eyed Beanie who had been hovering near the bedroom door. She must have just arrived. "Come on," she whispered excitedly. "I just got up. Let's go down and get the morning paper! I want to find out what happened last night!"

248

Tony eagerly agreed and grabbed his shoes. He had already pulled them on and was tying up the laces when he suddenly remembered. He couldn't go anywhere – not yet. He had to get his blood tested and take his insulin first. Rats, he thought, frustration bubbling up inside. Why couldn't he just be normal, like Beanie? He glanced back into the room, reluctant to awaken Andrea. She must be really tired.

"Come on," Beanie urged. "Let's go."

Tony was very, very tempted. He tried to push his medical needs to the back of his mind. He wanted to forget all about it. Today, especially, having diabetes was a total nuisance. "I-I can't go quite yet," he admitted grudgingly, looking uncomfortable. "I have to take my insulin first."

"And then you have to eat," Beanie said, a little unkindly. She was in a hurry to get to where the action was.

Tony bristled. "Look, then. Don't wait for me! I'll get there on my own! I didn't ask for this problem, you know. It just happened to me! I don't like it any better than you do."

Beanie thought about what she had said. "I'm sorry, Tony. I just get impatient sometimes." She patted his back. "I'll wait for you."

"Well, you could help, you know." he had a whiney tone in his voice. "Then it wouldn't take so long."

"Fine. I'll help. What do you want me to do?"

Beanie quickly added, "I'm not going to give you the needle!" She shuddered at the thought.

"Just make us each a peanut butter and banana sandwich and see if Rosie has any milk."

"Oh." Beanie was relieved. "Sure, I can do that." She headed to the kitchen table in search of the food. "And Tony," she called, "think about the parade instead of the needle!"

"Parade?" Tony looked puzzled, then he remembered the paper he had folded up and stuck in his pocket. "The parade! I'd forgotten all about it! That's on today! Yeah, I'll think about that instead!"

Walking back into the bedroom, he softly closed the door behind him. He stood uncertainly beside the bed, watching Andrea sleep. He could hear her soft breathing and see the even rise and fall of her body. It wouldn't be fair to wake her up just to have her give him a shot, but what were his options? He drew a trembling hand over his forehead, wiping away a tiny film of perspiration. Was this the day? Was he ready to take this huge responsibility on himself?

Out in the kitchen he could hear Beanie moving around. He knew how impatient she got. He didn't want to make her wait too long for him. He was excited to get out onto Main Street and find out what had happened last night.

Taking one more look at the slumbering Andrea, he dropped to the floor beside his backpack, taking a huge breath. Today was the day, he decided. Today he would grow up.

Digging into the little pocket in his knapsack, he pulled out everything he needed. He quickly got the swab and lancet all ready. With his mind more on Main Street than the procedure, he barely noticed the pain when he poked his finger. He smeared a dot of blood onto the electrode test strip and waited impatiently as the blood glucose sensor counted down the seconds. That was the easy part. Now for the final challenge. He heard Beanie begin to pace up and down in the kitchen area. She was waiting for him; he would have to hurry. Taking a deep breath, he carefully filled the syringe with the correct level of insulin and swabbed his leg. Licking his lips and concentrating, he placed the sharp needle against his skin. "Okay, here goes nothing," he said softly. He closed his eyes and pushed the plunger.

When he opened his eyes, the job was done. He carefully pulled the needle out of his leg and recapped it. A huge grin split his face and he punched the air in celebration. He had done it all himself! He had been thinking so much about last night that he hadn't fretted about giving himself the shot. There were much more important things to worry about in this world than having to have a little needle to stay healthy. He quickly gathered everything up and put it back into the sack for the next time, letting out a huge sigh of relief. "Wow, I did it! I really did it!" He laughed, making a soft sound that bounced against the walls of the narrow bedroom.

He burst out of the door and into the kitchen. "Let's eat," he announced. "I'm starved." His celebratory actions woke up Baby Alan. Tony could hear him cooing and gurgling in the other room. He munched on the sandwich Beanie had made, washing it down with a glass of lukewarm milk. He really missed having cold, cold milk to drink. Modern refrigeration was wonderful. He had to admit, too, he was getting very tired of peanut butter sandwiches. They had been his favourite food, but now he could barely stomach the idea of eating another one. He wondered what would happen when they ran out of the food Andrea had brought. They wouldn't starve, but it sure would be a lot harder to get a quick snack.

By the time he and Beanie had finished eating, everyone else in the house was moving around. "Tell us what happened last night!" they demanded in chorus as Rosie and Baby Alan came into the kitchen.

Rosie launched into the story, just finishing with the blurred photograph when Andrea stumbled into the room. "Wait for us," she pleaded as she tried to get herself into some semblance of order. She was really missing her daily shower.

"You can't wear that dress again," Rosie commented, studying the filthy blue dress Andrea had on. "Let me lend you something to wear. It might be a bit long, but I'm sure it'll do." She plopped Baby Alan into Beanie's waiting arms and returned to the bedroom. "What do you think of this?" Rosie asked as she came out of the bedroom a few moments later. It was a sailor style dress, a white long-waisted dress with wide navy pleats at the bottom. A double row of shiny gold buttons marched down the front of the outfit.

"I love it," Andrea said simply. "It's adorable. Thanks, Rosie." She gave her a quick hug and disappeared into the bedroom to change.

Watching her leave, Tony suddenly remembered something. "You know, I'd better pack some food," he said. "We don't know when we'll be back here and I'll need to eat."

"We can make a few more sandwiches," Beanie said, looking at the almost empty peanut butter jar. They got busy making and wrapping sandwiches, which Tony stored in his knapsack.

Rosie pushed her hair into an untidy bun and then plunked a small black hat on her head. "There," she commented. "Baby Alan has already nursed this morning and he and I are ready to go."

"Me too," Andrea called. "How do I look?" She walked into the kitchen and twirled around.

"Nice," Tony said as he pulled his backpack on.

Beanie agreed. "But those shoes are something else!"

Andrea grinned. "That's okay," she said, glancing briefly at her thick running shoes, then doing a few ballet steps across the kitchen. "I'm comfortable. Now, I'll just grab an apple for the road and let's get going! I can't wait to see what's happening on Main Street this morning!"

Mrs. Talbot caught up with the group as they turned onto Main Street. Everything sure looked different in the morning light, Andrea thought. Even the warehouse looked less foreboding with the sun shining on it.

Already groups of people stood together reading the paper and discussing the news. "It's even better than yesterday," Beanie noticed.

"Yeah," Tony said, looking around. "I can't believe how crowded it is! It's kind of neat seeing all the people standing around together talking about the news like this."

"Uh huh," Andrea agreed. "Too bad TV was invented. In our age no one does this kind of thing anymore. Everyone stays in their own house, by themselves. See what we're all missing in modern times."

"TV?" Beanie repeated. "That must be some new-fangled invention. What is it?"

Andrea punched Tony lightly on the arm. "They won't believe us when we tell them, will they?"

Tony shook his head. "Nope. We'll tell you later, when we have lots of time to explain it."

As they walked down Main Street toward the train

station, the crowds of people became thicker and thicker. "Boy," Andrea muttered, "some people are getting really upset by the story." She watched as one man shook his fist at another. Some people were arguing that the police couldn't possibly be involved, while others argued just as hotly that they were up to their armpits in the crime wave. Many names were being bandied about as possible suspects.

"Hurry," Tony urged them on. "Let's go get a paper from Vance and read what it says." They pushed through hordes of people on the last block, crossed Manitoba Street to the train station and huddled around Vance.

"I've been saving a paper for you," he told them, holding it out for them to read.

MAN CAUGHT WITH STOLEN GOODS: ARE MOOSE JAW'S FINEST INVOLVED? – *Reported by R.L. Saunders Last night the citizens of Moose Jaw slept soundly, a feeling of security easing their minds, certain of the fact that our fair city was being protected by its police force. They hoped that at last there was an end to the wave of crime which had been hitting businesses along Main Street....*

The article went on to explain the photograph and give details of the underground storage area, which was full of merchandise.

"You did a fabulous job," Andrea said, congratulating Rosie. Everyone agreed.

"I only have a few papers left!" Vance exclaimed. "I've been back to the newspaper office three times already to get more papers! The whole city is down here buying a paper today! It's selling faster than hotcakes!" He jingled the coins in his pocket. "I've made a lot of money, thanks to Rosie." He grabbed her arms and whirled her around in a victory dance. "It's a great article and the photograph is terrific!" He grinned at Rosie as she pulled away. "I'm really impressed! You did a great job – for a woman."

Andrea socked Vance hard on the arm. "What do you mean by that comment?"

"What?" Vance looked truly puzzled. "I just said she did a great job, didn't I, even if she is a woman?"

Andrea studied his face. He had a slightly hurt expression. "Oh, you really did mean that as a compliment."

"Of course I did," he replied, hurt making his voice husky. "I don't say that about women everyday, you know."

Andrea shook her head. Things sure were different in her world. She had considered Vance's comment an insult and yet the look on Rosie's face told her that Rosie was surprised and pleased by it.

"Mr. Smith wants to see you right away, Rosie," Vance informed her as yet another customer came by in search of a newspaper. "I've only got two papers left." One was almost snatched from his hand and the other quickly sold. "Okay, I'm ready, let's go."

It was difficult to skirt the groups milling along Main Street, discussing the morning news. Vance and Andrea led the way, breaking a trail for the rest of them. At the small newspaper office, the scene was the same. People who couldn't find the paper elsewhere had come directly to the office. Mr. Smith stood with a stack of papers at his feet and was passing them out as fast as people handed him the money. Isaac Hamilton was making change from a battered old cigar box.

Mr. Smith spotted Rosie walking in the group. "Good morning, young lady," he called out loudly. "What a marvelous article you wrote! I'm very impressed." He reached for her hand, shook it and then pulled a crisp white envelope out of his shirt pocket and handed it to her. "Here's your first paycheque!"

"Paycheque?" Rosie took the envelope in trembling fingers. "Did you say 'paycheque'?"

"Of course," Mr. Smith replied, a brusque tone in his voice. "When can you start to work?"

"W-work?" Rosie couldn't believe her ears. Was this man offering her a job?

"Yes," Mr. Smith replied kindly, grasping her hand in his. "I'm not going to let a crackerjack reporter like you out of my sight! That article is wonderful! You

covered all the basics and answered the most important questions: Who? What? Where? When? Why?
And how? And on top of all that, you made it an
interesting, attention-getting read. So, when can you
start?" When Rosie hesitated, Mr. Smith grabbed her
arm, pulling her to one side. "The thing is, this story
isn't over yet. We have the photograph showing two
men, but only one man is identifiable, although a few
of us know who the other person is. We need you to
investigate further. We need to get something on that
policeman, and we need it now!"

"Well, I have to find someone to –"

Mrs. Talbot touched Rosie's arm. "I'll look after
Baby Alan, don't you worry about that."

"You do want to work for me, don't you?" Mr.
Smith's voice was gruff and abrupt.

"Y-yes." Rosie smiled as tears of happiness glis-
tened in her eyes. "I really want to work for you!"

"Good." Mr. Smith clapped his hands together.
"Then that's settled. And here's your first assign-
ment." He looked around at the people jammed in
the office. "I've heard rumours of an unruly crowd
gathering at the courthouse. Why don't you go check
it out? And take Hamilton with you," he said, jerking
a thumb in his direction. "He could stand to learn a
lot from you. Actually, he can take the photographs.
You'll be too busy making notes and getting all of the
information down.

"By the way, what did you think of the way I put your name?" He pointed at the article, a long gnarled finger on Rosie's name. "I didn't know if you had a middle name, so I just invented one for you! I took your name, Rosalind Saunders and made it R. L. Saunders for Rosa Lind. How do you like that?"

She studied her name in print. "I like it, Mr. Smith," she said, her voice trembling. "I really like it!"

"Good." Mr. Smith patted her roughly on the shoulder and cleared his throat. He avoided any form of emotion. "Now, young lady," he said. "You have work to do. I don't pay you to stand around weepy-eyed, you know. You might be missing the scoop of the day! Go on over to the courthouse and find out what's happening there!"

Rosie stifled a giggle and resisted the urge to dance a jig as a bubble of happiness burst out of her. She threw her arms around the old man's shoulders and kissed his leathery cheek. "Thank you, sir. You won't be sorry you hired me!"

Mr. Smith stood still in the embrace for a moment and then untangled Rosie's arms from around his neck, his face beet red. "No, I won't be sorry, but you might," he bristled. "Now, get going!"

"Yes, sir!" Rosie saluted him, a grin lighting her face.

"Hamilton," Mr. Smith ordered, "get the camera equipment and go with Rosie."

"Yes, sir," Hamilton groused. He didn't like the idea of being usurped by a woman.

Rosie took off like a shot through the crowd, leaving everyone else to follow her.

"Wow," Tony said. "That's so cool! Rosie is a newspaper reporter."

"She'll probably make lots of money," Beanie decided. "Then she and Baby Alan won't have to be so poor all of the time."

Baby Alan rode contentedly on Andrea's arm, watching the colourful world pass by. Andrea kissed his cheek. "Your Mom is so lucky!"

"She made her own luck," Mrs. Talbot remarked, turning her head to address Andrea, and Andrea was left to ponder what that meant.

A Parade in
Little Chicago

It was a short walk to the courthouse, but squeezing through groups of people took a long time. The sidewalks were crowded, with men and women spilling into the street. Even with the sounds of hundreds of human voices along Main Street, the noise and rumblings in front of the courthouse could be heard before they rounded the corner. A huge crowd stood on the lawn and the steps.

"What do they want?" Rosie asked as the people pushed closer to the building.

"It looks like a mob to me," Vance pointed out, his face white with worry. "They want to blame this on Mr. Paterson somehow."

"Oh, no," Mrs. Talbot said. She swayed slightly, looking as if she might faint.

Suddenly a chant rose into the sky, leaving Rosie's legs weak with relief. "Pat-er-son! Pat-er-son! Pat-er-son!" The crowd called, and then: "In-no-cent! In-no-cent!" It became louder and faster each time they chanted.

"Wow," Vance said, staring at the huge number of men and women milling about on the lawn. White-gloved women made muffled sounds as they clapped. Some of the men tapped their canes on the sidewalks. "I'm glad they're all on our side. I'd hate to think what could have happened."

"Me too," Rosie agreed.

The crowd got larger and more boisterous until at last some important-looking men, dressed all in black, stepped out of the door of the courthouse. They waved their arms, but several minutes passed before the crowd was quiet enough for the men to be heard. "That's the mayor," Beanie whispered to Tony and Andrea.

"You have all seen the morning paper by now." A cry of tangled voices filled the sky. "Let me say that I am disgusted and angered by the signs of corruption in our police force. But I'm sure it's just one man."

"We want action," a voice in the crowd yelled, and the whole crowd cheered wildly.

The mayor again waited until the noise had died down.

"Paterson is innocent," another voice cried out.

The chant went up again. "In-no-cent! In-no-cent!" It boomed out into the morning air until the ground itself seemed to tremble.

"Hurry," Rosie ordered Hamilton, who had carried the camera from the newspaper office. "Set up the camera! We need to get some photographs!"

Hamilton fumbled with the camera. "Okay, okay," he mumbled. "I'm working on it."

The mayor and the other officials surrounding him held a brief conference on the steps while the crowd grew louder and louder. They broke apart and waved their arms for attention while two of the men opened the heavy wooden doors and disappeared into the building. When it was quiet the mayor spoke. "Constable Paterson is innocent of this particular crime," he declared to a rising cheer. He cut it off with a flamboyant wave of his hand. "Constable Paterson was in jail last night when that photograph was taken. The constable is being freed as we speak. You will see that for yourself in a moment...."

His voice trailed away as the door opened again and a haggard-looking Hugh Paterson stepped out onto the step, blinking in the bright morning sun. The crowd cheered.

"Ladies and Gentlemen!" The mayor's voice rang out over the noise. "I give you...Constable Paterson!"

Andrea shook her head. The mayor sounded more like a circus master announcing the next act than a concerned city official.

"There he is," Beanie yelled, bouncing up and down. "There he is!" She broke through the crowd and ran up the long flight of steps. Constable Paterson saw her rushing toward him. He bent down as she neared the top step and scooped her into his arms, hugging her close.

"Take the shot now," Rosie ordered, pointing as Constable Paterson patted Beanie on the back. He still held her tightly in his arms.

The crowd calmed down again while the mayor shook Mr. Paterson's hand and spoke briefly to him. "The Constable has accepted my personal apology for his being falsely arrested. He and the rest of the police force will work diligently to track down and arrest the real culprits in this unfortunate crime." The crowd cheered as the mayor and Mr. Paterson shook hands again. The mayor's voice rang out once more. "I am positive the newspaper photographer would like to capture this important moment in our city's history and then make sure it gets written up for all the good citizens of Moose Jaw to see," he said, still clutching Paterson's hand. "We're willing to wait while you ready the camera."

"Pompous bore," Mrs. Talbot muttered. "I never did like that man. He's always after attention. Poor Hugh, he looks so uncomfortable standing there."

"Go ahead and take the picture," Rosie sighed, "or we'll never hear the end of it. Hopefully it won't turn out."

Hamilton shrugged and snapped the photograph.

Beanie stood, beaming up at Mr. Paterson. Keeping one hand on her shoulder, he whispered in her ear. Beanie pointed excitedly to where the rest of her family stood on the steps below.

Suddenly Beanie and the constable were upon them. His big arms reached for Rosie first. "They were kind enough to shove a morning paper through the bars for me to read. Thank you," he said simply, pulling her into his arms for a bear hug, but his eyes were pinned on Mrs. Talbot. "It's wonderful to have friends like you." He released Rosie and reached for Mrs. Talbot, but the crowd closed in on the small group, demanding his attention.

Eventually the crowd dispersed, many people stopping to give Constable Paterson their well wishes and to shake his hand. He spoke briefly to each person, his eyes often returning to Mrs. Talbot and her family. Rosie caught his attention and managed to drag him away for a private conversation. He listened intently as she spoke, then appeared to ask a few questions. Andrea knew that it must be about the other police officers, especially the Sergeant. She hoped that Mr. Paterson would have ideas on how to catch them. Rosie kissed Baby Alan goodbye and disappeared with Isaac Hamilton to write the article about Mr. Paterson's release.

"Well, this calls for a celebration," Mr. Paterson said, a large smile on his friendly face. He took a large pocket watch out and looked at it. "The parade is scheduled to start soon. Let's head over to Main Street and get a good spot to stand."

"The parade!" Tony and Beanie cheered. Even Baby Alan looked excited by all the noise and laughter.

"In all the hullabaloo I'd forgotten about the parade," Mrs. Talbot said. "I'm afraid I'm not dressed appropriately for it."

"Nonsense," Mr. Paterson answered. "You look wonderful. Besides, the parade is due to start soon and I want to make sure that you have good viewing spots."

As they hurried toward the parade route, Mr. Paterson managed to pull Vance aside. "Fill me in on what's happened since I got arrested, Vance," he said. "Rosie told me a few things, but I'd really value your opinion, too." Vance felt proud to be singled out and jumped in with tidbits of information about Rosie and her determination to prove Mr. Paterson's innocence, and their dangerous mission to the storage area.

"You're going to have to show me these tunnels," Constable Paterson said as they marched along behind the others. "I should know about them, since they obviously led to the corruption of at least some of the officers on the night shift."

"I could do that," Vance offered. "I know them well."

"You do?" Mr. Paterson looked surprised and Vance blushed.

"Yeah, I guess you could say that I'm an expert on

the tunnels. I used to be a tunnel runner," he admitted. "I ran errands for the gangsters and guided customers through the tunnels."

"You mean they used kids to do their dirty work?"

Vance nodded, looking embarrassed. "They paid really well, but it wasn't always fun. I got beat up pretty badly once. That's why I quit."

Mr. Paterson thought for a moment. "I need to find a way to prove that the night shift was involved in the thefts."

"You know, I can identify some of the cops who were in the tunnel last night," said Vance. "And that one Sergeant is a bad seed, too. He almost killed Andrea. We had to rescue her. I hate to think what would have happened if we hadn't gotten there in time. But all those cops were stealing things. We saw them taking dresses and things last night."

"You said they stole ladies' dresses?"

Vance nodded. "Yes, they all took articles of women's clothing because that's about all there was left. They looked really comical, because they had the clothing stuffed inside their jackets. That's probably why I outran them so easily, too. They couldn't run fast for fear of losing the clothes."

Mr. Paterson thought for awhile. "Those women would probably save a fancy dress for a special occasion...like a parade! Those women, the wives, and sweethearts of the police on the night shift might be wearing the stolen clothes today. I'm told the officers' wives often get to ride in the automobiles in the parade! But we'd need to be able to identify the articles of clothing. Hmmm," Mr. Paterson thought. "I need to go see a few shopkeepers along Main Street about some stolen clothes. You be ready, Vance. I may need your help."

"What about us?" Beanie asked indignantly, having overheard the last part of the conversation.

Mr. Paterson nodded. "I may just need your help, too. Be on the lookout for anything suspicious."

"You'll miss the parade," Tony piped up. "Can't you look for the bad guys later?"

Mr. Paterson shook his head. "No. This gives me the element of surprise, I hope. I'll be back soon, don't worry."

"Okay," Tony shrugged. Hearing the clock tower chime the hour, he realized the time. Whipping off his backpack, he unzipped it and reached inside. "Anyone want a sandwich?"

"Tony!" Andrea said in horror, her face pasty white with fear. "I forgot all about your insulin!"

"That's okay," he said, grinning a huge grin. "I did it myself today."

"You did?" Andrea could barely believe her ears. "You really did?"

"Yep! I did!"

Andrea grabbed him in a huge bear hug and twirled him around so fast that his feet flew off the ground.

"Way to go, Brother! I'm so proud of you!"

"Yeah, me too," he said. He wriggled out of her grasp and grabbed a sandwich.

Andrea watched Mr. Paterson approach. "What I find suspicious is the fact that we haven't seen that Sergeant anywhere today," she said, scanning the large crowd. "But I sure feel as if someone's watching me." She shivered and moved closer to the group.

"I'm sure that Sergeant is miles away from here by now," Mrs. Talbot said.

Mr. Paterson looked doubtful. Scanning the crowd himself, he made his excuses to the group and left them to find a good viewing spot for the parade. The spaces were filling up quickly. It was a glorious day, and farmers and everyone from miles around had come to town for the big event. The sun shone brilliantly down on the street, not a cloud in the clear blue sky. The sidewalks were crowded with people of all shapes and sizes.

"Here comes the parade!" Tony shouted. He pointed down the street. A shiny black car was just travelling past the train station and turning the corner onto Main Street. It honked its horn, the people inside waving to the crowds. The car drew near, and a circus wagon, pulled by two Clydesdale horses, turned the corner. Clowns walked beside the wagon advertising the circus. The clowns shook hands with the people and chased one another around the wagon with baseball bats.

There was so much to see that Andrea wished she could lose herself to the parade. She loved the horses, large and small and all colours, but that nagging sensation of being watched wouldn't leave her alone. The hot-air balloon, being pulled on a wagon, caught her attention, too. The balloon's shell looked to be made of a thick material like leather and Andrea wondered how it managed to get up into the air and stay there. A sign on the wagon advertised rides in the balloon. Andrea wished she was up in the balloon right now. She would feel safer up there, away from that feeling of being watched, and she might be able to spot someone suspicious on the ground below.

Vance studied the brand new gas-powered combine lumbering down the street. It was one of the first gas-powered farming machines on the prairies and it was drawing loud exclamations and cheers from the crowds. A few minutes later he felt a tap on his shoulder and turned to find Constable Paterson standing behind them, a determined look on his face. He signalled Vance with a crook of his finger and Vance mutely followed him through the crowd. He could hear his mother talking baby talk to Alan as he walked away.

Standing against the general store, out of the way of the crowd, Mr. Paterson leaned toward Vance, talking softly. "Everything is set. We just need to make sure that the police wives and sweethearts are wearing the stolen material." He looked away and Vance followed his gaze, noticing the owner of the general store peering down the street toward the line of automobiles just turning onto the parade route. "It won't be long now," Paterson noted. "Here they come."

There were six automobiles in total. Three of them were brand new vehicles that were enclosed with windows that rolled down. These were rather high off the ground and had four doors. The other cars were older Model T runabouts with crank starters and large wheels. They were open cars that must have been miserable to drive on rainy days. Each car had a large sign on it announcing the official who rode in the car. The mayor and his wife were in the first car. The second car held the Chief of Police and his wife, and the cars following held several police officers and their wives.

As the cars rolled closer, Hugh Paterson made eye contact with the owner of the general store and pointed to Vance. The shopkeeper nodded. "If he recognizes anything, he'll signal to you. Meanwhile, I'm going to go jump into that car right there," he said, pointing to an open-roof Model T. "I think those women are looking particularly well-dressed today, don't you? If you find out anything, you could run and catch up to me. I have a feeling I'll be arresting those men before this parade is through."

Vance watched as Mr. Paterson dashed out into the street and caught up to the moving car. It was going slowly enough for him to open the door and climb in.

"Take a hike, Paterson," Vance heard one of the men say in a rough voice. "We don't want you in this car." Worrying, he watched as Paterson settled down in the already crowded seat. He sure hoped Mr. Paterson didn't have to defend himself. Those two officers were from the night shift, and they looked mad enough to string him up by his toes and drag him behind the car!

Police officers and officials and their wives filled the other automobiles. The men were from the night shift, since the day shift was working right now. Vance watched the cars pass by, the police officers and their wives waving and smiling. He even recognized some of the clothes. Glancing over at the shopkeeper, he found that the man wasn't paying attention to the parade at all! He was wrapped up in conversation with a man wearing a black trench coat with a black derby hat pulled low over his eyes. Who was that man, Vance wondered, and why wasn't the shopkeeper paying any attention?

Searching the parade, Vance saw that Paterson's car had already moved into the next block! He could be in danger and not even realize it! Vance looked once again at the shopkeeper and found him shrugging his shoulders, an apologetic look on his face. "That's a fine how-do-you-do," Vance muttered, wondering what to do now. He didn't know if he should chase the car down to see if Mr. Paterson was all right, or just keep watching the parade. He glanced over at the man in the trench coat, noticing a smirk of satisfaction creasing the man's thin lips. He glanced once again at the shopkeeper and saw his face turn white. The man's eyes nearly popped out of his head as he stared at the women in the car. He nodded his head, looking furious. That was all Vance needed. Tapping Andrea on the shoulder, he pointed down the street to Mr. Paterson's car. "Something's not right," he told her. "Come on, let's go." He took off running, Andrea following in hot pursuit.

Andrea was in trouble the moment she stepped into the street. Trying to run in a midi-length dress was ridiculous. The long material kept wrapping itself around her knees, threatening to trip her. Women lining the street gasped to see her jogging along, deciding that it was a most unladylike thing to be doing. Vance looked behind once and seemed to be slowing up to wait for her, but Andrea waved him on. It was more important to let one person catch up to Mr. Paterson than have two arrive too late to help.

Andrea pushed her way through the crowd and back onto the sidewalk, hoping to disappear behind the crowd. She hated making a spectacle of herself, and all she wanted to do was hide from the raised eyebrows and mocking eyes. Walking along Main Street, she stayed close to the buildings. A long row of human backs lined the edge of the sidewalk. Everyone was intent on watching the parade.

Slowing to a sedate walk, she realized that no one was paying the least bit of attention to her anymore. Fanning her face to cool her flaming cheeks, she suddenly thought how much she missed her parents. She wanted nothing more than to be at home in a world which she understood. If she'd had her jeans on she knew she would have been able to keep up with Vance. But girls in pants weren't common in this world. She just hoped she could get home, and soon. The rules of this old-fashioned world were beginning to wear on her.

The sound of heavy boots on the sidewalk caught her attention. She whirled around, tasting fear in her mouth, and found herself face to face with a man in a long black coat, a hat pulled low over his eyes. The man's lips curled into a cruel smile as his hand shot out, revealing a gun pointed right at her heart.

"You've caused me a lot of trouble, girlie, escaping from the warehouse like that! I know you were in on that little photograph in the newspaper, and now you're going to pay!"

WHERE'S ANDREA?

Vance quickly lost sight of Andrea in the mob on the sidewalk. Oh well, he realized that she would take care of herself. After all, it was midday, in Moose Jaw. What could possibly happen to her?

Putting Andrea out of his thoughts, Vance concentrated on catching up to Mr. Paterson. The parade seemed to pick up speed as it neared the end of the route, and his chest was heaving. He was running full out, his legs pumping, and he still couldn't catch up. He gathered up the last remaining energy in his body and squeezed out one more burst of speed, just managing to catch up to the constable's car. He nodded, signalling to Mr. Paterson. The parade vehicles began to pull to the side of the street and park, the people disembarking from floats, carts, and automobiles.

Officer Paterson jumped out of the car first, racing

over to four police officers standing on the parade route. He talked excitedly, gesturing toward the men in the cars. The officers looked skeptical at first, Vance thought, judging by the doubtful expressions on their faces. Understanding soon began to dawn and they dashed over to the cars, surrounding the men of the night shift within seconds. "You're all under arrest!" Constable Paterson called out loudly. The commotion in the street stopped dead. Even the animals seemed to realize that something important was going on, for they too remained silent.

"Come off it," an officer in a car mocked. "You're not going to listen to Paterson, are you?"

"Yeah, he's making a mockery of our police force."

"Don't you know, he's the guilty one!"

"He is not!" Beanie's young voice called out. Vance looked over to see her with their mother and Tony. They had obviously decided to follow along when he and Andrea had chased after the cars. Where was Andrea, he wondered. He scanned the silent crowd for her, but couldn't spot her. Oh well, he figured, she'd be along soon. Too bad she was missing the most exciting part of the day. Worry began to niggle at his brain, but he pushed it aside as he watched the events in front of him unfold.

The shopkeeper, who hadn't been very helpful at first, finally came through. "That woman, Officer Matthews' wife, is wearing a hat stolen from my store.

And Officer Hanson's wife is wearing a dress that was stolen as well. What more proof do you need that these officers are guilty of stealing from the very businesses they're supposed to be protecting?"

Convinced that Officer Paterson was right, the day shift arrested the members of the night shift. They tried to resist at first, but when the town's people began to step in to help with the arrests, the guilty cops subsided. Having no other way of transporting so many men to jail, the day shift marched them down the middle of Main Street while the parade goers gawked, some cheering and applauding. The wives, embarrassed and disbelieving, cried into new handkerchiefs that people speculated were stolen as well.

As the excitement began to die down, the crowds cleared away, leaving Vance growing more and more concerned about Andrea. He scanned the thinning crowd again. "Have you seen Andrea?" he asked Tony and Beanie.

Tony looked up in surprise. "I thought she was with you. I saw her running after you during the parade."

"She couldn't keep up," Vance explained. "She waved at me to go on ahead, and so I did. What could have happened to her? She should be here by now."

Anxious looks passed over their faces. "Let's go find Officer Paterson," Beanie said. "He'll know what to do."

"Good idea," Tony said. "He went to the police station to help arrest all those cops."

They hurried back along Main Street, each lost in private fears, wondering what could have become of Andrea. Dark images filled their minds, and Vance couldn't help but wonder about the suspicious character he had seen talking to the shopkeeper during the parade. Was he somehow involved?

"What if we can't find her?" Tony asked, a little whimper in his voice. His backpack bounced on his back as he walked.

Beanie patted his shoulder. "She'll turn up. She has to be around here somewhere."

They came face to face with a young couple and their baby, who must have just learned to walk. She tottered along, weaving all over the sidewalk, looking like one of the clowns in the parade.

When Vance stopped and stood aside to let the couple pass, the other two did the same. "Nice baby," Tony couldn't help commenting, "but she sure walks funny." Then he noticed that she was carrying something big and white. "Hey! Where did she get that shoe?"

The couple laughed. "Oh, she picked it up awhile back," the mother said.

"That's Andrea's shoe!" Beanie said. She bent down and tried to take the shoe away. The baby began to wail, pulling hard on the white object.

"Is it yours?" The father asked. "She's fallen in love with that. We'll have to distract her to get it back." He pulled a rag doll out and waved it in front of her.

"Please, little girl," Beanie pleaded. "Give us the shoe." The baby finally relinquished her hold on it in favour of the rag doll.

"Thanks a lot," Tony said, grabbing the shoe and hugging it to his chest.

"Where exactly did you find this?" Vance asked.

They pointed down Main Street. "At the end of the next block. We figured someone would come looking for it sooner or later. It is rather unique."

The trio took off down the street, terror in their hearts. "It's got to be Andrea's," Beanie breathed heavily. "No one else has shoes like that!"

"Beanie," Vance ordered, "you go get Officer Paterson now. Tell him it's an emergency. Tell him we think Andrea's been kidnapped! Hurry!" Beanie sprinted away, heading toward the police station.

The boys continued more slowly, searching for other clues to Andrea's whereabouts. "Why would she take off her shoe?" Tony asked.

"She wouldn't. Something has happened to her." Vance carefully studied the nearby building. Instinct took over. "I don't like where this shoe was found."

"What do you mean?"

"This is Jackson's Furniture building, the one with the warehouse and the tunnels," Vance said. "This is where the stolen goods were hidden. I'll bet someone has nabbed Andrea and taken her into the tunnels."

"That's a good theory," Officer Paterson puffed, coming up behind them. He studied the shoe and the building. "However, I suspect someone just wants us to think he's taken her into the tunnels, and I have a good idea who that someone is."

Vance thought of the suspicious-looking character talking to the shopkeeper. He quickly described him to Officer Paterson.

"It sounds like Sergeant Lyons," Mr. Paterson said. "I never did like the look of him. He's not to be trusted."

"Where would he take Andrea?" Tony asked tearfully, clutching the shoe.

Officer Paterson patted Tony's shoulder. "I think he's taken her as a hostage to ensure safe passage out of town."

"But he wouldn't take the train," Vance interjected. "The police can easily stop the train and search it."

"He'd just take a car," Tony said, with a sinking feeling in his stomach, thinking of the modern world.

Officer Paterson shook his head. "All of the cars in town were being used in the parade today. All he'd be able to get would be a horse and buggy, and even those were busy."

"I'll bet that's what he was talking to the shopkeeper about during the parade!" Vance said. "He was trying to find a way out of town."

"Well, if he can't take the train or a car, what else is there?"

Hearing a droning overhead, they all looked up. "An airplane!" they exclaimed together.

"I'll bet that's a barnstormer, at the exhibition to cash in on the crowds ready to spend their money," Mr. Paterson said. "The Sergeant's probably on his way with Andrea right now, to get a ride out of town."

"What's a barnstormer?" Tony wanted to know.

Mr. Paterson threw him a puzzled look and then replied, "They're men who fly around the countryside in biplanes. For two dollars you can go for a ride with them."

"But it's only a two-seater," Vance said, shielding his eyes from the sun as he studied the plane. "It couldn't take more than one passenger at a time."

"I don't think his plan is to take Andrea anywhere. I think once he's done with her he'll –" Officer Paterson stopped short. "Come on, let's see if we can get to the field before they do."

An old Model T from the parade was just trundling down the street. Officer Paterson quickly commandeered it, asking the surprised driver to move out of the driver's seat. The kids piled in and the car surged ahead, its gears grinding.

The trip up the long hill was very slow. Tony wanted to jump out and help push the car. He was sure he could make it go faster than it was moving. They were now out of town, heading into the long prairie grass at the exhibition grounds. The plane had been circling for several minutes to attract people's attention. "Look! It's landing!"

Officer Paterson cut the car engine well back from the crowds and the field. "I don't want to draw more attention than necessary to us," he said. "We need to surprise this man. I'm sure he'll use his gun if he feels trapped. He's in a deep trouble."

"I think I see him," Vance said, pointing into the distance. The figure wore a black trench coat and a hat.

"But where's Andrea?" Tony asked.

Officer Paterson squinted at the man. "Just in front of him, standing very close. I'll bet he's already got his gun trained on her. He's hiding it under his coat."

"What's the plan?" Beanie wanted to know.

Thinking for a minute, Officer Paterson wiped his brow and sighed. "Your mother will probably never speak to me again, but the only way I can see distracting him is to use you and Tony as decoys."

"Decoys?" they both asked.

"Yes. You need to run up to the plane, making a lot of noise and being excited. You need to push in front of the man. Someone's got to get on that plane first." He reached into his pocket, pulling out some bills and giving them to the children. "Whatever you do, don't let the Sergeant get on that plane."

"This sounds pretty dangerous for them," Vance protested. "Isn't there another way?"

"We're in a desperate situation, Vance. I just can't think of any other way to keep him distracted long enough for us to tackle him. See the way he keeps looking around? He's expecting us; he's expecting something to happen and he's ready for it. He'd spot us in a flash. We need the distraction of the kids to cover our moves. Do you think you can help tackle him and hold him down?"

"Yes," Vance agreed, thinking of the times Andrea had saved his skin. Now it was his turn to rescue her.

"Good!" Paterson clapped him on the shoulder. "Okay then, we all know our parts, let's go!"

The plane settled onto the hard-packed prairie soil and glided to a stop near the crowd of people. "All right, who's first?" the pilot called out, jumping lightly to the ground.

"Me! Me!" Beanie and Tony ran up shouting and pushing through the small crowd. Tony reached the plane first and clambered onto the wing.

"I won! I'm first!" he shouted.

The Sergeant protested, but Tony bravely drowned him out, ignoring the pleading look in Andrea's eyes. "I'm first!" he shouted, straddling the wing. "Take me first."

"I was here first," the Sergeant protested more loudly, his eyes throwing daggers of anger in Tony's direction. Balling one hand into a fist, he took a few steps in Tony's direction, dragging Andrea with him.

"I was here first," Tony pouted. "Don't hit me!"

The pilot turned to glare at the Sergeant, who moved back in line, his eyes narrowed slits of rage. "All right, all right," he said to Tony. "You're first."

Tony waited impatiently while the pilot pulled a beaten-up leather cap over his head and put thick goggles over his eyes. His arms were stuffed into an ancient leather jacket. Tony tried hard not to stare too much in Andrea's direction, although it scared him to see how pale she looked and how stiffly she stood in one shoe. Officer Paterson and Vance were sneaking up from behind, one on each side of the Sergeant. They seemed to be hiding behind the crowd, probably waiting for the roar of the engine to drown the sounds of their approach.

"Where's the money?" the pilot asked briskly as he did up the jacket. Tony handed it over and the pilot lifted him into the seat, strapping him in securely.

Tony hated the idea of being in the plane while the others took care of the Sergeant. He wanted to be on the ground helping, but this was his part of the job in saving Andrea. As the plane taxied away from the crowd, its engine revving loudly, Vance and Mr. Paterson made their move. They pounced on the Sergeant from behind.

The plane turned just then and began to pick up speed. Tony whipped his head around trying to see what was happening. The wheels bumped over the prairie field, jarring him until his teeth rattled. Just when he thought he couldn't stand it anymore, the wheels left the ground and the plane climbed into the sky. The wind stole his breath and caused his eyes to water, making it difficult to see the ground. He tried to peer over the side of the plane, but the pressure of the wind kept pushing him back into the seat. What was happening with the Sergeant? Was Andrea all right?

Finally Tony managed to sit forward in the seat and look over the edge of the plane. He saw Vance and Mr. Paterson struggling with the Sergeant. Who had the gun, he wondered. He felt so helpless, watching the scary scene taking place below him. If he was on the ground, he could help! The plane climbed higher into the sky and then began to perform a loop-the-loop above the crowd. The whole world seemed to be standing on its head.

Frantically he waited until the plane righted itself; then he peered over the edge of the plane. He saw, with relief, the Sergeant being marched away by Vance and Officer Paterson.

Tony sat back in the rear seat, his heart thumping, adrenaline pumping through his veins. He could relax now that he knew everyone was all right.

Suddenly he realized where he was. How had he gotten so lucky that he was able to get a ride in an authentic biplane? Who would believe the story? Tony smiled hugely, mostly in relief, the smell of gas and oil like perfume to his senses. The wind howled through the cockpit. It soon became tornado force as the plane gathered more speed. He looked down at the tiny Lego people waving up at him from the immense grassland. Moose Jaw was a tiny blip in the almost unbroken fabric of land that stretched in every direction as far as the eye could see. Small veins of brown led away from the buildings, like seams. Those were the roads.

The pilot waggled the wings and the plane tilted from one side to the other. Tony instinctively grabbed the sides of the airplane and hung on. Overhead he could see the upper wings and wondered how people ever actually got out of the seat to walk on them as he had seen in old photographs. He was glad that he wasn't that brave; he didn't even want to think about walking the wings.

Suddenly the plane began to climb higher and higher into the bright sky and he knew another loop-the-loop was coming. Now that his thoughts weren't pinned on Andrea, he was petrified. Holding on for dear life, he tried to keep his eyes open. His body was forced back into the seat as the pilot turned the plane and suddenly Tony was suspended for what seemed like an eternity. Something small hit him on the head and then fell to the earth. A bigger object followed, fluttering briefly and then vanishing. What was that, he wondered. Then the plane straightened and was once again flying upright. What a thrill! "Yahoo!" Tony shouted as the plane's wheels touched down and it taxied to a stop. He would never forget that as long as he lived!

On slightly wobbly legs, Tony descended to the ground and straight into Andrea's arms. He squeezed her tightly around the waist and hung on. "I was so worried," he admitted. "Then I saw Vance leap on the bad guy's back and I knew you'd be okay." He noticed that she was wearing two shoes again.

"I'm glad you had fun on the plane," she said. "You've always wanted a ride in one. You should have left your backpack on the ground," she observed. "It's open. I hope you didn't lose anything."

The two objects flashed through Tony's mind. Grabbing his backpack from his shoulders, he set it on the ground and rifled through it. Oh no, he was in big trouble now.

Rosie and Hamilton hurried up to the group, camera in tow. "I just heard the news of that wonderful tackle and arrest. I want a picture of the whole group, since you all helped get that Sergeant arrested!" Rosie announced. "It's going to be the lead story tomorrow and I want a picture to go with it."

"That means you'll have to be in the photograph too," Officer Paterson told Rosie, grinning down at her. "After all, you're the one who got me out of jail so that I could track down the Sergeant and arrest him."

"Let's get the whole family in on it," Rosie said. "We all played some part in ridding Moose Jaw of corruption." Just then Mrs. Talbot strode up with Baby Alan and everyone agreed that they needed to be in the shot, too.

"Please hurry up," Andrea said between gritted teeth. "I don't feel well." It was a feeling she hadn't had for a few days, that strange sense of being compelled to travel through the tunnels again. Only this time the feeling was so intense she wondered how she could ignore it. Tony stood mutely at her side and she nudged him with her elbow. "You okay?" he shrugged, smiling weakly.

"It's no surprise you don't feel well," Beanie said, "after what you've been through."

They shuffled together, standing stiffly in a row, all looking stern and serious. "Why doesn't anyone smile?" Tony whispered as he and Andrea found their places.

Andrea shrugged her shoulders. "I don't know. Maybe their photographs are very expensive and they don't want to waste them." The group squeezed together, Beanie and Tony standing in front with the others behind. Rosie held Baby Alan facing the camera. Mrs. Talbot and her police officer stood together with Vance and Andrea on either side of them. Mr. Paterson's hand was resting on Beanie's shoulder. "Hold still," Hamilton warned. "What a fine family you make." And he took the picture.

As soon as the photo was taken, Tony dragged Andrea aside. "I lost my insulin on the plane ride," he said, his eyes huge and panic-stricken. "My backpack was open and it fell out. I lost my new comic book too. What are we going to do?"

"We have to leave now," Andrea decided. "We have to try to get back into our own world. I'm having that weird feeling again, the one about the tunnels. Something is telling me we need to get back right away, especially since your insulin is all gone. I don't think we have much time to spare."

"But can't we even say goodbye?"

"I guess we could," Andrea agreed, "but we'd better hurry, Tony. I'm afraid that if we don't go now we'll be stuck in this time forever."

"I don't think it would be that bad," Tony said, "except for the insulin." That scared him. He knew that he would be in big trouble without it.

"Probably not," Andrea agreed. "But I miss Mom and Dad, and Grandpa and Grandma Talbot and Aunt Bea."

"But they're right there," Tony said, pointing to Vance and Beanie. "How can you miss them?"

"What's the matter?" Vance wanted to know.

Andrea wondered how she could explain it in front of everyone and get the cryptic message across. "Ah-h-h, our time is up," she stated. "We really need to be getting back."

She turned to study the police officer. "Thank you for saving me, Mr. Paterson," she said, remembering her manners. She nudged Tony in the ribs with her elbow.

"Yes," Tony said quickly. "Thank you. You were great! And I loved the plane ride!"

"You can come by to visit us anytime," Mrs. Talbot said. She frowned slightly, her eyes narrowing. "Where did you say you lived?"

"Oh uh-h-h," Andrea hesitated. "Somewhere far away," she replied vaguely. "We really do have to be going now," she said, backing away from the group. "I wish we could stay."

"Well, let us see you home, at least," Mr. Paterson said.

"That won't be necessary," Andrea replied, almost laughing at the absurdity of it. "You stay and enjoy your evening."

"Bye, Aunt Bea," Tony whispered in Beanie's ear as he gave her a bear hug. "I'm going to miss you."

Beanie clung to him for a minute. "What am I like as an old person?"

Both Tony and Andrea stood for a moment studying her bright blue eyes and quick smile. "You're still the same old Beanie," Andrea said truthfully, "only a little older. When I look at you as Aunt Bea, I just see – Beanie." She gave her a quick hard hug. "It's been fun, Aunt Bea. It's been really great getting to know you and Grandpa Talbot better. I can't wait to talk to the older you all about this time travel trip." She turned and gave Vance an awkward hug and then backed away. "Come on, Tony. We'd better go now."

"Goodbye, Tony," Beanie called. "Goodbye, Andrea Talbot!"

"'Bye," Tony called. He made a quick detour for his backpack lying in the grass, then followed Andrea across the field. "I hope we can come back again some time.

"Where do you think we should get back into the tunnels?" Tony asked. They had raced down the long hill and reached the business part of Main Street.

Andrea had been thinking about that. "We should enter through that stairwell at Rosie's – I mean Grandpa's house."

"How long have we been here?" Tony asked. "It feels like a lifetime."

"It has been a lifetime. But actually, it's only been a few days."

Tony watched the Model T cars chugging by on the street. "You know," he said as they hurried along, "I could get used to living here – if we got stuck here, I mean. It wouldn't be that bad. I could be a newsboy like Vance."

"Not for long, you couldn't," Andrea said. "You'd probably die, Tony, without your insulin. Oh, I don't even want to think about that. I hope we can get into the tunnel and back to the present." Suddenly the need to hurry felt stronger. "Come on, Tony. I don't want you to be stuck here. I'm scared for you. I know insulin was discovered right around this time, by some Canadians, but I don't think it's in use yet. Let's hurry, Tony!" She grabbed his hand as they raced toward the town.

Ominica Street came into view and she and Tony turned toward Rosie's house. They sprinted around to the backyard toward the heavy wooden door. "Help me lift this," she said.

They tugged on the door and got it open just enough to slip inside, feeling that familiar electrical current tickle their fingers and toes. Tony went in first with Andrea following closely behind. They both worked to close the heavy door quietly behind them and then scooted down the few steps to the other door. They opened it and stepped inside. "Sh-h-h," Andrea cautioned, just in case the tunnel wasn't empty.

The feeling was intense now. It was a magnet drawing them into the black tunnel. She felt her body being pulled, almost against her will, farther into the tunnel. "It's almost as if the tunnel knows that we belong in the other world. It's as if it's trying to set everything right; it's trying to send us back."

"That's what I think too," Tony whispered. He put a clammy hand into hers and hung on tightly. It felt weird down here and he was glad of the company.

"Where's the flashlight?" Andrea asked. Without waiting for an answer, she reached around behind Tony and unzipped the pocket on the backpack, rummaging inside. "Here it is." She fastened the sack after switching on the powerful light. It bounced around the walls of the tunnel and then settled into a straight line right down the centre, beckoning the duo forward.

They moved quickly along, Andrea letting the light travel the side of the tunnel wall, looking for that elusive caved-in area. Lanterns shone down weakly, providing some light. The dirt walls looked the same, and she was afraid that they wouldn't be able to find the spot where the cave-in had taken place. "Please be there," she whispered as they hurried along the tunnel. "Please." Slowing down, she directed the beam of light against the base of the dirt wall.

"There!" Tony called out, pointing at loose dirt against the wall. "This might be the spot." It looked as if part of the wall had given way. A hollowed-out space was visible at shoulder height. Tony fell to his knees and began to shovel the dirt away with his bare hands.

Dropping the flashlight, Andrea leaned in beside him, helping to pull the earth away. "I feel a breeze," she said. She bent lower and stared along the floor. "It's coming from the other side. This is the place! Keep digging, Tony."

Within a few minutes they had made the hole wide enough. "Crawl through, Tony," she ordered. He did as he was told and she quickly followed him, staying close. She was fearful of another cave-in and didn't want to be caught in it.

Snaps and crackles of electricity wrapped around them and the tiny hairs on her body stood straight up. The force field felt intense and painful. "We're almost there," she noted as they made the last turn into the tunnel that led into Grandpa's office.

"I don't like this," Tony said, clinging to her hand. "It's much worse than it was before. It hurts and my hair feels funny. What if we don't make it? What if we can't get the armoire moved again?"

"It won't happen," she said with more confidence than she felt. It had to be open. "Let's hurry, Tony."

They struggled forward, pushing into the force field. She felt the electrical current wrap around her body. Like a giant python it began to squeeze until the breath was almost choked out of her. Looking ahead, she said, "Hurry, Tony! I think the armoire's closing!"

Tony stumbled and tripped. "I can't make it," he cried.

"Come on, Tony," she shouted, the sound being whipped out of her mouth and into the black hole of time. "We're almost there."

"I can't," he whimpered. "It hurts too much; it's too hard."

"Oh no," she moaned, trying desperately to pull him to his feet. The tunnel grew darker and darker. The armoire was closing! Would they be stuck in this bizarre time-warped world forever?

EPILOGUE

Suddenly strong arms were reaching out to them, pulling them up the few wooden steps and into the office. Andrea struggled to catch her breath, sinking to the floor where Tony already lay in a heap. Together they watched the armoire slide firmly against the wall as the electrical current slipped in behind it.

"It's all right. You're safe now."

"Grandpa?" Andrea looked up. The crinkly blue eyes of her dear old grandfather beamed down at her. "Oh, Grandpa! Am I ever glad to see you!" She climbed to her feet and flung herself into his outstretched arms.

"I didn't think we were going to make it," she said, a shudder of fear going through her at the thought.

"That's why I was here," Grandpa replied in his gravelly voice. "I knew you needed me."

"We did need you," Tony replied. "I don't think we would have made it without you."

Aunt Bea came slowly into the office, looking tired but happy. "So, how are my time-travelling relatives?"

"Beanie!" Both Tony and Andrea tried to hug her at once. "How are you feeling?"

"I'm fine," Aunt Bea replied, blue eyes sparkling between delicate wrinkles. "Those pesky doctors can't keep me down. I'm as strong as an ox! And I now have a defibrillator and it's working well! I'm going to live to be one hundred and twenty!"

"But you have to take it easy for now, Beanie," Grandpa warned, gently taking her arm and guiding her to a chair. "Sit down and rest for awhile. Grandma's making lunch."

"It was a great adventure," Tony said, puffing up his chest importantly. "I'm a hero, now. I helped save Moose Jaw from those bad cops and I helped save Andrea – twice!"

"What happened to Constable Paterson?" Andrea asked.

"My stepfather, Hugh Paterson – your great-grand-father, got promoted to police Sergeant for his part in catching the crooked cops. He became a hero, too."

"Stepfather." Andrea smiled. "I thought they made a cute couple, Viola and Hugh, I mean; my great-grandparents. And what about Rosie?"

Grandpa smiled, his grin wide and joyful. "Rosie became the best newspaperwoman in the province. She really had a nose for news, and the people in the town came to respect her, too." He cleared his throat uncomfortably and changed the subject. "Bea and I have been saving this old photograph for you to see."

"What do you mean, old?" Tony blurted. "It was only taken a few minutes ago! It's probably not even developed yet!"

"It was developed some seventy years ago." Bea reminded him. "Look!" Andrea peered over her Grandfather's shoulder as he stared at the old picture, which was grainy and yellowed with age.

"It's the same photo that's in my book!" Tony said. Rummaging quickly through his backpack, he pulled it out. "See!"

"I sure wish I understood how time travel works," Andrea said, gently running a finger along the page. "Was I really there? It almost seems like a dream."

"No one can really begin to understand time travel, Andrea," Aunt Bea said, "even Vance and I, with all of the reading and studying we've done on it. But maybe things, events of the past can be changed, especially if you think about them a lot. I still believe it was all my doing, Andrea, getting you to come back in time. Remember, I called you back by thinking about you so much for so long."

Andrea nodded. "I know you said that, but I wonder if it's true. I wonder if it would have happened anyway."

"Well, we'll never know," Grandpa Talbot said, drawing Andrea and Tony close to his side. "I'm just glad you're home safe and sound, that you had a great experience and you helped rid Moose Jaw of those crooked cops. And I have something for you, Tony," Grandpa added, pointing to the desk. There Tony saw a new set of walkie-talkies and a remote control car.

"Thanks!" Tony smiled. "I wonder what happened to the ones that we left in the warehouse."

"We'll never know," Grandpa Talbot replied. "I never went back in there searching for them."

"We did have a great time, even if parts of it was scary and dangerous," Tony said, still looking at the old photograph. "I sure learned a lot about myself. I'm the one who has to live with diabetes and I guess I just have to make the best of it." He laughed aloud as he got swept up into first Grandpa Talbot's and then Aunt Bea's bear hugs. "Now I know I can take care of myself!"

"Your parents will be really proud of you." Grandpa tousled his hair.

"You know," Tony studied the old photograph again. "We should get this enlarged and hung up in the living room, just to remind us all of the fabulous time we spent together."

"Good idea, Squirt," Andrea said, "but don't you think someone might recognize us and wonder how we managed to do it?"

"Nah," Tony shook his head. "We could just say those two people were shirttail relatives in town for a brief visit. After all, it's the truth, isn't it?"

ANDREA TALBOT.

TIME TRAVELER. CRIME STOPPER?

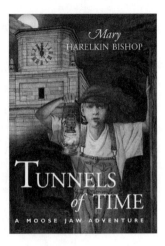

Thirteen-year-old Andrea doesn't want to hear about some dumb old tunnels from the old days in Moose Jaw. But then she finds herself in those tunnels, in that past! Can she outwit the gangsters who rule this underworld full of secrets? Can she escape back to the present?

TUNNELS OF TIME: A MOOSE JAW ADVENTURE. If you loved *Tunnels of Terror*, you'll want to find out how it all began.

Available from fine bookstores everywhere
TUNNELS OF TIME — CAN $7.95, US $6.95

COTEAU BOOKS
WWW.COTEAUBOOKS.COM

ACKNOWLEDGEMENTS:

To The Snowbound Road Queen

Snowstorms in May, and Time-share option clothes;
Bazaart and Sundog;
High bridges, long walks, and laughter.

Not to mention book launches;
A little rubber ducky in my pocket for luck,
And tea (or cocoa) served with quiet conversation.

For all of this, and
So much more,
Eileen,
This one's for you.

With special thanks to Sarah Phillpot for sharing her journey with Juvenile Diabetes; to Logan, who reminds me of Tony; and to Joan Cochrane for helping with the medical technicalities.

To the staff and students of Roxmore School, in Avonmore, Ontario, with heartfelt gratitude for my wonderful visit, May 25, 2001.

Especially to Brenda Quesnel and her fabulous class, for a magical day, and for writing letters to the publisher to help get this book published.

And with deep gratitude and affection to Adele, Erin, MacKenzie, Olivia, and Steve for opening their home and hearts to me. You truly are special.